2

BEST

"A cheek... themselves laughing throughout."

—*Publishers Weekly*

"*Single White Vampire* is a wonderfully funny, fast-moving story that's an absolute delight to read. . . . Fans of humorous romance won't want to miss this one, even if vampires aren't their cup of tea."

—*RT Book Reviews*

LOVE BITES
"Readers will be highly amused, very satisfied, and eager for the next Argeneau tale."

—*Booklist*

"With its whip-smart dialogue and sassy characters, *Love Bites* . . . is a great romantic comedy worth tasting!"

—Romance Reviews Today

TALL, DARK & HUNGRY
"Delightful and full of interesting characters and romance."

—*RT Book Reviews*

"*Tall, Dark & Hungry* takes us on a heartwarming journey of healing hearts and sizzling attraction as Bastien and Terri race through New York and around the world in search of love."

—A Romance Review

BITTEN

The man was obviously mad. Beautiful but mad, Rachel thought grimly as she crossed the room to the set of double doors she hoped was a closet.

"Look," he said soothingly. "I realize this is upsetting, confusing and perhaps—"

Rachel spun. "Confusing? Upsetting? What could be confusing or upsetting? You're a vampire. There's a madman out to get you, but he accidentally axed me, so you turned me into a vampire too. Now I'm a soulless bloodsucker damned to walk the night and suck neck." Rolling her eyes, she turned back to the closet. "I have to get out of here."

LYNSAY SANDS

LOVE BITES

AN ARGENEAU NOVEL

AVON
An Imprint of HarperCollinsPublishers

AVON BOOKS
An Imprint of HarperCollins*Publishers*
10 East 53rd Street
New York, New York 10022-5299

Copyright © 2004 by Lynsay Sands
ISBN 978-0-06-201974-5
www.avonbooks.com

First Avon Books paperback printing: July 2010

Avon Trademark Reg. U.S. Pat. Off. and in Other Countries, Marca Registrada, Hecho en U.S.A.
HarperCollins® is a registered trademark of HarperCollins Publishers.

Printed in the U.S.A.

10 9 8 7 6 5 4 3 2

For Deborah MacGillvray,
a good friend and the lady who came up with
the brilliant title Single White Vampire

LOVE
BITES

Prologue

Pudge squinted through the scope of his rifle. Not just any rifle. A Tac Ops Tango 51, the ultimate tactical precision rifle. It weighed 10.8 pounds, was 44.3 inches long and had a guaranteed accuracy of .25 MOA. Its stock incorporated a semiwide beavertail—

He paused in his mental recitation of the Tac Ops catalog description to peer at the weapon, not quite sure what a beavertail was. It sounded almost sexy the way it read. A semiwide beavertail. Beaver tail. Beaver. Tail. The whole description of the weapon was sexy. For instance, it was suppose to have "dual palm swells." He wasn't sure what those were, but it made him think of boobs. Of course, most things made him think of boobs.

Yep. He was holding "beavertail" and "dual palm swells." Awesome.

The sudden blare of a horn made him start and nearly drop his rifle. Grasping it protectively to his chest, Pudge glared down at the dark street below. He'd chosen the rooftop of this building because it afforded a bird's-eye view of the parking lot across the street. It had never occurred to him that it would be completely unsheltered up here on the roof and cold as an Alaskan winter. If Etienne didn't hurry, Pudge was going to freeze to death waiting for him. He scowled at the possibility. How long was the jerk going to be in there, anyway? It was already past midnight. This was—

"Shit!" The toothpick he'd been chewing on slipped from his lips as the man in question exited the building and started into the parking lot. Etienne Argeneau. And he was alone.

Pudge froze for one moment, then scrambled into position. He peered through the scope, got a bead on the guy, then hesitated. He was suddenly aware that his breath was coming fast. He was panting as if he'd been running for miles, and despite the cold he was sweating heavily. Norman Pudge Renberger was about to kill a man. And not just any man. Etienne Argeneau. His nemesis.

"Bastard," Pudge muttered. With a slow grin, he directed the laser sights of his gun onto his target's chest. There was no sound as he pulled the trigger. He had outfitted his Tango 51 with a Tac Ops 30 suppressor, a silencer, so the only noise was a *pfft* of air. If it weren't for the way the rifle jerked in his hands, he might not have believed it fired.

Hurrying to focus on Etienne again, Pudge squinted through the scope. The man had stopped dead, staring down at his chest. Was he hit or not? For a moment Pudge was afraid he'd missed altogether, but then he noted the blood.

Etienne Argeneau raised his head. His silver eyes found and focused clearly on where Pudge was positioned on the rooftop, then the light in them faded and the man fell flat on his face on the pavement.

"Yes," Pudge breathed, a shaky smile coming to his lips. He worked clumsily to dismantle his rifle, ignoring the sudden trembling of his muscles as he replaced the pieces in their case. His sexy Tango 51 with dual palm swells and beavertail had cost him nearly five thousand dollars, but it had been worth every penny.

Chapter One

"Yo, Rach. I'm gonna grab a java. You want anything?"

Rachel Garrett straightened and wiped the back of her gloved hand across her forehead. She had been bouncing between the chills and fever since arriving at work two hours earlier. At the moment, she was in a hot phase. Sweat was gathering across her back and along her scalp. She was obviously coming down with something nasty.

Her gaze slid to the clock on the wall. Almost one. Two hours down, six to go. She almost groaned. Six more hours. The way this flu bug was coming on, it was doubtful she'd last half of that.

"Hey! You feeling all right, Rach? You look like hell."

Rachel grimaced as her assistant moved to her side

and felt her forehead. *Like hell?* Men could be so tactful.

"Cold. Clammy." He frowned and asked, "Fever and chills?"

"I'm fine." Rachel pushed his hand away with embarrassed irritation, then reached into her pocket for some change. "Okay, Tony. Maybe you could get me some juice or something."

"Oh, yeah. You're fine."

Rachel stilled at his dry words, suddenly realizing she had pushed her smock aside and shoved her hand into her pants pocket without removing her bloody rubber glove first. Great.

"Maybe you should—"

"I'm fine," she said again. "I'll *be* fine. Just go on."

Tony hesitated then shrugged. "Okay. But you might want to maybe sit down or something till I get back."

Rachel ignored the suggestion and turned back to her cadaver as Tony left. He was a nice guy. A little weird maybe. For instance, he insisted on talking like a Goodfella from the Bronx when he had been born, raised, and never left Toronto. He also wasn't Italian. Tony wasn't even his real name. The name he'd been given at birth was Teodozjusz Schweinberger. Rachel had complete sympathy with the name change, but she didn't understand how the bad accent came with it.

"Incoming!"

Rachel glanced at the open door to the main room

of the morgue. Setting down her scalpel, she stripped the rubber glove from her right hand and walked out to meet the men propelling a gurney inside. Dale and Fred. Nice guys. A couple of EMTs whom she rarely saw. They generally delivered their clientele to the hospital alive. Of course, some died after arrival, but it was usually after these two had already been and gone. This patient must have died in transit.

"Hi, Rachel! You're looking . . . good."

She crossed the room to join them, politely ignoring Dale's hesitation. Tony had made it more than plain how she looked. "What have we here?"

Dale handed her a clipboard with various sheets of paper. "Gunshot wound. Thought we got a beat before transporting from the scene but might have been wrong. For the record, he died in transit. Doc Westin pronounced him gone when we got here and asked us to bring him down. They'll want an autopsy, bullet retrieval, and so on."

"Hmm." Rachel let the paperwork fall back into place, then moved to the end of the room to grab one of the special stainless steel gurneys used for autopsies. She rolled it back to the EMTs. "Can you switch him over onto this while I sign?"

"Sure."

"Thanks." Leaving them to it, she moved to the desk in the corner in search of a pen. She signed the necessary papers, then walked back as the EMTs finished shifting the body. The sheet that had covered it for the trip through the hospital was now missing. Rachel paused and stared.

The latest addition to the morgue was a handsome man, no more than thirty, with dirty blond hair. Rachel took in his pale chiseled features, wishing she'd seen him while he was alive and that she'd known what he looked like with his eyes open. She rarely thought of her work as having been at one time living, breathing beings. It made her job impossible if she considered that the bodies she worked on were mothers, brothers, sisters, grandfathers. . . . But this man she couldn't ignore. She imagined him smiling and laughing, and in her mind he had silver eyes the likes of which she'd never seen.

"Rachel?"

She blinked in confusion and stared up at Dale. The fact that she was now sitting was a bit startling. The men had apparently rolled the wheeled desk chair over and urged her into it. Both EMTs were hovering over her, worry on their faces.

"You nearly fainted, I think," Dale said. "You were swaying and all white-faced. How are you feeling?"

"Oh." She gave an embarrassed laugh and waved her hand. "I'm fine. Really. I think I'm coming down with something, though. Chills then fever." She shrugged.

Dale placed the back of a hand to her forehead and frowned. "Maybe you should go home. You're burning up."

Rachel felt her face and was alarmed to note that he was right. It crossed her mind to hope that the speed and strength with which this bug had hit her wasn't an omen of how bad it was going to be. And if it was bad, she hoped it would burn out as quickly as it had come. She hated being sick.

"Rachel?"

"Huh?" She glanced at the concerned faces of the EMTs and forced herself upright. "Oh, yeah. Sorry. Yes, I might go home early when Tony gets back. In the meantime, I signed for the body and everything." She retrieved the necessary paperwork and handed back the rest. Dale accepted the clipboard, then exchanged an uncertain glance with Fred. Both appeared reluctant to leave her alone.

"I'm fine, really," she assured them. "And Tony just went out to grab us some drinks. He'll be back shortly. You two go on."

"Okay." Dale still sounded reticent. "Just do us a favor and keep your butt in that chair till he does, huh? If you faint and hit your head . . ."

Rachel nodded. "Sure. You two go on. I'll just rest till Tony gets back."

Dale didn't look like he believed her, but he had little choice. He followed Fred to the door. "Okay. Well, we're out of here then."

"See you later," Fred added.

Rachel watched them leave, then sat still for a moment as promised. It wasn't long before she became impatient, though. She wasn't used to being inactive. Her gaze slid to the body on the gurney. A shooting vic. Those were rare. It meant there was a shooter out there running around Toronto. It also meant this man had become her top priority. The police would want the bullet for forensics testing, which meant she wasn't going home after Tony came back. At least, not until she had removed the bullet. The official autopsy wouldn't be done until morning, but retrieving the bullet was her job. As head coroner at night, it was her responsibility.

Straightening her shoulders, she stood and moved to the table. Peering down at her newest customer, she said, "You picked a heck of a night to get shot, my friend."

Her gaze slid over his face. He really had been a looker. It seemed a real shame that he was dead—but then it was always a shame when people died. Shrugging such thoughts aside, Rachel grabbed her tray of equipment and rolled it over. She looked the body over once more before setting to work.

The EMTs had ripped his shirt open, then laid it back across his chest. He was still fully clothed and in a rather sharp—not to mention expensive—designer suit. "Nice duds. Obviously a man of taste and means," she commented, admiring the cut of the suit and the body beneath. "Unfortunately, your suit has to go."

Picking up the shears from the equipment table, she

quickly and efficiently cut away the suit coat and shirt. As the cloth fell back, Rachel paused to take in what was revealed. Normally, she would have simply moved on to remove the cadaver's pants and underwear, but the fever was affecting her strength. Her arms felt all rubbery, her fingers limp and awkward. She decided a change in routine wouldn't hurt. She would start recording her findings of his upper body before she moved on to try to remove the clothing from his lower body. With any luck, Tony would be back by then to help.

Setting the shears aside, she reached up to swing the overhead light and the microphone directly over his chest. Then she switched the microphone on.

"The subject is . . . Oh, shoot!" Rachel flicked the microphone off. Quickly retrieving the paperwork Dale and Fred had left behind, she scanned the information in search of a name. She frowned. There wasn't one. He was a John Doe. Well-dressed, but without identification. It made her wonder if that was the reason behind the shooting. Perhaps he'd been shot and robbed of his wallet. Her gaze went to the man. It seemed a real shame he was dead for nothing more than a couple of bucks. What a crazy world.

Setting the paperwork down, Rachel flicked the microphone back on. "Dr. Garrett examining shooting victim John Doe. John Doe is a Caucasian, male, approximately 6-foot-four," she guessed, leaving actual measurements for later. "He is a very healthy speci-men."

She turned off the microphone again and took her time looking him over. "Very healthy" was an under-statement. John Doe was built like an athlete. He had a flat stomach, a wide chest, and muscular arms to go with his handsome face. Picking up one arm then the other, Rachel lifted each to examine its underside be-fore stepping back with a frown. He hadn't a single identifying mark. No scars or birthmarks. There was nothing that could be considered an identifying fea-ture on the man. Other than the gunshot wound over his heart, the man was completely flawless. Even his fingers were perfect.

"Strange," Rachel muttered to herself. Usually there were at least a couple of scars—an appendicitis scar, small ones on the hands from past wounds, or some-thing. But this man was completely unmarred. His hands and fingers were even callous free. Idle rich? She wondered and peered at his face again. Classi-cally handsome. No tan, though. Jet-setters usually had tans from the sunny spots they visited or from the tanning salon.

Deciding she was wasting time on such supposi-tions, Rachel gave her head a shake and turned the microphone back on. "Subject has no identifying fea-tures or scars on the front upper body except for the gunshot wound. Death, upon first glance, appears to be due to exsanguination caused by the aforementioned wound."

She left the microphone on as she reached for the forceps to remove the bullet. The recorder was sound-activated, so it would only record what she said anyway. Later she would use the tape to write up her report, leaving out any muttered comments it caught that were irrelevant to the case.

Rachel measured and described the size of the gunshot wound, as well as its placement on the body, then set to work cautiously easing her forceps into the hole, moving slowly and carefully to be sure she was following the path of the bullet and not pushing through undamaged tissue. A moment later, she had reached and grasped the missile and was drawing it carefully back out.

Murmuring a triumphant "Ah ha!" she straightened with the bullet caught in the spoon of the forceps. Turning toward the tray, Rachel paused with irritation when she realized there was no container for it. Such things weren't normally needed, and she hadn't thought to grab one. Muttering under her breath at her lack of forethought, she moved away from the table to the row of cupboards and drawers to search.

While looking, Rachel pondered where Tony had got to. His five-minute trip in search of beverages had become a rather lengthy absence. She suspected it was a certain little nurse who worked on the fifth floor who was holding him up. Tony had fallen hard for the girl and knew her schedule like the back of his hand. He usually arranged his breaks around hers. If she was in the cafeteria when he arrived, Rachel could count on his taking his full break now. Not that she minded. If she did go home after removing this bullet, he would have no one to relieve him for the rest of the night.

Finding what she'd been looking for, Rachel packaged the bullet, then carried it to her desk to make out an identification tag. It wouldn't do for evidence to get misplaced or to be left lying around without a label. Of course, she couldn't find the labels right away and wasted several minutes looking for them. Then she messed up three before getting one right. It was all a good indication that Rachel wasn't on the ball tonight, and that going home was a good idea. She was a perfectionist, and such little mistakes were frustrating, even embarrassing.

Exasperated with herself and her weakened state, Rachel smoothed the label onto its container, then paused as she caught movement out of the corner of her eye. She turned, expecting Tony to have returned, but the room was empty. There was just herself and John Doe on the gurney. Her feverish mind was beginning to play tricks on her.

Rachel shook her head and stood. Alarm shot through her as she noted that her legs were a touch shaky. Her fever was skyrocketing. It was as if a furnace switch had been flicked on, taking her from cold and clammy to burning up in a heartbeat.

A rustle drew her attention back to the gurney. Was that right hand where it had been the last time she looked? Rachel could have sworn she'd laid his hand back palm down after examining it for identifying scars, yet now it was palm up, the fingers relaxed.

Her gaze travelled up the arm to the face, and Rachel frowned at its expression. The man had died with a blank, almost stunned look, which had remained frozen in death. But now he wore more of a pained grimace. Didn't he? Maybe she was imagining things. She *must* be imagining things. The man was dead. He hadn't moved his hand or changed his expression.

"You've been working the night shift too long," Rachel muttered to herself. Slowly she moved back to the gurney. She still had to remove the rest of the corpse's clothes and examine his lower front body.

Of course, she would need help from Tony in turning the man to examine his back. His lower front could wait until Tony returned too, but Rachel decided against it. The sooner she got out of there and went home to bed, the better. It was smarter to get as much done as possible now, before her assistant returned. Which meant cutting away the shooting vic's pants. To that end, Rachel reached for the shears— then realized she hadn't checked for head wounds.

It was doubtful he'd been shot in the head. At least, she hadn't seen any evidence. Fred and Dale would have mentioned it too. And despite their claims of thinking they'd got a heartbeat, then losing it, the man would have died instantly when the bullet hit his heart. Still, she had to check.

Leaving the shears where they were, Rachel moved to stand at the top of the gurney and did a quick examination of the vic's head. The man had lovely blond hair, the healthiest she had ever seen. Rachel wished her own red locks were half as healthy. Finding nothing, not even a small abrasion, she gently set his head back down and returned to the side of the gurney.

Retrieving the shears, Rachel opened and closed them as she eyed the waist of the man's suit pants, but she didn't immediately start cutting. Oddly enough, she was rather hesitant to do so. She hadn't felt shy about cutting off a guy's pants since medical school, and had no idea why she was now.

Her gaze slid up over his chest again. Jeez, he was really built. His legs were probably as muscular, Rachel supposed, and she was chagrined to note that she was more than just a little curious. Which was probably the reason for her hesitation, she decided. She wasn't used to feeling anything like this while examining a subject, and she felt embarrassed. Man, this fever was really playing havoc with her thinking.

Even pale and lifeless, John Doe was an attractive man. Mind you, he didn't appear quite as pale and lifeless as the usual clientele. He looked as if he were simply napping.

Her eyes traveled back to his face. She found him

really appealing, which was alarming. Being attracted to a dead man seemed a little sick. But Rachel reassured herself that it was just a reflection of how dry her social life had been. Her work hours made dating difficult. While most people were going out and having fun, she was working. Yes, the nightshift had put a real crimp in her lovelife.

Well, in truth, her lovelife had never been very exciting. Rachel had shot up in height as a pre-teen and remained taller than all the other kids in her age group through high school. It had left her shy and self-conscious, and had managed to ensure that she grew into something of a wallflower. Getting the job on the nightshift at the morgue had merely increased her difficulties. But it had also been a handy excuse when people asked about her non-existent lovelife. She could easily blame her job.

Things were getting pretty bad, however, when she began finding herself attracted to corpses. It was probably a good thing she was trying to get off the nightshift. All this alone time couldn't be healthy.

Forcing her gaze away from the corpse's too pretty face, Rachel let her gaze slide over the instruments of her job and once again marvelled that she had chosen to work in this field. She had always hated anything having to do with doctors and doctor visits. Needles were a nightmare and she was the biggest wuss on the planet when it came to pain. So, of course, she'd got a job in the morgue of a hospital where needles and pain were a constant companion. Rachel supposed it was a subconscious rebellion of sorts, a refusal to allow her fears to hold her back.

Despite herself, Rachel eyed John Doe's chest, pausing abruptly at the gunshot wound. Had the opening grown smaller? She stared at it silently, then blinked as the chest appeared to rise and fall.

"Eyes playing tricks," Rachel muttered, forcing herself to look away. She'd pulled a bullet out of the guy's heart. He was definitely dead. Dead guys didn't breathe. Determined to get this over with quickly so that she could refrigerate him and stop imagining things, she turned back to his pants and slid one blade of her shears under the material.

"Sorry about this. I hate to ruin a perfectly good pair of pants, but . . ." She shrugged and started to slice through the material.

"But what?"

Rachel froze, her head jerking toward the man's face. The sight of his eyes—open and focused on her—made her shriek and leap back. Almost tumbling to the ground on shaky legs, she gaped in horror. The corpse stared back.

She closed her eyes and reopened them, but the guy was still lying there looking at her. "This isn't good," she said.

"What isn't good?" he asked with interest.

His voice sounded weak. But, hey! For a dead guy,

even a weak voice was a neat trick. Rachel shook her head in awe.

"What isn't good?" the corpse asked again, sounding a little stronger this time.

"I'm hallucinating," Rachel explained politely, then noticed the stranger's eyes. She paused to stare at them. Rachel had never seen such gorgeous eyes. Like her earlier imaginings, they were an exotic silver-blue. She had never seen eyes that shade before. In fact, had she been asked, she would have said they were a scientific impossibility.

Rachel relaxed, and the fear and tension slipped out of her. She had never seen silver eyes before. They didn't exist. Earlier she'd imagined his eyes were silver, and she was obviously imagining now that they were wide open and that color. There was suddenly no doubt in her mind; she was hallucinating, and it was all due to her skyrocketing temperature. Jeez, it must have hit dangerous levels.

The corpse sat up, drawing Rachel's attention back to him. She had to remind herself, "It's a hallucination. The fever."

John Doe's eyes narrowed on her. "You have a fever? That explains it."

"Explains what?" Rachel asked, then grimaced as she realized she was talking to her hallucination. Which maybe wasn't much worse than talking to dead people, she reasoned, and she did that all the time. Besides, the stiff had a really nice voice, kind of warm and whiskey smooth. She wouldn't mind some whiskey. Tea, lemon, honey, and whiskey. Yes, a hot toddy would fix her right up and nip these hallucinations in the bud. Or simply make it so she didn't care about them. Either way would be fine.

"Why you won't come to me?"

Rachel glanced back at the corpse. He wasn't making much sense, but then who said hallucinations had to? She tried to reason with him. "Why would I come to you? You aren't real. You aren't even sitting up."

"I'm not?"

"No, I just think you are. In reality, you're still really lying there dead. I'm just imagining you sitting up and talking."

"Hmm." He grinned suddenly. It was a nice grin. "How do you know?"

"Because dead men don't sit up and talk," she explained patiently. "Please lie back down now. My head is starting to spin."

"But what if I'm not dead?"

That stumped her a minute, but then Rachel recalled that she was feverish and he wasn't really sitting up at all. She decided to prove her point by stepping forward and swinging out, expecting her hand to sail through thin air. Instead, it slammed into a hard chin. The corpse cried out in surprised pain, but Rachel hardly noticed—she was busy shrieking and leaping away again. Her hand stung, but she was too busy yelling to care. The dead man was sitting up.

The room that had been spinning moments before suddenly stopped. It began to darken. "Darn. I'm going to faint," Rachel realized with horror. She told her corpse almost apologetically, "I never faint. Really."

Etienne watched the tall redhead slip to the floor, then slid carefully off the cold metal table and peered around. He was in the morgue. The realization made him grimace. This was not somewhere he'd ever, in three hundred years of living, aspired to be.

Giving a shudder he knelt to examine the woman. The moment he bent to touch her forehead, though, the room immediately began to revolve. It was a result of his weakened state. He'd lost way too much blood—first to the chest wound, then to healing it. He would have to replace that blood soon, but not with this woman's. She was obviously ill, which meant her blood would do little good. He would have to find another source, and soon. But for the moment he would have to ignore his need and weakness the best he could. There were things he had to do.

Etienne brushed the hair away from the woman's face and took in her pallor. Her head had hit the floor with an audible crack. He wasn't surprised to find a bump and an abrasion there. She would have a terrible headache when she awoke, but otherwise she would be fine. Reassured that she was relatively unscathed, he concentrated on attempting to ensure that she wouldn't recall his arrival—that memory, com-

20

bined with his disappearance from the morgue, could raise all sorts of questions he didn't need. Etienne sought her mind with his own, but found her oddly elusive. He couldn't seem to get into her thoughts.

He frowned over the turn of events. Most minds were open books to him. He had never run into this problem before. Except for Pudge, he admitted with a touch of regret. He had never been able to get through the pain and confusion in that boy's head to reach his thoughts and eliminate his knowledge of Etienne's family's special situation. Had Etienne been able, things would have never reached this juncture.

He blamed himself. Etienne considered his inability to sort through the pain and loss in Pudge's mind as a personal failure. Pudge had suffered greatly in the last six months or so: the loss of Rebecca, a woman he had loved and been engaged to marry. Etienne had known her. She had been a processor of high caliber and as sweet as a sunny summer day. She had been something special. Her death in a car accident had been tragic. For Pudge, it had rocked his world. The subsequent death of the man's mother had finished pushing him into a world of pain.

Etienne simply wasn't strong enough to suffer with the lad. The one time he had tried, the loss tearing at Pudge's thoughts had touched Etienne in ways he wouldn't even admit. He didn't know how anyone could suffer the heart-sore state Pudge did without losing his mind. Etienne had barely touched those feelings and had come away both sad and terribly depressed. Pudge experienced it twenty-four hours a day on a daily basis. Etienne fully understood how the other man would seize on the knowledge he had garnered regarding Etienne's supernatural status and use it to give him a purpose in life. It gave the boy something of a shield between himself and his loss.

Etienne had experienced such pain and compassion for the fellow, he had refused to try to sort through his thoughts and try to eliminate the more dangerous memories. But that had left him wide open to attack by the man, which wasn't the most ideal scenario—as tonight's latest murder attempt proved. It was time to try a different tactic. The problem was, Etienne didn't know what that should be. Eliminating the problem seemed easiest, but such a solution was always a last resort. Besides, Etienne couldn't accept the idea of killing someone who was suffering so horribly. It was rather like kicking a dog when it was down.

Shrugging away his upsetting thoughts, Etienne contemplated the redhead again, wondering why he couldn't seem to get into her mind. Loss and pain and teetering on the verge of insanity were not what he was sensing from this woman. The only sensation he had felt was an infinite sense of loneliness, something Etienne was used to feeling himself.

His difficulty now must be because he was so weak, he decided. Well, the woman's fever combined with the knock on her head should convince her she had hallucinated. The woman had claimed he was an hallucination while still conscious, so perhaps that was enough.

Etienne's fingers were smeared with blood when he set her head back on the floor. After a moment's hesitation, he lifted his fingers to his nose, sniffed the sweet scent, then chanced a lick. He frowned. The poor woman needed vitamins or something; she was bordering on anemic. Or perhaps that was just a result of her illness.

Despite himself, his gaze went to her neck. He was *so* hungry. Etienne fought the temptation to bite her. He needed blood, but it wouldn't help him to take it from someone who was ill. And this woman was definitely ill. Her skin had felt on fire under his cool hand, and her face was flushed with blood. The scent of it was driving him wild and making his body cramp with hunger. His body didn't care that she was ill and would do him little good, it smelled blood and wanted some.

Forcing his basest instincts away, he straightened, grabbing weakly at the edge of the table he had been lying on to keep his balance when the room again swayed. He was waiting for his legs to regain some strength when the swinging doors behind him suddenly opened. Etienne turned his head slowly. A man had entered and stood frozen just inside the room.

"Who—?" The guy's gaze went from Etienne to the

woman crumpled on the floor, then back to Etienne's naked, bloodstained chest. "Oh, man!"

Much to Etienne's amusement, the guy glanced around wildly, then held out the coffee he carried as if the hot liquid were a deterrent. "What did you do to Rach? What are you doing here?"

"Rach?" Etienne glanced down at the woman on the floor. Rach. Short for Rachel, no doubt. A pretty name for a pretty lady. A pretty sick lady, from what he could tell. The woman should be home in bed. He glanced at the newcomer. "Are you sick too?"

"Sick?" The fellow straightened somewhat, bewilderment crossing his face. Apparently that was the last thing he'd expected to be asked. "No."

Etienne nodded. "Good. Come here."

"I—" The man's mouth froze in the refusal he'd been about to make, then his hands lowered and he moved forward as if compelled. Which, of course, he was. Allowing the orange juice he held in one hand and the coffee he carried in the other to hang at his side, the man continued forward until he stood directly before Etienne.

"I need some of your blood. I need a lot of blood but will only take a bit from you," Etienne explained. Not that it really mattered or he expected permission; the man stood silent and still, his gaze unfocused.

Etienne hesitated. He hadn't bitten anyone in a long time. In years, really. Doing so was frowned upon by his people now that there were blood banks. Still, this was an emergency. He had lost a lot of blood, and it

24

had left him extremely weak. He needed to feed to restore himself enough to get home.

He cast an apologetic glance at his victim, then used a hand at the back of the man's neck to tilt his head, nicely exposing the throat. The man stiffened and made a slight sound of protest as Etienne's teeth pierced his skin, but he relaxed with a moan as Etienne began to drink. The blood was warm and rich, nourishing. It was also much tastier than the cold bagged blood he'd become used to. It reminded Etienne of days gone by, and he partook of a bit more than he intended. It wasn't until his donor sagged weakly against him that he forced himself to stop. Easing the fellow into the rolling chair next to the woman crumpled on the floor, he checked him to be sure he hadn't done any lasting damage. He hadn't.

Relieved to find the man's heartbeat steady and strong, Etienne took the time to wipe his memory clean, then straightened, his glance catching on a container on the desk. He immediately recognized the object inside: a bullet. His hand moved to his chest to absently rub the still healing wound, then he reached out for the container and checked the label.

This was the bullet that had stopped his heart. The woman's removal of it had allowed his body to heal. Otherwise, he'd still be on the table. It was proof of his existence and couldn't be left behind.

Pocketing the bullet, Etienne did a quick search of the room. Finding the paperwork left behind by the EMTs, he realized he would have to find them, clear the memory of the incident from their minds, and get their paperwork as well. He supposed there would be police reports and other things he would have to take care of too. It was going to be a bigger project than he liked, and one with which he would need help. The thought made Etienne grimace. He'd have to ask Bastien, which meant the family would find out, but there was no help for it. This incident had to be removed from public memory.

Resignation overwhelming him, Etienne collected his shredded shirt and suit jacket, and did one more quick search of the room to be sure there was nothing of his left behind. Then he borrowed one of the lab coats hanging from a peg by the door. He donned it, found a garbage bag for the bullet and his ruined clothing, then quickly left the morgue.

Bastien would have to be called in to help clean up. Etienne just hoped his older brother wouldn't tell their mother. Marguerite would have fits if she caught wind of this. She had gotten a taste of Pudge's suffering from Etienne shortly after his attempt to read the other fellow and, a very soft-hearted woman, she had agreed with Etienne that Pudge shouldn't be killed. But she hadn't had an alternative solution, and she'd been annoyed with Etienne for being unable to come up with more useful ideas himself.

Etienne grimaced as he made his way quickly out of the basement of the hospital. He hated failure in any form.

Chapter Two

"Well, that was depressing," Etienne commented as he led the way out of the crowded theater.

"It was supposed to be a comedy," his mother Marguerite said apologetically. "It was advertised as a comedy."

"Well, it missed that boat by a mile at least." He clapped Bastien on the back. "Still, happy birthday, brother."

"Thank you."

Bastien sounded less than enthused, but Etienne couldn't blame him. After four hundred years, celebrating birthdays was probably a bit of a drag. Hell, after only three hundred, Etienne would gladly let his own pass without notice, but he knew he would be no more fortunate than Bastien at avoiding some sort of celebration. Their mother would insist on marking their births every single year, no matter how many accrued. Marguerite Argeneau loved her children. She was glad they had been born and believed life was to be celebrated. Etienne supposed he should be glad she bothered. It was good to have family.

"Oh, dear. It's raining," Marguerite said as they joined the milling throng under the building's awning. The theatergoers were obviously reluctant to brave the downpour.

"Hmm." Etienne glanced out into it. His gaze flickered with disinterest over the autos moving slowly by, but halted rather abruptly on a car parked across the street. Recognition struck him like a bolt of lightning. It looked very like the car with which Pudge had run him down. That incident had occurred a couple of weeks before the shooting, but Etienne had walked away from it. His body had repaired in a few moments the broken femur and fractured skull he'd suffered. Fortunately, no one had witnessed the attack or his spontaneous healing.

As he watched, Pudge's vehicle's engine started, the driving lights came on, and it pulled into traffic. Etienne had just relaxed when his mother asked, "Was that him?" He immediately tensed again.

His mother knew everything. She had been fretting over the situation since the shooting. After being asked several times what he intended to do about his assailant, Etienne had been forced to admit that he didn't know. He had tried to reassure his mother by promising he would be more careful and that it was all really amusing, but she hadn't taken the comment well at all. Now, here was Pudge making his life more difficult.

"No. I'm sure it wasn't," he reassured her, then attempted to head off another lecture. "You two wait here, and I'll bring the car around."

He left before they could debate the matter. The theater had no valet parking, but Etienne had been fortunate enough to find a spot a bare half a block away. He was grateful for that now, escaping as he was any chance of a lecture by rushing off through the rain. He nodded at the lot attendant as he passed the booth, then rushed to his car, pushing the button on his keychain to unlock the doors. He then pushed the second button to start the vehicle for him, a nifty little gadget he'd had installed just the week before in preparation for the coming winter. Winters in Canada could be bitterly cold, and there was nothing as nasty as getting into an icy vehicle.

He was only a few feet away when he started the car this night. He was reaching for the door handle when it revved to life, and that's what saved him. Had he been inside the vehicle, the explosion might very well have finished him. As it was, he was caught by the blast, a red hot wave that picked him up and threw him back several feet. Etienne smelled burnt flesh, pain radiated through him, then he felt and knew nothing.

"Hey, you're back!"

Rachel glanced up from her overdue paperwork and smiled at Fred and Dale, who wheeled in a covered gurney. It was her first day back since the night she'd been so sick she'd fainted on the job. She'd woken some time later to find Tony kneeling over her, weak, pale, and claiming he'd caught her flu bug because he didn't feel well, either.

Rachel didn't recall much about fainting. She had a vague dreamlike memory of Dale and Fred bringing someone in, but didn't recall anything more than that, and there had been no new bodies about when she regained consciousness. Positive that it had all been part of some fever-induced hallucination, Rachel had decided bed was the place for her and called in a replacement. She'd asked if Tony wanted a replacement as well, but he'd felt better after a couple of moments and insisted he would be fine.

Rachel had been sick as a dog for a week. She'd suffered some of the strangest dreams too, filled with handsome, silver-eyed corpses that sat up on gurneys and spoke to her. But those had stopped as she started to feel better, and for the first time since she'd got the job on the hospital morgue night shift, Rachel was glad to be coming to work.

Well, mostly glad. She was a morning person and

genuinely hated working nights. She liked daylight. Working all night then sleeping all day was annoying and made her moody, and she couldn't seem to sleep in the evening. It was only after her shift, when Rachel dragged her exhausted self home, that she was able to sleep, and then it was interrupted slumber, up and down, waking then falling back to sleep.

"I hear you were pretty sick. This isn't much of a welcome back. Sorry," Dale said as Rachel grabbed a table and wheeled it over next to the stretcher.

"What is it?" she asked curiously.

"Crispy critter." Fred tugged the sheet free to reveal the charred remains of a burn victim.

"House fire?" Rachel asked with a grimace.

"Car explosion. He was caught in the blast," Dale answered.

"Yeah." Fred stared at the body, then shook his head. "Strange thing was, we thought there was a heartbeat. We got him in the ambulance, no beat. Then, halfway here, there's another beat. Then no beat again. The guy couldn't decide if he was dead or not, I guess. The doc pronounced him dead when we got here."

Rachel glanced curiously at the corpse, then took the clipboard Dale held out.

"Where's Tony?" the EMT asked as he watched her sign the necessary papers.

"He's off. Sick."

"Caught your flu bug, did he?" Fred chuckled.

"Not from me. From his nurse friend." Rachel watched them shift the body to the steel table, then she returned the clipboard.

"So, I hear we're not going to have your smiling face around here at night anymore," Dale said. "Congratulations."

"Congratulations?" Rachel stared at him blankly.

"On getting the assistant coroner job. Tony told us about it last time we were here."

Rachel's jaw dropped. "What?"

Fred and Dale exchanged glances, but it was Fred who finally said, "Er . . . Tony said Bob was going to tell you as soon as you got back to work. Bob told you, right?"

Rachel just stared. Bob was Robert Clayton, the coroner. He worked the day shift but often dropped in to give instructions and get reports at the beginning of the night. He hadn't done so tonight. "Jenny told me he called in sick today too. I guess it's his turn to have the flu," she said.

"Oh, shoot, we ruined the surprise."

Rachel continued to stare, but she found herself grinning. She had gotten the assistant coroner's job. She would be off the night shift soon. She'd got it! "Guys!" Rachel began excitedly, then hesitated and asked, "This isn't a joke, right? You aren't pulling my leg?"

Both men shook their heads but looked apologetic. "Nope. You got the job. Just try to act surprised when

Bob tells you. I don't want to get Tony in trouble."

Dale grunted as she launched herself at his chest. Catching him in a hug, she squeezed as tight as she could and laughed happily. "I got the job! Thank you, thank you, for telling me. Man! This is great news. No more nights. No more trying to sleep through buddy next door mowing his lawn. No more not being able to go out with friends 'cause I have to work. This is brilliant!"

"I take it you're happy, then?" Fred laughed as she released Dale and turned to hug him.

"Oh, you'll never know," Rachel said blissfully. "I absolutely, positively *hate* the night shift."

"Well, we'll miss your smiling face," Dale said. "But we're glad you're happy."

"Yup. Just remember to act surprised when Bob tells you," Fred said, patting her shoulder. He glanced at Dale. "We should get back to work."

Rachel stood, smiling as they left, then turned to the gurney and surveyed her guest. She would have to remove his belongings if there was anything left intact, then strip him, tag him, and move him to one of the freezer drawers. She couldn't do it by herself; she'd need help moving the body.

A glance at her watch showed it was nearly midnight. Beth should be arriving soon, a part-timer who filled in when someone was ill. The woman was really getting the hours lately. Normally Beth was the most dependable of workers too, arriving early and willing to work late, but today she'd had car trouble and called in to warn Rachel she'd be late. The woman was waiting for a friend to pick her up and drive her.

She'd be in within the half hour. Once here, Beth could help strip the body, but in the meantime, Rachel herself could remove his possessions and tag him. She glanced down at the unfortunate fellow, then stilled. He didn't seem to be in quite as bad a shape as he had first appeared. In fact, he seemed a *lot* better. When she had first glanced at him, he had seemed almost completely charred, with very little flesh. Now, a lot of the charred color seemed gone. In fact, Rachel realized, it was flaking off, and a lot of it now lay on the metal tabletop. Reaching out, she brushed at the skin on his face, fascinated to see the blackened flesh crumble, revealing healthier skin beneath. She'd never seen anything like it. He was shedding dead flesh like a snake.

Rachel straightened and stared, her heartbeat accelerating. How was this happening? Or was what she thought happening at all? Perhaps that wasn't charred flesh brushing away; perhaps something had been blown onto him by the blast. Perhaps he hadn't been badly burned at all, he just looked as if he had. Rachel knew it was silly; Dale and Fred were excellent EMTs. Still, she found herself looking for a pulse in his wrist. When more of the charring crumbled beneath her fingers, she feared it might interfere with getting a pulse, and she bent to press her ear to his chest instead. At first she felt foolish looking for life in a dead man, but then a thump sounded. Rachel straightened with amazement, then lowered her ear again. Silence followed for an extremely long time, then another thump.

The door banged behind her. "Get away from him! He's a vampire!"

Rachel straightened and whirled gaping in surprise at the man standing in the open doorway. He looked quite mad. It wasn't just the army fatigues he wore under the huge trench coat he opened, or the fact that he had a rifle swinging from a strap over his shoulder and dangling under one arm, or the ax that hung from the other. All of it, plus his wild eyes and his very expression, screamed escapee from the booby hatch.

Rachel eyed him warily and raised one hand. "Now, look, friend," she began in reasonable tones. It was as far as she got. The man charged forward and shoved her aside.

"Didn't you hear me? Get away, lady, get away! He's a vampire. A monster. A beast of the night. Demon spawn. A hell-breathing bloodsucker. I have to dispatch him."

Rachel grabbed the gurney to keep from stumbling, her eyes wide as the man unstrapped his ax and hefted it over his shoulder with both hands. She couldn't believe it. The fool really intended on cutting the head off her corpse. If he was a corpse, she reminded herself. She had heard a heartbeat. Her gaze shot to the man on the table to see that even more of the charring had flaked onto the table. Rachel could make out his features more clearly and he appeared familiar to her.

Without stopping to consider the action, Rachel threw herself between them and shouted "No!" even as the crazy man brought the ax down. She realized her mistake at once. It really would have been smarter to have pushed the man off balance or something. His swing barely slowed, and Rachel's breath left her in a stunned "Unh" as the ax struck. It happened so fast, she hardly felt any pain.

Her attacker cried out in shocked horror and pulled his ax free, but it was too late. Rachel knew as she sagged back against the table, it had been a killing blow. She would bleed to death very quickly.

"I'm sorry. I didn't mean . . ." The man shook his head in horror, then stumbled forward.

Despite herself, Rachel instinctively flinched away from his reaching hands. Regret and sadness covered his face.

"Let me help you. I want to help you. I really never meant to hurt you. Why didn't you stay out of the way? It's him I . . ."

The man's voice died abruptly as a familiar squeak reached Rachel's ears. She recognized the sound of the door to the hall opening, and guessed by the gasp that sounded—not to mention her attacker's expression—that she was right. The squeak sounded again and was followed by the tap of rushing footsteps in the hall.

"I *am* sorry," her attacker said as he turned a tortured expression back to her. "I really am. I never meant to hurt you. Help is on the way, but I have to go. Hang in there," he ordered as he stumbled away. "Whatever you do, don't die. I couldn't live with that."

Rachel stared after him, wanting to cry out, but she didn't have the strength. A moan from behind made her instinctively try to turn. She managed, but that was where her strength gave out. She found herself slumping over the explosion victim's face.

Blood, sweet and warm. Etienne sighed as he swallowed. It eased the agony cramping his body. He needed the nourishing fluid trickling into his mouth, and even his guilt at this woman taking the blow meant for him didn't stop his enjoyment of it. He needed her blood desperately and was grateful.

"Etienne!"

He recognized his mother's voice but couldn't seem to see where it was coming from. Then the warm body lying across him was suddenly lifted away, and he opened his eyes in protest to see his mother bending over him.

"Are you all right, son?" Worry crowded her face as she felt his cheek. "Give me one of those bags of blood, Bastien," she ordered. She turned back to Etienne. "Bastien insisted on stopping at the office on the way to pick some up. Thank God he did." She punctured the bag with one long fingernail, then held it over his open mouth. She did this with three bags before he felt strong enough to sit up.

Grimacing at the sight of his charred flesh peeling away and shedding all around him, Etienne swung his legs off the table and sat up of his own volition. He hadn't lost any blood in the explosion, but his body had used a lot to repair his flesh. A couple more bags and he would be fine. He accepted the next bag his mother handed him and chugged it. As she opened the last for him, Etienne spotted the woman Bastien knelt beside.

"Is she going to be all right?"

His older brother frowned and shook his head. "She's dying."

"She can't die. She saved my life." Etienne ignored the blood his mother held out and forced himself off the table.

"Sit down. You aren't strong enough yet," Marguerite said, her voice sharp.

"I'm fine." Etienne knelt beside the girl, ignoring his mother's muttered, "Sure you're fine. And 'Pokey isn't a real threat, this is all in fun.' Everything's all fun and games until someone gets an ax in the chest."

"Pudge, not Pokey," Etienne corrected, reaching out to check the dying girl's pulse. He recognized her from his last trip to the morgue. She was beautiful and just as pale now as she had been on his last visit—but that time her pallor had been caused by illness. This time she was suffering from blood loss. Etienne was very aware that some of her blood had gone down his throat. The woman had saved his life. He had been weak, but he had seen her leap between him and the ax Pudge wielded.

"I tried to stop the bleeding, but I'm afraid it's too late," Bastien said quietly. "Nothing can save her."

"One thing can," Etienne countered. He tried to roll up his sleeve. The brittle cloth broke away in his fingers, so he just ripped it off.

"What do you think you're doing? You can't turn her," his mother said.

"She saved my life," Etienne repeated.

"We have rules about these things. You can't turn people willy-nilly, and you can't do it without permission."

"I'm allowed to turn a life partner."

"Life partner!" His mother sounded excited rather than upset. Bastien looked worried.

"You don't even know this woman, Etienne," his brother pointed out. "What if you don't like her?"

"Then I won't have a life partner."

"You would give up a life partner for this woman?" Bastien asked.

Etienne paused, then simply nodded. "Without her, I wouldn't have life." He bent his head and bit himself on the wrist. Red liquid bubbled to the surface, and a moment later he took his teeth away and pressed his bleeding flesh to the dying girl's mouth.

"There, all we can do now is wait." Marguerite straightened and turned to her son. "Now we have to tend to you."

"I'm fine," Etienne muttered. His gaze fixed on the woman in his bed. They had taken her from the hospital and brought her here to his home. His mother and Bastien had stripped her, strapped her to the bed, and fit an IV into her arm to feed her the blood she would need to facilitate the changes. Etienne didn't know what to expect. He'd never witnessed a turning. He wasn't too sure it was going well. The woman had been silent and still after he poured his own blood down her throat, but in the car on the way home, she'd started moaning and thrashing about. Etienne still wasn't sure he hadn't been too late, but he was a little more hopeful.

"You're not fine. You're still shedding burnt skin and you're terribly pale. You need rest and blood."

"I can have blood here."

"You need to lie down," his mother insisted. "You're swaying on your feet."

"I'll see to him," Bastien announced and took Etienne's arm.

Etienne considered arguing, but he didn't really have the energy, so he let his brother lead him without protest.

"Which room?" Bastien asked, pausing in the hall outside. "Have you finished furnishing the spare rooms yet?"

"No." Etienne grimaced. "But my coffin is in my office."

"Good Lord! Do you still have that thing?" Bastien shuddered in disgust. "I got rid of mine the moment they were no longer necessary. I don't know how you stand having it."

"It helps me think," Etienne said. "I come up with some of my best ideas in there."

"Hmmm." Bastien led him along the hall, downstairs and to the back of the house. The stairway to the basement was situated in the back corner of the kitchen. His brother urged him down it, holding his arm as his swaying increased. Soon he had Etienne in the coffin in the corner of his office. "I'll be right back," he announced.

Etienne murmured a weary response and closed his eyes. He was exhausted and growing achey. He needed more blood and knew Bastien was fetching him some.

Despite the growing pain of his body attacking itself in search of more blood, Etienne fell asleep. He woke up several moments later to feel a poke in his arm. Opening his eyes, he found Bastien leaning over him, inserting an IV in the vein below his elbow.

"Do I look like Lissianna to you?" he asked irritably.

He tried to move his arm away, but Bastien was stronger.

"No, you don't look like Lissianna. Her face isn't peeling off," his brother responded dryly. "I would have brought you ten nubile virgins to feast on, but I couldn't find any. Virgins are in short supply nowadays, you know."

Etienne gave a weary laugh and relaxed.

"More seriously," Bastien said as he worked, "you need a lot of blood, a lot of rest. It's easier this way. I'll change the bag while you sleep. You'll be back to normal by morning."

Etienne nodded. "Do you think the girl will live?"

Bastien was silent for a moment, then sighed. "We'll have to wait and see. I'll wake you if . . . anything happens," he finished.

Etienne closed his eyes unhappily. "If she dies, you mean. And if she does, it will be all my fault. I should have done something about Pudge."

"You can't blame yourself, Etienne. It's hard to know how to deal with such a fellow. I haven't come up with any ideas myself, and I've been pondering the problem since the shooting. We definitely have to deal with him, though." He straightened and frowned. "I'll call Lucern and see if he has any ideas. We'll brainstorm later, when you're feeling better. You just rest for now."

*　　*　　*

It was morning when Etienne awoke. He was back to his old self and feeling a hundred percent again. Lying in the still darkness, he could sense the presence of his mother and brother in his home. He could also sense *her* presence. She lived.

Easing out of his coffin, he removed the IV from his arm, collected the IV stand, and carried it upstairs with him. He stashed it in the kitchen closet where he kept it for emergencies or visits from his sister, then continued through the dark silent house and upstairs.

He found his mother and brother in his bedroom, watching over the woman.

She was writhing and moaning on the bed. Her hair was a damp tangle around her flushed, feverish face. Etienne frowned. "What's wrong with her?" he asked anxiously.

"She's turning," his mother said simply.

Marguerite's calm attitude soothed him somewhat; then Etienne noted the empty bags of blood stacked on the bedside table. There had to be a dozen. Even as he noted this, his mother stood and began to remove yet another empty bag from the IV stand. As if they had done this several times, which they obviously had, Bastien also stood and moved to the small bar fridge Etienne had placed in a corner of the room. He returned with fresh blood.

"Why is she taking so much?" Etienne asked.

"There was a lot of damage, son. She lost a lot of

blood from the wound, and there are also thirty years of living to be repaired."

Etienne relaxed a little more. "How long does this go on?"

Marguerite shrugged. "It depends."

"On what?"

"On what damage needs repairing."

Etienne scowled. "She looked healthy enough, maybe a tad anemic, but—"

"She could have had anything in her system, son," Marguerite said gently. "Cancer, leukemia, anything. You can't always tell from outside appearances."

Reassured, Etienne settled himself on a corner of the bed.

"You look better," Bastien commented. "How are you feeling?"

"Fine." Etienne peered down at his hands. Every trace of black was gone; fresh, healthy pink skin covered his hands and arms. He knew the rest of him would be the same. He'd have to vacuum out the coffin later, though, as he'd left most of the damaged skin inside. "Were you able to get hold of Lucern?"

Bastien nodded. "He's coming over tonight, so we can brainstorm. In the meantime, there's a lot of damage control to do."

Etienne's eyebrows flew up. "What happened?"

"She made the news. Apparently, someone witnessed Pudge in the coroner's office and went for help. That help must have arrived after we left with the two of you, because the news report states they suspect this 'camouflaged, armed man' kidnapped her. They've put out a sketch and description of Pudge. They don't know who he is, but they're looking for him."

"That could work in our favor," Etienne said.

"Yes. If we can get her to go along with a kidnapping story, it could solve the problem of Pudge for you."

Etienne nodded, then glanced to his mother. She was nodding off in her seat. It was well into morning, past the time that they would usually have gone to bed. "I can watch over her now. You two should get some rest."

"Yes." Bastien stood, then moved to urge his reluctant mother to her feet. "We'll come back tonight," he said as he ushered her to the door.

Marguerite turned sleepy eyes back to Etienne. "She shouldn't need much more blood. Perhaps a bag or two. The fever should end soon. I think she's very close to being done. Her wound is pretty much healed. She will probably wake up this evening sometime."

"Yes, Mother." Etienne followed them to the door.

"And you should be able to remove the straps soon. You don't want the poor girl waking up to find herself a prisoner."

"Yes. Of course."

"Etienne," Marguerite added in a solemn voice that

45

signaled what she was about to say was important. "You've never witnessed a turning before, so I should warn you—Rachel's thinking processes won't be very clear for a little while after she first wakes up."

"What do you mean?" Etienne asked.

"Turnees are often confused and closed-minded upon awaking. They have trouble accepting the evidence before them as to their new state and they fight it—and their mind is often in such an uproar that their reasoning skills fly out the window. She may come up with all sorts of excuses for what's going on here, a lot of them outlandish. Just be patient with her until her mind clears and she's able to accept it. Try not to agitate her too much."

Etienne nodded slowly, digesting his mother's words. "Okay. I'll do my best."

"I know you will, son." His mother patted his cheek affectionately, then followed Bastien to the door. "We'll come back early to help," were her last words as the door closed behind her.

Etienne smiled to himself. Family was good, he thought as he turned back to his patient.

Chapter Three

Rachel ached everywhere. Her body was a mass of pain and, for one moment she felt sure she was still suffering the flu that had brought her so low. But when she opened her eyes, Rachel saw at once that she wasn't bundled up in her bed at home. In fact, she'd never before seen the room she was in.

She was struggling to understand how she'd got there, and where exactly *there* was, when memory swamped her—random and confusing memories, a blond-haired man bending over her, holding her half upright and urging her to drink, though there was no glass to drink from. Yet she recalled fluid warm and thick on her tongue. Rachel also had a flash of a madman in khakis and a trench coat wielding an ax. She recalled a horrible pain in her chest, which was followed by a memory of Fred and Dale telling her that she'd got the assistant's job and would soon be off the night shift. The memories seemed out of order, but the last was good and made her smile as she drifted in and out of consciousness. Then Rachel remembered a confusing conversation she'd heard—one that had made very little sense to her at the time and still didn't, but had something to do with life partners and turning. Turning what, and how, she couldn't recall. All in all, the memories were scattered and made very little sense.

Rachel opened her eyes again and glanced around the room. It was blue, with a tasteful modern decor, abstract paintings and silver lamps on either side of the bed. Rachel still wasn't sure where she was or how she'd got there, but she was so weak and exhausted she decided she didn't care and would rest. The moment her eyes drifted closed, though, she had a flash of an ax swinging at her.

Rachel popped her eyes open, and horror consumed her. She'd been struck down by an ax blow, and she had been sure it was a killing one. At least, without aid it would have been. But Rachel had a vague recollection of her attacker, then a silver-eyed man bending over her, telling her to rest and conserve her strength while he checked her wound. He had been similar in looks to the man who had haunted her dreams while she had the flu, but this man's hair had been dark where her dream man was blond.

Obviously, help had come. Rachel just wished her thoughts were a little less murky. While the memory of being brought down by the blow of an ax explained the pain in her chest, it didn't explain the pain through the rest of her body. It also didn't explain where she was. She really should be in a hospital. This definitely wasn't a hospital.

Rachel peered toward the blinds covering the windows. They glowed at the edges with a hint of the sunlight attempting to enter. It was obviously day out. She wished the blinds had been left open so she could perhaps figure out where she was.

Pushing aside the blankets that covered her, Rachel struggled to a sitting position, then peered down at herself. She was completely nude. That was interesting. She never slept in the nude, and hospitals generally put those awful gowns on. Well, this was a wrinkle, and she had no idea what to make of it.

She shifted restlessly on the bed, then glanced down curiously when something pulled at her arm. The sight of an IV near the crook of her elbow made her pause. Her gaze followed the clear tube leading from it to the bag hanging from the IV stand. The bag was deflated and empty, but a drop or two of liquid remained behind—enough for Rachel to recognize it as blood. She had obviously needed a transfusion.

The thought made her glance down at her chest again in search of her wound. She distinctly recalled the ax slamming into her body, yet there were no bandages, and no sign of injury other than a thin scar that marked her chest from her shoulder blade down to the top of one nipple. Her eyes widened incredulously on the scar, and she went still as its meaning struck her: Weeks, perhaps even months, had passed since the attack.

"Dear God," Rachel breathed. How long had she slept? Had she been in a coma? Was she in a special facility for coma cases? That was almost reassuring, until she recalled the promotion she had just got at work. If she had been in a coma for months, she might have lost the position to someone else. Hell, she had probably lost her job altogether. But then why the blood? she wondered, and glanced at the empty IV bag. She could understand the need for a transfusion directly after the attack, but if it had been months, surely she wouldn't need it again now?

Her mind awhirl with questions, Rachel tugged the tube free, leaving the IV itself in place in her arm, then slipped her feet off the bed and tried to stand. It took a great deal of effort to do. Once she had managed, Rachel stood weak and exhausted and gave her idea second thoughts. It was a very short thinking session. As much as her body seemed to want to crawl back into bed and rest and recuperate, it also yearned for something that bedrest couldn't give. She didn't know what it was, just that she had a hankering that needed fulfilling. Even if she had been able to ignore that hankering—though Rachel very much suspected she couldn't if she tried—her mind had a hankering as well. It wanted to know where the heck she was, along with what had happened to the man who attacked her, and whether the man on the steel table really had been alive as she had suspected, or if she had risked her life for a dead man.

It would be just her luck if she had suffered the wound, lost months of time to a coma, and now had a lovely scar for a dead man. Feeling a tad cranky, and strengthened by it, Rachel started for the door, then stopped suddenly as she recalled she was naked. She could hardly walk around in the nude.

A check of the drawer in the nearest bedside table turned up nothing but a couple of books Rachel had already read. Someone had good taste, or at least taste similar to her own.

Her gaze slid around the shadowed room to the three doors leading out of it. There was one to her right along the wall the bed backed onto, and one straight ahead in the wall parallel to the bed, both of which were normal-sized doors. Directly across from the foot of the bed, however, was a double set of doors that were most likely to the closet. They seemed an awfully long distance away, and while Rachel was sure she could reach it, she would be embarrassed to be caught naked halfway there. Besides, she had no guarantee that there would be clothes in it.

After a moment's thought, she tugged the bedsheet out from under the comforter and wrapped it around herself like a toga. Then she moved toward the door in the wall parallel to the bed, deeming it the one most likely to lead to a hall and some answers.

As she had hoped, the door led out into a hallway, but it definitely wasn't the hallway of a hospital. She appeared to be in a house—a rather well-decorated house. Her gaze drifted over the neutral earth tones of the hallway with appreciation. She had used the same colors in her apartment and found them warm and inviting.

But the decor wasn't her main concern at the moment, Rachel reminded herself. The room she had just left was at the end of the hall. Several doors led off the hallway that stretched before her, but there was no evidence of anyone else in attendance. Rachel shifted from one foot to the other in the doorway and considered what to do, but in the end there seemed little choice. She could either stay where she was and wait for someone to come to her, or she could seek out someone to get answers to her questions.

That hankering she was suffering decided for her. Rachel moved out of the door and made her way along the hall. She didn't think to check the doors she passed. The house was so silent, it seemed to scream of emptiness, at least on this floor.

Things didn't appear much more hopeful when she reached the landing. Peering down into the entry below, she frowned at the darkness and silence reaching up to her. Surely she wasn't alone in this house? Someone had to have been changing her IV bag.

Her legs were still a tad shaky, but Rachel was able to manage the stairs without incident, then she stood in the entry and peered about. Every window was covered. This part of the house was as shut against the sun as the bedroom. Rachel instinctively tried the knob of what appeared to be the front door but found it locked. It was an old-fashioned lock, needing a key to open. There was no key around, though she checked the table nearby.

Giving up on the door, Rachel started along the hall in search of someone, anyone, who could explain where she was. She passed unknown rooms full of darkness and shadow, but obviously empty of human inhabitants. At the end of the hall, she pushed open the door and found herself in what appeared to be a kitchen. There she paused and peered around at the dark shapes of a refrigerator, stove, table and chairs. She was about to back out of the room when she noted the soft glow of light coming from under a door on the opposite side.

Excitement coursed through Rachel at this first sign of someone besides herself being present. It was quickly followed by trepidation. But she pushed fear aside and moved to the door. It led to another stairwell, she noted with dismay when she opened it. There was a light on. Rachel hesitated on the landing, unsure what to do. Her strength seemed to be waning again, the cramps returning. It was like the flu, but more intense and pervasive of every portion of her body.

"Hello?" she called out hopefully.

Of course there was no answer. No one came rushing to explain or help. Rachel was creeping through a dark and empty house, trailing a sheet like some old-fashioned gown.

"I've stepped into a Gothic novel," she muttered to herself with amused disgust but couldn't laugh. It truly felt like she had. It made her suffer some pretty weird thoughts—like, perhaps she was dead and this was Hell. Or it could be Heaven. Rachel was relatively sure that she hadn't done anything in her life to land herself in Hell. Unless . . . Perhaps she hadn't got last rites. The priests said if you died without those . . .

Rachel pushed such depressing thoughts aside and started down the stairs. Better to know what she was dealing with than to not. Ignorance wasn't bliss.

She managed the stairs, though just barely. Pain and weakness were really setting in now. Her legs were almost rubbery with the combination by the time she descended the last step onto the carpeted basement floor. This can't be Hell, she decided as her feet sank into the plush carpeting. Surely Hell wasn't so well appointed.

Perhaps it was a dream. Perhaps she hadn't really woken up yet. That idea was a lot easier to accept. Rachel even liked it. It certainly beat the heck out of being dead. Dreams could be entertaining. As long as they didn't turn into nightmares.

Shrugging that disquieting thought aside, she allowed her gaze to slide over the doors available to her. The first door was open and revealed what appeared to be a laundry room in the bit of light that spilled from the hallway. The second door opened onto what turned out to be a wine cellar of all things. That left the third door, the only one with light spilling out from behind it.

Rachel took a deep bracing breath, then pushed that door open. At first glance, the room beyond appeared to be some sort of security room. Computer equipment lined the large L-shaped desk that covered two walls. There were at least four computers all told, and as many monitors. But the idea that it was a security room slipped away when she realized the images on the screens were not of this house.

She moved into the room to get a better look at the images. One was a freeze-frame of a spooky night forest. Another was an image of an old house even creepier than this one. The third held a frozen computer image of a beautiful woman clutching a cross she held thrust out as if to ward off evil. The last monitor was blank.

Fascinated by the woman, Rachel ignored the rest of the room and moved to stand in front of that monitor. She was beautiful, with long, dark hair and large silver eyes. She also looked familiar.

"I know you," Rachel murmured to the image. "Where do I know you from?"

The woman seemed to be part of the menage of memories floating loose in her mind.

"Where do I know you from?" Rachel repeated a little louder, as if expecting the monitor to answer. It didn't, but a sudden creaking from behind her did. Rachel whirled, the hair on the back of her neck standing on end. There was an old-fashioned coffin along the wall next to the door that she hadn't noticed upon entering, and now its lid was slowly pushed upward until a pale hand propelling it could be seen. It continued to creak all the way open, revealing a wrist, an arm, and then a shoulder.

A moment passed, seeming to stretch into hours; then Rachel's breath left her in a whoosh and her legs gave out as the coffin's occupant sat up. Rachel crashed to the floor, kneeling, mouth agape as the blond man from her dreams peered around until he spotted her.

"Oh." He seemed surprised by her presence. "Hello. I thought I heard someone talking, but I didn't sense your presence, so I wasn't sure I wasn't simply dreaming. I should have known. I worried that you might awake on your own and be afraid."

"Oh, fudge," Rachel breathed as the room began to spin. "I'm going to faint."

"Really?" he asked. "You seem to do that a lot."

Rachel dropped weakly onto her butt with a thump

as the muscles in her thighs turned to putty. However, she didn't faint, and after a moment the room's spinning slowed and steadied. She was even able to ask, "Who are you?"

"Sorry." He made a face and bounded out of his coffin in one smooth move, then let the lid fall closed. "Rude of me not to introduce myself. I'm your host," he announced with a courtly bow. "Etienne Argeneau, at your service."

"You're the dead guy!" Rachel gasped as he moved closer. She noted his silver eyes.

"You remember me." He seemed pleased by the news, though she couldn't imagine why. Rachel certainly wasn't pleased to find herself talking to a dead man—a man who had, in fact, died twice, she realized. He was easily recognizable as the gunshot victim she had managed to convince herself had been a fever-induced hallucination, but it had taken her a few more moments to recognize him as the crispy critter from last night . . . or whenever it was she had stopped the armed guy from hacking his head off, she corrected herself. She frowned as she recalled the attack.

"Get back, he's a vampire," the madman had yelled.

Rachel's gaze slid to the coffin, then back to her self-proclaimed host. There were no such things as vampires. Yet this guy had just leapt out of a coffin and apparently got up twice and walked away from death.

"Vampire?" He echoed the word with amusement,

making Rachel realize she had spoken aloud. "Now, what would make you think I was a vampire?"

Rachel gaped at him, then glanced toward his coffin. Her host followed her gaze, and his expression turned slightly sheepish. "Well, I realize sleeping in a coffin must seem odd, but it helps clarify my thoughts. Besides, you were in my bed and I didn't think you'd appreciate my joining you."

Rachel shook her head. No. She wouldn't have been happy to awake with a stranger in bed with her. Especially a dead stranger. That was taking the idea of bringing work home with her a bit far. Not that she was home, she reminded herself.

"Where am I?" That seemed the obvious question at this point.

"My home," her host answered promptly. "Mother wanted to take you to the family manse, but I insisted we bring you here."

"Ah." Rachel nodded as if her question had been answered, then asked, "Your mother?" Did vampires have mothers? She supposed they must. They were made, not hatched. Or was it turned rather than made? Rachel was a little fuzzy on the point.

Aware that he was moving toward her, she instinctively reached for the cross that usually hung around her neck. It wasn't there, of course. Silly to imagine it would be, Rachel supposed. Her host would hardly ignore such a threat to his well-being. Without the cross, she did the only thing she could think of—she

58

made a cross out of her pointer fingers and thrust them out. She was most amazed when it worked and her host paused.

He didn't look properly horrified, however. Tilting his head, he appeared more curious than cringing. He said, "I just thought you might be more comfortable in a chair." Apparently unaffected by her makeshift cross, the man then swept her into his arms.

Hooking the desk chair with his foot, he tugged it out, and before Rachel could draw enough breath to either protest or scream, he set her in it. He then stepped back to lean against the L-shaped desk. "So, tell me a little about yourself," he suggested in a chatty tone. "I know your name is Rachel Garrett and you work in the hospital morgue, but—"

"How did you know that?" Rachel snapped.

"It was on your hospital ID card," he explained.

"Oh." Her eyes narrowed. "How did I get from there to here?"

"We brought you."

"Why?"

He seemed surprised. "Well, they couldn't help you, and we knew you'd need time to adjust."

"Adjust to what?"

"To your change."

"Change?" she squeaked. Rachel was beginning to get a very bad feeling. Before he could respond, she blurted, "Some crazy man hit me with an ax."

Her host nodded solemnly. "You saved my life taking that blow. Thank you. I could hardly do any less in return."

"You couldn't?" She frowned at his statement, almost asking how he had saved her, but she suddenly wasn't sure she wanted to know. After all, the man hadn't denied being a vampire.

Recognizing the ridiculous nature of her thoughts, Rachel shook her head. There were no such things as vampires, and even considering it . . . Well, that way lay madness. Instead, she asked, "When was that? The attack, I mean?"

"Last night."

Rachel blinked in confusion. "Last night, what?"

"Last night is when you were injured," he explained patiently.

Rachel immediately began to shake her head. This was impossible. The wound had healed into a scar. She glanced down and tugged her makeshift toga aside just to be sure she hadn't imagined it, then froze, her eyes widening. The scar was gone. Reaching beneath her sheet, she prodded the unbroken skin with disbelief, as if touching it would make the scar suddenly reappear, but it was gone.

"We heal more quickly than mortals."

"We?" Rachel echoed. "Mortals?" Her tongue felt fat and dry. Unwieldy. Yet, somehow she formed the words. At least, he seemed to understand them.

"Yes. I'm afraid there was only one way to save you, and while we generally like to receive permission before we turn someone, you weren't really capable of the decision. Besides, I couldn't simply let you die after you had sacrificed your life for mine."

"My life?" Rachel's tongue felt as if it was made of cotton.

"Yes. Your life."

"Turned?"

"Yes."

"Turned into what, exactly?" Her cotton tongue made the question "urned inoo ut aghactly," but again he understood.

"An immortal."

Immortal. Rachel felt a moment's relief. She had very much feared hearing the word vampire. Immortal sounded much better. *Immortal.* It made her think of that movie with that actor—what was his name? Good looking, cool accent, Sean Connery had played another immortal . . . Oh, yes. Christopher Lambert, and the movie had been *Highlander*. And in it immortals weren't evil bloodsucking demons, but . . . well . . . immortal. It seemed to her that there had been some evil immortals, though—and some nastiness about cutting off heads. Some nonsense about there could be only one. She didn't care for the idea of having her head cut off.

"Not immortal like Sean Connery and Christopher Lambert in *Highlander*," her host explained patiently, making her realize that she had been muttering her thoughts aloud. "Immortal like . . . well, the closest thing you would understand is a vampire."

"Oh, jeez." Rachel was suddenly on her feet and running. Time to go. She had heard enough. This had moved beyond a cool dream and into the nightmare realm. Unfortunately, her legs were no more steady now than they had been. They gave out halfway to the door, and her head spun. She fell back, limp.

Her host scooped her into his arms. Saying something about it being time for her to go back to bed, he carried her out of the room and upstairs. All Rachel could think to say was a plaintive, "But I don't want to be a bloodsucking demon. How will I do my makeup if I don't have a reflection?"

He said something in response, but Rachel wasn't listening; she was thinking of the few episodes of *Buffy the Vampire Slayer* she had caught on TV as she prepared for work and added, "Those facial lumps and bumps are so unattractive."

"Facial lumps and bumps?"

Rachel glanced at the face of the man carrying her. He didn't look anything like she imagined vampires would look. He wasn't really pale—that must have been an effect of the lighting in the computer room. Here in the lighted stairwell, his skin looked natural and even flushed with color. He looked like a typical healthy male, not a dead man. He also smelled vaguely of some rather expensive cologne, and not like a rotting corpse.

"Facial lumps?" he repeated.

"Like Angel and Spike and the rest of the vampires on TV. Their faces reshape and contort into these really unattractive demon faces," she explained absently. She wondered if he was mad. There were no such things as vampires; thus, this man thinking he was one . . . On the other hand, she distinctly recalled an ax entering her body, yet there was no longer any sign of injury. Had she really been injured? Perhaps she had imagined the scar earlier in the bedroom. Or perhaps this was *all* a dream.

"Your face won't contort," he assured her. "You won't look like a demon."

"Then, how do your teeth extend?" Rachel asked. It was a test pure and simple, to see if he was mad.

"Like this."

He opened his mouth, but the fake vampire teeth she had expected weren't there. In fact, his teeth looked perfectly normal—for the count of a heartbeat; then his canines began to lengthen as if sliding along oiled hinges.

Rachel moaned and closed her eyes. "It's just a dream," she reassured herself as Etienne stepped out of the stairwell and carried her through the kitchen. "Just a dream."

"Yes. Just a dream." His voice was warm and soothing by her ear.

Rachel relaxed a little at his words, but only a little. She remained in his arms as he carried her up the second set of stairs and along the hall. At last he set her in the bed she had so briefly left.

Opening her eyes, Rachel snatched at the blankets and tugged them up to her chin. Not that she needed to be defensive. He seemed to have no interest in attacking her and he was instead walking away toward a small fridge. He bent to open it and retrieved a bag of what was unmistakably blood.

Rachel's eyes narrowed suspiciously and she tensed when her host walked back to affix the blood bag to the IV stand. "What are you doing?" she asked. She tried to snatch her arm away when he took it, but he was much stronger than she.

"You need this." He slid the tube back into the IV in her arm with the skill of a nurse. "Your body is going through changes, and healing took a lot of blood. This will ease the cramps so you can sleep again."

Rachel wanted to argue, but the moment the blood slid down the clear tube and began to pour into her body, some of the aching she had suffered since awakening began to ease. So did the odd hankering she'd been experiencing. Apparently, this was what her body had yearned for.

"You will sleep now."

It sounded more like an order than a suggestion. Never having cared much for being ordered about, Rachel wanted to argue . . . but she was suddenly quite weary. Her exhaustion and lassitude were growing in proportion to the blood entering her. She felt much as she did after a big carbohydrate-rich holiday meal.

"This is a dream, remember?" her host said soothingly. "Just sleep. All will be well when you wake up."

"Sleep," Rachel muttered.

Yes, sleep would be good. And when she woke up for real, she would find herself in a hospital, or perhaps snoozing at her desk. Perhaps it was *all* a dream—the crispy critter, the ax-wielding madman, everything. It was such a reassuring thought that she closed her eyes and let her mind drift. Rachel did have one regret just before she gave in to sleep: If it was all a dream, then the handsome, vital man who had carried her upstairs was a dream too, and that was rather a shame.

Etienne watched Rachel's face relax into sleep. She was a beautiful woman—nearly as tall as him too, which he liked—but her life had obviously been a stressful one. There were vague tension lines around her eyes and mouth. Those would disappear once she'd had enough blood, but they were signs that her life had not been an easy one. He brushed a fiery red curl away from her cheek, smiling when irritation flickered on her face and she brushed his hand away like a pesky fly.

Yes, Rachel was an interesting woman. She showed signs of being prickly. He liked prickly, and he had always enjoyed challenges.

His smile faded as he considered Rachel's reaction. She would be resistant to the change at first. The woman obviously had all sorts of preconceived ideas about his people. Lumpy faces? Bloodsucking demons? He would have to clarify matters when next she awoke. Vampire wasn't a label he liked, but it was expedient, and one most people could at least understand. It would serve as a starting point in the conversation to come.

Stifling a yawn, Etienne glanced around his room. He would have liked to remain here, didn't want to leave her alone, but sleep was creeping over him. From her pallor, he estimated she needed another two or three bags of blood, and cramps would wake her again when this bag ran out. He didn't want her wandering around weak and shaky—she could fall and hurt herself.

After a hesitation, Etienne stretched out on the bed. He crossed his ankles and clasped his hands behind his head, then turned to glance at her. He would stay, catnap, and change the bags as needed. Her restless stirring when the bag ran out would wake him to the task.

Chapter Four

The room was dark and silent, but something awakened her. Rachel lay still for a moment, simply listening, collecting her thoughts. It wasn't *completely* silent. Outside, it was obviously windy. She could hear the soft rush, the battering of the building and the rustle of blown branches. Those were the only sounds, however; there was nothing to signal where she was—nothing except the memories crowding her.

Those memories were horrific, not to mention confusing. They came to her in order this time. Rachel distinctly recalled Fred and Dale arriving with the burn victim and telling her she'd earned the position she'd sought. Then, she recalled her confusion at the burn victim's state and the wild-eyed madman bursting into the room. Rachel had a very clear memory of his ax slamming into her. Yet now she was feeling no pain.

She wanted to believe her feeling of health was because she'd been given some excellent drugs, but she also recalled waking up earlier, meeting the handsome blond man with silver eyes. Etienne. He was the same man who had haunted her dreams while she'd been sick the week before the ax attack. She distinctly recalled waking up and him claiming to be a vampire, then showing her his extendible teeth. Which should only convince her that all her memories were nothing more than a dream. There were no such things as vampires, after all.

Rachel shifted cautiously where she lay, mentally prepared for a burst of pain to rip through her chest from the wound she'd sustained, but there was none. The hospital had obviously given her some pretty strong drugs. No doubt those drugs were leaving her confused as well as warding off the pain she should feel.

Amazing drugs, Rachel decided. She hadn't felt this strong or healthy in years. At least, not since she'd started working the night shift.

Moving carefully to avoid disrupting the IV she could feel trailing out of her arm, Rachel sat up and blinked several times, trying to bring the surrounding dark shapes into better focus. The room seemed large in the blackness, much larger than a hospital room should be.

Rachel was frowning over this when she realized that, from the shadows and shapes she could make out in the darkness, the room very much resembled the bedroom from her dream. A light had been on then, revealing a draped bed and blue decor. She recalled creeping down through an empty house to a basement where that silver-eyed man had risen from a coffin.

Definitely a dream, she decided.

Unable to see herself in the darkness, Rachel ran her hands over her upper body. She wore no clothes, and there was no sign of injury—just as it had been in her dream. Had she been hurt at all? What was dream and what was reality?

"Oh, jeez." Feeling a little panicked, Rachel thrust the blankets aside, hardly noticing as the IV tore from her arm. She paused long enough to feel around for the bedsheet, which she had been lying on top of rather than under. Pulling it from the bed, she fashioned it around herself toga style. Again? She was suffering a definite sense of déjà vu.

Don't even think like that, Rachel ordered herself firmly, suddenly desperate to find someone, anyone, to verify what had happened. She had a vague recollection of the setup of the room, but since she had already decided it was a dream she remembered, she couldn't go by it. Instead, she crept along the bed toward the wall it should back onto, arms extended.

Once she felt the wall, Rachel eased her way carefully along it in search of a door.

The first thing she found was a piece of furniture. Actually her knee found it—with a crack to her shins. Rachel paused to rub her aching leg before she felt the outline of the item was a chair.

"Nice place for it," she muttered irritably, then forced herself to pause and take a deep breath. She should have turned on the bedside lamp. But, then, she hadn't felt one, or even a bedside table. Of course, her arms had been extended and she'd probably missed it because of that. Every room had bedside tables, didn't they?

Rachel briefly considered returning the way she'd come, but it seemed an awfully long way back. In the end she decided to keep going and eased around the chair to continue forward. Her breath caught at the sudden feel of wood beneath her fingers. Then she found a doorknob and quickly turned it. She thrust the door open. Black yawned before her, more absolute than that of the room in which she stood. After a hesitation, Rachel felt along the wall until she found a switch. She flicked it on.

Light exploded from overhead, forcing her to close her eyes. When she could open them again, Rachel found herself standing in the doorway of a bathroom. A large sauna tub lay directly before her. There was also a toilet and a bidet. The owner of this establishment obviously had European taste, which proved more than anything that she was definitely not in a hospital. Unless it was a hospital in Europe.

Which was a possibility, Rachel supposed. She might be in a special clinic for coma patients. Although the bathroom was larger and more luxurious than the average hospital bathroom, and she didn't think that European clinics—even expensive European clinics—would waste this kind of space on a comatose patient. Besides, Rachel's health insurance wouldn't cover such expensive care, and her family was middle class, hardly able to pay for such extravagant accommodations.

More confused than before, Rachel started to turn away but paused as she glimpsed herself in the mirror. Caught, she eased closer until the vanity counter halted her progress.

She stood for several minutes, staring. She looked good. Darn good. Her hair was shiny and vital—a dark red with its natural wave and not the usual flyaway orange-red that needed a good oil treatment. She hadn't looked this good since she was a teenager. The fast-paced, stress-filled life of University, then the working world had not been kind. Her face was flushed and healthy now, however, hardly the complexion of someone recovering from a chest wound. Nor like the pale undead. A wry smile tugged at her lips. Vampires had no reflection. She was not a vampire.

Not that she had believed she was, Rachel assured herself. She grimaced then admitted, "Okay. For one minute I was afraid those dream memories of a silver-eyed man telling me I'd been 'turned' to save my life were true.

"Silly girl," she chided. But she also lifted her lips into a snarl so that her teeth showed. They were normal, and Rachel could have sobbed with relief. "Thank you, God," she breathed.

Sucking in a fortifying breath, she unwrapped the sheet she wore for the final test. She found her upper chest and the mounds of her breasts smooth and unblemished. Shoot. Not that she wanted to be wounded, but it would have been better for disproving the validity of her dreams.

It was then that Rachel also realized the sheet she wore was the same pale blue as she'd dreamt. A moment of panic swamped her, but she forced herself to control it.

"Okay. Stay calm," she ordered. "There is a perfectly sensible, sane explanation for all this. You just have to find it."

Reassured a little by the sound of her own voice, Rachel turned away from her reflection. Peering back into the bedroom, she surveyed the furnishings now visible in the light. Her heart sank. It was indeed the room from her dream.

Her gaze went to the IV stand. The bag was mostly empty, but as before there was a drop or two of red liquid remaining. Blood.

"Oh, jeez." Rachel shifted from one foot to the

other, then walked to the other door and out of the bedroom. She had to know what lay beyond. Surely not the hall from her dream?

"Damn," she breathed as the door opened onto just that—the long, empty hall she remembered so well. This was getting spooky. Taking a deep breath, she tried for rational thought. Okay, so the hallway and even the bedroom had been in her dream. That was simple enough to explain. Perhaps she hadn't been totally comatose when she'd been transferred here. Perhaps she'd been semiconscious, or feverish or something, and awake enough to see and remember the hall and the bedroom.

Ignoring any flaws in that reasoning, Rachel stepped out into the hall and walked to the landing. In what she had thought was a dream, the entry below had been dark and empty. It was still empty, but no longer dark. Light spilled out of one of the adjacent rooms, and she could hear the faint rumble of voices.

After a hesitation, Rachel moved down the stairs. She squeezed her toes into the hardwood with each step, an effort to prove to herself that this time she wasn't merely dreaming.

"You told her it was a dream?"

Rachel slowed as that question came clearly to her ears. A woman's strident voice continued, "Etienne! What were you thinking?"

"I was thinking that she needed to rest, and that this was the easiest way to calm her," a male voice answered in slightly defensive tones. "She was a bit freaked out, Mother."

"Understandably so," came another voice, similar to that of the dream man who had claimed to be her host, but deeper, more solemn somehow, despite its present amusement. "Especially since she caught you sleeping in that coffin of yours."

"Oh, Etienne!" the woman exclaimed. "Surely you don't still have that nasty old thing?"

"I don't normally sleep in it"—he was now definitely defensive—"but I've had some of my best ideas resting in that coffin, Mother. Besides, she was sleeping in my bed."

"Well, surely you have other beds here, son. You *have* finally gotten around to furnishing the spare rooms, haven't you?"

Etienne's answer wasn't really audible from where Rachel stood. Realizing she had stopped, she eased herself forward to stand outside the door. Then she hesitated, waiting until the woman spoke again before peeking around the door frame at the room's occupants.

"Well, you are going to have a lot of explaining to do when she comes in here, Etienne. And now that you've already lied to her, she may not trust anything you say." The woman sounded annoyed. She also looked perturbed, Rachel saw, as she gaped at the speaker. The woman was beautiful, incredibly beautiful, the kind of woman other women hated to be seen around. She was also the living image of the woman Rachel had seen on the monitor downstairs. Long wavy hair, large silver eyes, a pouty mouth.

Mother, the man named Etienne had called her? Rachel shook her head in denial. This woman looked to be in her late twenties. Thirty at the most. She was definitely not the blond man's mother. Mother had to be a nickname, perhaps chosen because she was a worrier and a fusser.

"I know."

Rachel glanced to the speaker, Etienne. The woman had addressed him as son. Impossible. Her gaze roamed over his perfect face and tawny hair. He was the man from her dreams—sexy, blond, and strong. If her dream had been reality, he had carried her up two flights of stairs as if she weighed nothing. Yes, he was definitely strong.

"And she has negative notions of what we are, of course," Etienne continued.

"Of course she does," the second man said. He was a darker-haired version of Etienne, though the two men appeared the same age. "Most people do."

"How negative?" The woman sounded wary.

"I believe the phrase she used was 'bloodsucking demons,' " Etienne said.

"Oh, dear." The woman sighed.

"And she thinks our faces contort like on *Buffy the Vampire Slayer.*"

The dark-haired man grimaced. "Nasty show. Gave us all a bad name."

"You've seen it, Bastien?" Etienne sounded surprised.

"No, but I've heard of it. There are a couple of fans at the office. Have you seen it?"

"Yes. It's quite entertaining, really. And Buffy is an interesting little package."

"Can we get back to the subject at hand?" the woman asked—a bit archly. "Etienne, how are you going to explain?"

"I'll just tell her it was the only way to save her. Which it was. I couldn't let her die after she saved my life."

The woman harrumphed, then turned to Bastien. "Did you handle the hospital officials?"

"I didn't have to," the man announced. "We went unseen. We're just lucky they decided Pudge made off with her."

"What about the hospital paperwork on Etienne's corpse?"

"I took that before we left, while Etienne was turning the girl. All I had to do this morning was help the EMTs forget his name, and take the paperwork they had. Oh, and get the paperwork on Etienne's car from the police station."

"Is that all?" the woman asked.

Bastien shrugged at her amusement. "It could have been worse, Mother."

The woman made a face, then turned back to Etienne. "You really have to deal with this Pudge fellow."

"I know." The blond man sounded unhappy. "If you have any ideas, I'd be happy to hear them."

The woman's expression relented somewhat. She patted his knee in a both soothing and affectionate gesture. "Well, I shall think about it. We all will. We'll come up with something."

"Yes," Bastien agreed. "And Lucern will get here later. Between the four of us, we should be able to figure out a solution."

"When is he coming?" Etienne asked.

"A little later. He's working on galleys for his latest masterpiece but promised to come after dinner."

"Which means about midnight," the woman grumped. "In the meantime, I think we should offer our guest a drink."

Rachel ducked quickly out of sight, but she caught a glimpse of the startled expression on Etienne's face as she did. Her heart thumped near her throat. None of them had looked her way, but somehow she must have given away her presence.

"She's been standing outside the door for several minutes," Rachel heard Bastien announce.

"No, she hasn't," Etienne replied.

He suddenly stepped out into the hall, surprising her. Rachel's first instinct was to run. Unfortunately, her body apparently didn't agree. It seemed to be frozen to the spot.

"You *are* up." He paused a foot away and stared at her.

Rachel stared back, a squeak slipping from her lips.

"Why didn't I sense her approach?" He looked behind him, obviously asking one of his companions.

The question managed to free Rachel's frozen limbs somewhat, enough so that she was able to ease along the wall until she bumped into a table. There, she stopped and smiled nervously as the man glanced back at her. Crossing her fingers, she prayed he wouldn't notice she had moved.

"Didn't you?" The woman's voice floated out from the other room. "How interesting."

Her apparent fascination only increased Rachel's nervousness, and it seemed to annoy Etienne. He turned and scowled back at her. The moment he was no longer looking, Rachel eased around the hall table and sidled toward the front door. She paused again when he muttered something under his breath.

He'd turned and seen she was almost at the door, and he frowned. Gruffly he informed her, "It isn't a good idea to go outside."

Rachel scowled. Anger overcame her panic. "Why? Because you've turned me into a bloodsucking demon, and the light of day will kill me?" she sneered. She didn't really believe any of this was happening . . .

but, at the same time she had an irrational fear that it just might.

"It's nighttime," he pointed out gently. "But it's also uncommonly cold for late summer. Too cold to be gadding about in nothing but a sheet."

Reminded of her lack of proper clothing, Rachel gasped. She made a run for the stairs, half fearing her host would give chase, but much to her relief she made the upper hall unpursued. Still, she didn't slow her steps but ran straight back to the bedroom where she'd woken and rushed inside, slamming the door behind her.

Inside, Rachel simply stood, breathing heavily, her eyes darting around in search of something with which to barricade the door. Unfortunately, there didn't appear to be any options. She briefly considered dragging the dresser over from against the opposite wall, but then she decided that if she had the strength to drag it over, he probably had more than enough to push the door open, barricade and all. What she really needed was a way to lock herself in. But, of course, there wasn't any.

Giving up on the idea, she forced herself to move away from the door in search of a weapon. Rachel didn't know where she was or who those people were, but they had taken her from the hospital, messed with police files, and at least one of them thought he was a vampire. Self-defense seemed an important consideration.

*   *   *

Etienne frowned up the stairs. Rachel didn't appear to be taking this very well. She'd rather resembled a scared rabbit fleeing to its hole, a reaction from her that he hadn't expected. Redheads were usually feisty. Of course, she wasn't sobbing hysterically or anything annoying like that.

"She isn't frightened so much as confused and embarrassed," his mother said.

Etienne tossed an irritated glance her way, and she joined him in the hallway. He hated it when she read his thoughts. He also didn't much care for the fact that she could obviously read Rachel's. He himself couldn't.

"I'll have to find her something to wear and explain the situation to her," he said absently. "I have some joggers that might do for now."

"She'll hardly wish to wear your joggers," Marguerite said dryly. "She needs her own clothes. Something familiar to make her feel more in control. Bastien?" She turned to peer back at Etienne's brother. "You brought her purse when we left the hospital, didn't you?"

"Yes." He joined them in the hall. "I left it in the kitchen."

Marguerite nodded. "Go fetch her keys then, and we shall go retrieve some proper clothing for the girl."

Etienne felt himself relax. His mother's suggestion would give him a little more time alone with Rachel, hopefully enough to at least explain things. It would be less difficult than with his mother and Bastien there.

When Bastien returned with the keys, Etienne ushered his mother and brother out of his home. Then he turned to survey the stairs.

Rachel. Rachel Garrett. He straightened his shoulders and headed up to explain the situation to her. He was sure once she realized it had been the only way to save her life—and once he had extolled the benefits of this new life he had given her—she would be grateful for what he had done.

Chapter Five

"You what?"

Rachel gaped at her handsome host, her hands squeezing the loofah-on-a-stick she had hidden under the blankets. It was a pretty pathetic weapon, but the only one she'd managed to find. Thinking that even a pathetic weapon was better than none she'd crawled back into bed hoping that a loofah combined with a surprise attack would be enough to save her from anything untoward. She'd huddled under the blankets until a knock had sounded at the door.

Her "Yes?" had held a startled note. It had revealed her surprise at the courtesy of him not barging in.

The blond man Etienne had entered, and Rachel had watched him warily. Much to her relief, he'd come alone. Then he launched into a long drawn-out story about how he was indeed her crispy critter, as well as the rifle-wound victim from work. She had sat in amazed silence as he explained that she had indeed been felled while trying to save him from the ax-wielding madman Pudge, and that he had saved her in return by turning her into a vampire like himself and the rest of his family.

"I turned you to save your life," Etienne repeated, a hopeful expression on his face.

Did he expect a thank-you? Rachel stared at him blankly for a moment, then gave up her huddled position under the blankets. She swept irritably from the bed.

Etienne Argeneau, as he had reintroduced himself, took a wary step back, but Rachel had no intention of going near him. The man was obviously mad.

Beautiful but mad, she thought grimly as she crossed the room to the set of double doors she hoped was a closet. And she was not now a bloodsucking demon.

"Not a bloodsucking demon," the man agreed with exaggerated patience, making Rachel realize she was muttering her thoughts aloud again. "A vampire."

"Vampires are dead people. Soulless dead people who continue to exist," Rachel snapped. She dragged the double doors open to reveal that beyond was indeed a closet. She surveyed its contents as she continued, "They are soulless bloodsucking demons. And they are fiction. They aren't real."

"Well, the soulless bit is fiction. We are— What are you doing?" he interrupted himself to ask.

She was sorting through the clothes on hangers. "Something I should have done a long time ago. Looking for something to wear." She dragged out one of his dress shirts, considered it, then tossed it onto the bed.

"I could—"

"Stay where you are!" Rachel warned. Glaring at him until he stopped, she turned back to the closet.

"Look," he said soothingly, "I realize this is upsetting, confusing, and perhaps—"

Rachel spun. "Confusing? Upsetting? What could be confusing or upsetting? You're a vampire. And there's a madman out to get you. But he's not a madman, because you really are a vampire," she pointed out grimly. Then she added, "Oh, and we musn't forget he accidentally axed me trying to get to you, so you turned me into a vampire too. Now I'm a soulless bloodsucker damned to walk the night and suck neck." Rolling her eyes, she turned back to the closet. "I have to get out of here."

"We don't 'suck neck'," he said, as if the very suggestion were asinine. But when Rachel turned to arch an eyebrow at him, he added reluctantly, "Not much, anyway. Only in emergencies. I mean, we do everything to avoid— Well, there is the occasional rogue vampire who . . ." He came to a halt, looking distressed.

Rachel shook her head and muttered, "Completely bonkers. Looney-bin boy."

"No, really," he said. "What I mean is that we all invested in blood banks when they came into existence. In fact, it was one of our kind who came up with the idea of blood transfusions. He mentioned it to Jean Baptiste Denis, and the fellow tried it and . . . Well, it doesn't matter. The point is, we have our blood *delivered*. See?"

"Look, I . . ." Rachel paused as she turned toward him. Her gaze landed on the minirefrigerator he had opened. Her eyes widened incredulously. There had to be a dozen bags of blood inside.

"Bastien stopped and picked up a couple dozen pints on the way here last night," Etienne explained. "For you and I both. We weren't sure how much you'd need for the change and healing and such. We figured you would need four or five bags to heal, but the full turning can be tricky. How much you need for that depends on how much damage your body has sustained over the years. You seemed relatively healthy, but there are always cancers, heart disease, et cetera." He eyed her stunned expression warily, then took out a bag and explained, "It isn't as pleasant as fresh, warm blood from the source, but it can be consumed much the same way."

As she stared in disbelief, he lifted the bag and opened his mouth. Rachel gasped in horror as his teeth extended, and he plunged them into the bag.

The blood immediately began to disappear as if drawn up through the teeth.

Still drinking, Etienne reached down and retrieved another bag, to hold out for her. "Unh?"

She supposed it was an invitation. Rachel wanted to laugh. She wanted to howl hysterically at this madness and return to ignoring him and ransacking his closet, but that unnamed yearning from earlier was again clenching and cramping her belly. Even worse, as the tinny scent of blood wafted around her, she could feel something odd happening inside her mouth. There was a strange sensation of shifting—not painful, more just a sort of pressure, but strange to say the least. Then she felt a sharp prick on the edge of her tongue. Startled, Rachel opened her mouth and felt around.

"Oh, God," she breathed as she felt her canines protruding down from between her other teeth. Lurching away from the closet, she rushed for the bathroom and hurried to the mirror. Horror coursed through her at the sight.

"It must be a trick," she said desperately.

"It's not a trick," Etienne assured her. He'd followed her into the bathroom. "Bastien looked into it today and said that sometimes the turning is relatively fast. The teeth are the first major change. Soon you'll be able to see better in darkness, hear better, and . . . stuff," he finished vaguely.

Rachel shifted her gaze to his reflection in the mirror, then paused, distracted by the realization that she could see it. Etienne stood directly behind her, and his shoulders, neck, and head were plainly visible.

"Vampires don't have reflections," she argued. It was a rather desperate point to make, but Rachel was desperate.

"A myth," he informed her, then smiled. "See? You *can* do your makeup."

Somehow that didn't seem very reassuring. Rather than relax, Rachel felt herself slump unhappily. "I'm dead."

"You aren't dead," Etienne said patiently. "I turned you to *save* your life."

"Oh—thanks a lot, buddy. Kill me to save me. Perfect male logic." She cursed. "I guess that trip to Hawaii is off. Shoot! And I just found a swimsuit that didn't make me look like Godzilla."

"I didn't kill you," Etienne repeated. "Pudge—"

"Pudge? The guy in army fatigues?" she interrupted. The man's image rose in her mind, wielding his ax, and Rachel frowned. She glared at Etienne in the mirror. "Jeez, I should have let him hack your head off. At least then I wouldn't be dead and soulless."

"You are not soulless," Etienne argued. His patience was obviously beginning to fray. "Pudge wounded you mortally. To save your life, I had to turn you."

"I don't feel soulless." Rachel leaned close to the mirror and pulled her lips back in a snarl, then poked at her new teeth.

"You *aren't* soulless."

Rachel ignored him and began to search the vanity. What she wanted was pliers, but of course, she had no expectations of finding any. The best she could do was a pair of nail clippers. She found a small one and a large one. Rachel chose the larger pair and leaned into the mirror.

"What are you doing?" her host shrieked. He snatched the clippers from her when she tried to catch the end of one of her new teeth and pull it out.

"I don't want to be a vampire," she snapped. She would have grabbed the clippers back, but he was holding them out of reach.

Turning away, Rachel searched the drawer again, this time coming up with a nail file. She turned back to the mirror and began trying to file down one of the teeth.

"It will just repair itself," Etienne said with irritation. "And it isn't so bad being a vampire."

"Ha!" Rachel grunted and continued to file.

"You'll never age," he pointed out hopefully. "You'll never get sick, never—"

"Never see the light of day," she interrupted sharply. Turning to glare at him, she asked, "Do you know how long I've been trying to get off the night shift? *Three years*. Three years I've been working through the night and not able to sleep during the day, and just when I get promoted to a day position, you turn me into a night walker!" Her voice rose with each word until

Rachel was shrieking. "You have doomed me to an eternal night shift! I *hate* you!"

"You can go out in daylight," Etienne said. But he didn't sound very sure about it, and Rachel concluded that he was just trying to calm her down. She didn't bother to call him on the lie. Her mind had already moved on to other vampire do's and don'ts.

"Garlic!" Her eyes widened incredulously. "I absolutely *love* garlic, and now I can't—"

"You can eat garlic," he interrupted. "Really, that's just another myth."

She couldn't tell if he was lying or not and so she eyed him consideringly. "What about church?"

"Church?" He looked blank.

"Can I go to church?" she asked slowly, as if he were an idiot. "My family has attended mass together every week for my whole life, but vampires—"

"You can attend church," he assured her, seemingly relieved. "That's another myth. Religious articles and places have no ill effects on us."

He had obviously expected this news would please her. It didn't. Rachel's shoulders slumped again. "Great," she said. "I was hoping to have a good excuse to miss mass from now on. Father Antonelli is way long-winded, but even Mom wouldn't have insisted on my going if I was going to burst into flames or something equally embarrassing the minute I walked through the doors." Rachel heaved out a dejected breath. "I guess there are just no positives to this deal."

Etienne frowned. She suspected he had preferred her anger. "Of course there are positives," he said. "You're alive. And you'll live for . . . well, a long time. And you won't age, and—"

"You already said that," she pointed out dryly. Pushing past him, she walked back into the bedroom.

"What are you doing?" Etienne sounded anxious, and he followed her.

"Finding something to wear." Rachel paused halfway across the room. "Unless my clothes happen to be around here somewhere?"

He shook his head. "They were blood-soaked. Ruined, I'm afraid."

"Hmm." Rachel turned back to the closet. "Then I'll just have to borrow clothes of yours. I'll replace them."

Etienne frowned but remained silent as Rachel ransacked his wardrobe. Apparently forgetting she had already chosen one, she snatched another long-sleeved white dress shirt and a pair of pants, then marched back to the bathroom. Out of pure instinct, Etienne started to follow, only to nearly get his nose broken when the door slammed in his face.

"I'll wait out here," he muttered.

"Good thinking," she responded through the barrier.

Etienne scowled at his bathroom door and listened to the rustle of clothing. He supposed she was stripping. A quick image flashed in his mind of her untying the sheet and letting the material drop down over her pale round breasts, her belly, her hips, her . . . He shook himself.

Etienne knew exactly what she looked like naked. He hadn't been strong enough to help when they returned home with her from the hospital, but neither had he been strong enough not to watch as Bastien and his mother undressed her, tended her wounds and cleaned her up, then put her in his bed. He had a very good idea of what she would look like now beyond that door. Her pale skin and red hair would be complemented by the blues of the bathroom. Her muscles would stiffen and tense as she tossed the sheet aside and began to don the overlarge shirt, his favorite. . . .

Etienne was really getting into the vision when the door suddenly opened. Rachel stopped abruptly and scowled when she found him standing there.

He cleared his throat and offered a crooked smile. "That was fast."

"Move."

"Yes, of course." He stepped quickly to the side and watched her pass. The pants were far too large and hung like a sack from her hips. She had tucked the shirt inside, then tied the waist of the pants into a knot, but as she walked back to the closet, the material unknotted and dropped from around her waist.

Etienne's eyebrows flew up as the pants fell down. Rachel stopped walking, and he was sure she scowled as she peered down at the garment now pooled around her ankles. He was scowling himself—not at the pants falling, but because the shirttail had dropped just as quickly, obstructing his view. It was rather disappointing. He still got a nice view of her legs, however. Lovely legs.

Muttering under her breath, Rachel stepped out of the pants and continued forward. "I'll need shoes."

"No, you don't."

"Yes, I do."

"Why?"

"I can hardly leave barefoot. Could you call me a cab?" She bent to survey the shoes in his closet.

"No."

Rachel glared at him rebelliously. "Then I'll call one myself."

"I mean, no, you can't leave," he explained.

She turned to face him fully, her eyes narrowing to slits. There was no doubting her irritation. "Look, I was thinking while I changed."

"It must have been a fast think," he commented.

She ignored his sarcasm. "And you know, while you had me going at first, I've realized that none of this is true. The jig is up. It's over. You might as well let me go."

"None of what is true?" he asked with surprise.

"The vampire bit. I can't be a vampire. There is no such thing."

"Yes, there is. I'm one."

"No. *You're* crazy. You just think you're a vampire, like those people who think they're werewolves but are really suffering from lycanthropy. You're obviously suffering from a vampire version of that. Vampanthropy or something."

Etienne rolled his eyes. "I see. So . . . what about your teeth?"

Her mouth tightened, and she looked uncertain for a moment.

To press the point, Etienne moved to the small refrigerator and grabbed the bag of blood he had offered earlier. He used the long nail on his baby finger to slit it open and moved closer.

When the smell reached her, what Etienne had expected happened: her teeth slid out, lapping over her lower lip—a usual reaction in the newly turned, from what he had heard. It would take her a while to gain control of her body's new instincts. Gasping, Rachel covered her mouth and ran for the bathroom.

Etienne followed. He stood behind her as she examined herself in the mirror, and he knew there was trouble when she suddenly relaxed.

"What?" he asked warily.

"Vampires don't have reflections," she repeated. "But I do." She met his gaze in the mirror and smiled. The expression looked rather evil with her new canines.

"A myth," he reiterated.

93

"No. It's proof that I'm not a vampire." She sounded incredibly firm on the point.

"And the teeth?" Etienne asked.

That point seemed to stymie her for a moment, then she relaxed again. "I'm dreaming," she answered. "This isn't happening at all." She turned to face him, her smile brilliant. "I'm dreaming of you, because I found you attractive when they brought in your corpse. I made you a vampire in this dream because it's the only way a dead man can live. Well, sort of live."

She frowned over that paradox, then added, "And in the dream, I've become a vampire too, so that I can be with you."

"You find me attractive?" Etienne asked, pleased.

"Oh, yes," she admitted airily. "It's the first time I've ever found a dead man attractive. Perhaps that's part of the reason for this dream too. It's rather weird to be attracted to a corpse, so maybe I had to give you life in this dream to deal with the fact that I found you so attractive." She tilted her head, considering. "Anyway, you are the most gorgeous corpse I've worked with."

"Really?" Etienne smiled. No one had ever told him he was a gorgeous corpse before. Of course, he wasn't a corpse and he should really explain, he told himself.

"Well," she sighed. "What do we do now?"

Etienne blinked. "Do?"

"Yes. What happens next in my dream?" She examined him with interest. "Is this a wet dream?"

"What?" He gaped at her.

"Sorry, I suppose you don't know any more than I do, since you're just a part of my mind symbolizing my attraction to the real you—but I'm not really sure how this works. I've never had a wet dream before. My friend Sylvia has them all the time, but I haven't . . . that I recall," Rachel said. She smiled wryly and added, "Too repressed. Catholic girl, you know. Confessing wet dreams to old Father Antonelli would just be too embarrassing." She frowned. "This one ought to be a doozy. Might give the poor old guy a heart attack."

"Er . . ." Etienne found himself suddenly incapable of speech.

Rachel wasn't. "So"—she glanced toward the bed— "since most of this has taken place in a bedroom, I gather it *is* a wet dream." Her gaze remained on the mattress. "And I presume the fun will take place in this bed. It seems pretty pedestrian compared to Sylvia's dreams, but I suppose that since this is my first one, I subconsciously decided to start slowly."

Etienne choked on his reply.

Rachel went on with a huff of breath, "Since you're not making any moves, you must represent my less aggressive side." She sounded disappointed, then perked up a bit as she added, "Well, at least this isn't a rape dream. I don't think I'd care for that."

"Uh," Etienne said.

"Oh, wait! This makes perfect sense. I'm a control freak. I probably need to be in control for a wet dream to work. That's probably the only way I'd be comfortable having one." She glanced at the bed again, then nodded. "Well, let's get to it. I can hardly wait to tell Sylvia. She's always so smug about her dreams. The guy does exactly what she wants, and it's always terribly exciting. The best sex ever. Real men can't compare."

Rachel moved toward him as she spoke but looked a bit at a loss when Etienne took a nervous step back. She spoke again, some irritation in her tone. "I know I have some control issues, but a *little* aggression wouldn't go amiss."

"I don't think—"

"Don't think, then," she suggested. She leaned up to kiss him.

Etienne froze at the feel of her soft lips moving over his. Hunger rose in him, but he didn't dare act on it. Rachel was confused, thinking she was asleep. He had to convince her otherwise—as much as that sucked.

"I've figured out I'm supposed to be the aggressor, but a little help would be nice," Rachel muttered against his lips. Giving up on kissing him, she grabbed his hand and dragged him to the bed. "Perhaps it would help if we were horizontal."

"I . . ." Etienne's words died in a surprised gasp as she tugged, then pushed him over. He barely bounced once on the mattress before she climbed on top and settled down on his groin. She immediately leaned forward, obviously intending to kiss him again.

Fending her off with a desperation born of the fact that he didn't want to fend her off at all, Etienne grabbed her shoulders and stopped her forward progress. "No! Wait. It's not really a dream."

"Sure it is," she countered. "You're my dream guy."

He weakened a bit. She leaned closer, but he caught himself and stopped her again. She broke free, and he struggled to ignore the hands that ran busily over his chest then set to work on the buttons of his shirt. "No, really. I—Oh, you're good at that."

Rachel had his buttons undone and his shirt already open. Her cool hands ran greedily over his chest.

"Lots of experience," she explained. "Often we just cut clothes off, but sometimes we have to undress our corpses. Wow, you have a great body," she commented.

"Well, thank you. Yours is very nice too," Etienne said. His eyes fixed on her straining chest as she slid her hands over him. The top three buttons had come undone and a good deal of cleavage was showing. It was nice cleavage. *Very* nice. His tongue slid out and ran along his lips when what he really wanted to run it along was the swell of those breasts.

"Well, I don't know if you had such a nice chest in real life," she commented, "but in my dream I definitely gave you a perfect one."

Etienne was congratulating himself over the fact

that she found his chest perfect when he felt her hands move to his waistband.

"You must be really hung too. Let's see."

"No!" He let go of her shoulders and grabbed her hands.

Rachel peered at him with disappointment. "No? You aren't well hung? But I want you to be. And it's my dream," she whined.

"No, I meant—" She looked so disappointed that Etienne decided to reassure her. "The men in my family are all well endowed."

"Oh, goody!" Rachel shrugged his hands away and set to work on his pants.

"But *we can't do this*," he managed to get out. It was almost painful to say.

"Of course we can. It's my dream and I want to," she said reasonably.

"Yes, but . . . Look, I can't in good conscience allow you to do this while you think it's a dream."

Rachel paused and stared at him, then blew her bangs out of her eyes with a heavy sigh. "Only I would have a wet dream where the guy fights me off."

"It's not a dream," Etienne repeated. "And if you would just accept that this is all real, we could—"

"Okay," Rachel agreed. "It's not a dream." She grinned.

Etienne eyed her warily. "What?"

"It's not a dream, it's a nightmare. But the best darned nightmare I've had in a long time."

"No, it's not a nightmare."

"It certainly is," she disagreed. "It's every woman's nightmare. Waking up in a sexy man's bed only to find he doesn't want you? Definitely a nightmare."

"I *do* want you," Etienne assured her.

"Oh, good. Maybe it's not a nightmare after all, then." She claimed his lips with her own.

This time, Etienne had no fight left. After a moment's hesitation, he gave in to his desires. The passion that burst to life between them was startling.

Etienne had lived a long time, and sex had become old hat. In fact, his passion for most things had waned over the ages. He'd grown deadly bored with life until recently—until the advent of computers. Those wonderful machines had caught his interest and passion with a vengeance that women hadn't for a long while. But this woman stirred feelings he hadn't enjoyed for centuries. And all with just a kiss?

Etienne was so startled by his body's enthusiastic response, he gave in to it at once, his gentlemanly urges overwhelmed by lust. He released his hold on Rachel's shoulders and slid his hands over her body with hungry caresses impatient at the clothes she wore. With a primitive growl, he caught fabric and tugged, uncaring that he was snapping buttons off his favorite shirt. He didn't possess any bras for her to have pinched, so Rachel wasn't wearing one. It left him free to first gawk at, then cover the round globes of her breasts with his hands.

Rachel broke their kiss with a moan and arched forward into the caress.

"Oh, yes," she breathed, head thrown back and eyes closed. She covered his hands with her own. "I'm good."

"You are, are you?" Etienne asked with a chuckle. He sat up until he could reach her breast with his mouth. Closing his lips over her nipple, he sucked it into his mouth and rubbed the hardening nub with his tongue.

"Oh, Gawdddd I'm good," Rachel gasped. Shifting on his lap, she ground against the erection burgeoning inside his jeans. "Sylvia said wet dreams could be good, but Gawdddd!"

Etienne felt a moment's guilt, but he quickly pushed it aside. She was obviously enjoying her dream, and he had tried to tell her the truth.

His self-justification ended as her hand again found his waistband. This time Etienne didn't try to stop her, instead finding himself sucking in an excited breath, his stomach muscles contracting as she unsnapped the button then lowered the zipper. Her hand had just slipped in when the bedroom door opened. Marguerite stepped inside.

"Well." Etienne's mother's voice was full of dry amusement. "I gather you two are getting along all right."

Etienne groaned. His eyes went to Rachel, who sat up to glance around. Her expression was perplexed when it landed on his mother. "What are you doing in my wet dream?"

"Wet dream?" Marguerite Argeneau shifted her gaze back to her son.

"Er . . ." was all Etienne said.

Chapter Six

"You were supposed to convince her that she *wasn't* dreaming, son."

"I know," Etienne said soothingly. He'd never seen his mother so annoyed. She had been sweet and nice to Rachel, ignoring the wet-dream comment and acting as if she hadn't just walked in on an awkward moment. Presenting Rachel with a tote bag filled with clothes collected from her apartment, Marguerite had then suggested Rachel might be more comfortable in them than Etienne's cast-offs. Then she had asked Rachel to come below when she was ready.

Next, she had ushered Etienne out of the room, her silence along the hall and down the stairs warning him that she was more than a little peeved. Now, in the living room, he tried to defend himself. "I tried to convince her it wasn't a dream. I really did."

"Well, you apparently failed," Marguerite snapped. "The girl thinks she's having an erotic dream, for God's sake!"

"An erotic dream?" Bastien echoed. His tone was half-amused, half-horrified.

"Fascinating." Lucern—a carbon copy of Bastien, except taller—pulled a pen and pad out of his pocket and jotted something down.

Etienne glared at his older brothers, then took a deep calming breath. Turning back to his mother, he said, "She's really resisting the idea of being a vampire. I mean, *really* resisting, Mother. She's twisting her brain and contorting her thoughts in the most convoluted ways to avoid accepting it."

"Perhaps you haven't presented it properly."

That deep male voice drew Etienne's attention to the bar, and he raised an eyebrow in surprise at the couple standing there. The man had spoken, but Etienne's gaze found his sister first. Except for the fact that she was blond, Lissianna was an exact replica of their mother. She always looked beautiful, but now, as she crossed the room toward him with a drink, she positively glowed. Being engaged obviously agreed with her.

Etienne glanced at the man following her. Gregory Hewitt. Tall, dark-haired, and good-looking, Lissianna's fiancé smiled at him in greeting.

"I didn't realize you two were coming over," Etienne said. "I thought you were busy with wedding preparations."

"Never too busy for family," Lissianna murmured. She hugged him. "Besides, I had to meet your life mate."

Etienne slumped. His life mate was fighting him tooth and nail—when she wasn't doing completely outlandish things like insisting this was all a wet dream and jumping him.

"As I said," Gregory reiterated, slipping his arm around Lissianna. She released Etienne and stepped back. "Perhaps you simply haven't presented it in the right light."

"Of course he hasn't," Lissianna agreed, smiling. "Once she knows all the benefits, she'll take to it fine."

"I *told* her the benefits," Etienne insisted.

"Bet you didn't tell her all of them." Lissianna's grin somewhat soothed his irritation at her questioning his abilities.

"Bet I did," he countered.

"We shall see."

Lissianna shrugged and smiled, but the smile was aimed over his shoulder, making Etienne aware of someone else—Rachel, of course. He turned, his eyes widening as he took in her outfit. She had been wearing dress pants, a blouse, and a lab coat both times he'd seen her in the morgue. She had been naked, wrapped in a sheet, or wearing one of his shirts here in his home. Now he found himself gaping at her in a pair of tight, faded jeans and a T-shirt that barely reached her midriff. Her hair was pulled back into a ponytail and and her face was makeup free. Altogether, she looked about eighteen. A very sexy eighteen.

Etienne was wowed.

"Umm, these aren't . . . er . . ." Rachel shifted on her feet, tugging nervously on the bottom of her T-shirt in an effort to draw it down to hide her belly. "I don't suppose you brought any other clothes back from my apartment, did you?"

"I'm sorry. No, dear. Are they wrong?" Marguerite asked. Getting to her feet, she approached. "Aren't they yours? I got them out of your closet. They were the only casual clothes I could find."

"Yes. Yes, they're mine," Rachel said quickly. "But they're old. I mean, I haven't worn jeans since graduating University, and I've obviously outgrown them." She frowned down at herself and tugged on the top again. "I should have thrown them out, really, but I'm something of a packrat."

"No, you look wonderful." Marguerite took her hand and drew her to the couch. Once she was seated, the woman patted her hand and said, "From what Etienne has told us, you appear to be a little confused."

"I'm not the one confused," Rachel said, though she was no longer sure that was the case. This dream had taken a surreal twist. She wasn't sure what was happening. Dream? Nightmare? Feverish imaginings? Was it all just bad drugs?

"Ah. Well." Marguerite smiled widely. "Perhaps if you tell me the last thing you recall before waking, we could work from there."

"The last thing," Rachel pondered. The logic was comforting. Marguerite wasn't claiming to be a vampire or insisting Rachel was, either. Maybe this would all work itself out.

She ran her tongue over her upper teeth, relieved to find them perfectly normal. This all had to be the result of bad drugs. She rubbed absently at her chest where the ax had severed skin but left no scar. She was probably comatose right now and a bad morphine drip was giving her weird dreams. Not necessarily bad dreams. Those few heated moments in the bedroom hadn't been bad at all. In fact, the only bad part to her mind was that it had ended so abruptly— and without satisfaction.

"The last thing I remember . . ." she repeated, pushing other thoughts aside. "I was at work for the first time after being sick for a week."

"Uh-huh." Marguerite nodded encouragingly.

"Tony was off, and Beth was late." She glanced up and added, "Car trouble."

Marguerite made a murmur of possible sympathy for the unknown Beth and her car.

"Fred and Dale, a couple of EMTs, brought in a crispy critter."

"A crispy critter?"

Rachel glanced at the man seated across from her. He, like the man from earlier, looked a lot like a brunette Etienne, but a little grumpier. And he had a pad he seemed to be making notes on. She stared curiously at the notebook on his knee and answered, "Burn victim."

"You call them crispy critters?" Bastien, the first brunette, asked in distress.

Rachel heaved an inward sigh. It was difficult to explain such seeming coldheartedness to people not in the industry, but she gave it a try.

"Death can be pretty grim. Sometimes we use such terms to . . . well, basically, to distance ourselves from the tragedy. And every case is a tragedy, whether burn victim or heart attack. Every individual is loved by someone and will be grieved over. We're aware of that, but we have to push it to the back of our minds or we simply couldn't do our jobs." She could tell by the expressions of those around her that they didn't really understand. She supposed no one really could. Her job was difficult work, both technically and emotionally. She and her co-workers did their best to respect the dead, but some of their coping mechanisms . . .

"So this Fred and Dale brought in a burn victim," the young blond woman prompted.

"Yes." Rachel glanced curiously from her to the woman who'd collected her clothes. The two could have been twins but for the difference in their hair colors. Then Rachel's gaze slid to Etienne again, and confusion filled her. "Yes, a car explosion victim. Fred and Dale left, and I started to process the burn victim and noticed that the burnt skin seemed to be coming away as if it wasn't burnt skin at all but something blown onto him by the explosion. Then I thought I saw his chest move. So I tried to take a pulse, but as I did . . ." She hesitated. This was where things got murky. Not because she couldn't recall—Rachel would never forget that ax entering her body—but because there was no wound now and nothing made sense.

"But as you did . . ." the man with the pad prompted.

"The door to the morgue slammed open." She forced herself to continue. "A man was there, dressed in khakis and a trench coat. He whipped the trench coat open and had a rifle hanging on a strap from one shoulder and an ax from the other. He yelled at me." Her gaze flicked with uncertainty to Etienne again, then away.

"He yelled to get back, that the burn victim was a vampire. Then he rushed forward, raising the ax as he came. I realized he meant to cut off my burn victim's head, but I couldn't let him. I wasn't sure the man was really dead. I moved between them, hoping to stop him, but he was already committed. He couldn't stop, and the ax . . ." Her voice trailed off, and she reached absently to rub below her collarbone.

Silence reigned for a moment, then Rachel cleared her throat and finished, "He was horrified by what he did. He tried to help me, but I was in shock and scared, then I think someone started to come into the morgue. He spooked, told me help would soon arrive, told me to stay alive, then turned and fled."

"Bastard," Etienne breathed. He turned to the others. "I definitely say we call the police and claim he kidnapped her. Let them lock him away."

"But he didn't kidnap me," Rachel said.

"That doesn't matter," Etienne claimed. "It'll be your word against his, and someone saw him enter the hospital with weapons. They'll believe you."

"But he didn't kidnap me," she repeated.

"No, he just tried to kill you," he replied sarcastically. Turning back to the others, he added, "We can have her call the police from a phone booth near his house and claim she just escaped, then—"

"I'm not doing that," Rachel interrupted. "I'll tell the police that he accidentally hit me with the ax while aiming for you, and that he seemed to regret it at once, but I will not claim he kidnapped me. That would be lying."

Her host huffed with exasperation. "Rachel, he tried to *kill* you."

"Actually, no, he didn't," she argued. "That was an accident."

"Okay. So he tried to kill me," he snapped.

"Well, if you're a soulless bloodsucker like you claim, who could blame him for trying to kill you!"

Everyone gasped. Then Marguerite burst out laughing.

Etienne gaped at her. "Mother! How can you laugh at that?"

"She's so delightful, dear," she excused, then turned to pat Rachel's hand. "He isn't soulless, child. None of us are. Neither are you."

Rachel looked mutinous. Marguerite apparently decided not to convince her, but to take a different approach. She said, "Let me introduce my children. You've met Etienne, of course."

Etienne offered an encouraging smile, but he doubted Rachel noticed it. Her gaze skated nervously to him, then away as she nodded and blushed.

"And this is my daughter Lissianna, and her fiancé Gregory." Marguerite smiled as she gestured to the pair, then waited for Lissi and Greg to shake Rachel's hand and welcome her. She next turned to her elder sons. "And these are my oldest boys—Lucern and Bastien. Stop grinning like that, boys. You'll make Rachel uncomfortable."

Etienne's head snapped around. A glare covered

his face when he saw the way both men were leering.

"Umm, excuse me," Rachel interrupted, her confused gaze on Marguerite. "Did you say your *children?*"

"Yes." Marguerite smiled.

"But you're far too young to—"

"Thank you, dear," Marguerite interrupted with a laugh. "But I am much older than I look."

Rachel's eyes narrowed. "How much older?"

"I'm seven hundred and thirty-six."

Rachel blinked, then cleared her throat. "Seven hundred and thirty-six?" she echoed.

"Yes, dear." Marguerite nodded.

Rachel nodded.

They all nodded.

Then Rachel shook her head, closed her eyes, and Etienne distinctly caught the words, "I'm still dreaming. But it's turned into a nightmare again."

Much to Etienne's surprise, his mother burst out laughing again and patted her hand. "It's not a dream. Or a nightmare. Or even a wet dream," she explained. "This is all really happening. We are—though we don't much care for the term—vampires, and I really am seven hundred and thirty-six years old."

"I see." Rachel nodded again, then closed her eyes and shook her head.

Her eyes blinked open and she cried out in surprised pain as Marguerite reached over and pinched her. "You aren't dreaming," the woman said. "That pinch would have woken you up. This is all really happening. We are vampires. And you are now, too."

"You say that like it's a good thing," Rachel muttered. Then she added, "This whole family is loony."

"Perhaps if Bastien were to explain the scientific basis of it," Greg said suddenly. He wore a sympathetic look that reminded Etienne he had only recently dealt with all of this himself.

"Yes." Bastien stood and moved to join Rachel on the sofa. Etienne watched Marguerite get up and move to the bar to poke around in the fridge. He suspected his mother was having a little drink from his private stock of blood. He doubted if any of them had stopped to feed before coming over. They were all concerned about this matter. Pudge's knowledge and obsession was a threat to them all.

"You see," Bastien began, taking Rachel's hand and smiling at her in a way Etienne didn't care for. " 'Vampire' is a term that we didn't choose. It was applied to us, and we accept its expediency when dealing with mortals—er . . . non-vampire types, I mean. But it isn't quite correct."

"It isn't?" Rachel sounded wary.

"No. At least not in the way that vampires have come to be known. We aren't this way due to any curse," Bastien explained, "or because God shunned us. Hence the reason religious symbols have no effect on us."

"I see," Rachel said slowly.

"We are not possessed by demons who contort our

facial features and who feed on or delight in torturing people."

"Uh-huh."

"There is a scientific explanation and basis for our state."

That caught her attention. She was listening, Etienne noted with relief.

"You see, our ancestors are very old," Bastien explained. "They're from before Roman times, before the birth of Christ. Before recorded history, actually."

"Oh?" Rachel was looking uncertain again.

"Yes. Our original home was a place some people refer to as Atlantis."

"Ah." Etienne knew from Rachel's tone of voice that Bastien was losing her again. She had that skeptical look on her face once more.

"Our scientists there were quite advanced. They developed . . . well, the easiest explanation is a sort of nano."

"Nanos?" She relaxed, back on sure scientific footing again.

"Yes. And they combined it with some tricky bioengineering to create specialized nanos that act as a sort of benign parasite."

"Parasites?" Bastien definitely had her interest now, and Etienne felt his hopes rise that she would finally accept what was happening.

"Yes. They feed off the blood we produce."

"So it's a science experiment gone wacko," she clarified, relaxing a little when Bastien nodded. "But how did these nanos get into your people?"

"They were deliberately introduced," he admitted. "You see, they were engineered to reside in the bloodstream and to help repair damage done by injuries—rather like microscopic surgeons working from the inside, so to speak. But once these nanos were introduced to the bloodstream of our ancestors, it was found that not only did they repair tissue, they regenerated it as well, and fought illness."

"I see. So they repair and regenerate your body, in effect keeping you young and healthy, and in exchange then feed off blood?" she asked slowly.

"Exactly." Bastien smiled.

Rachel seemed to consider for a moment, then she commented, "I imagine it takes a good deal of blood to constantly repair and regenerate tissue."

"Yes," he admitted. "More than a normal human body can possibly produce."

"Hence the need for sucking neck," Rachel guessed.

Etienne cleared his throat, and everyone in the room gave a start.

"Well, don't look at me," he said irritably as they turned toward him. "That's not my phrase."

"We don't 'suck neck' anymore," Lissianna said soothingly. She moved to take up position on Rachel's other side. "It's true that in the past there was some necessity, and occasionally health issues or . . . er . . .

phobias"—she glanced at Greg and the couple exchanged smiles—"have made one or two of our kind revert to the old ways. However, biting people has been frowned upon since the advent of blood banks."

"Blood banks." Rachel's eyes widened. "Jeez, they'd be like fast-food restaurants, a McDonald's for vampires."

"More like a deli than McDonald's. All cold cuts." Lissianna grimaced with distaste. She had been forced to "suck neck" up until recently due to a bad case of hemophobia. There was nothing more debilitating to a vampire than to be unfortunate enough to faint at the sight of blood—something Lissianna had suffered since childhood. She was cured now, but Etienne knew she was still trying to get used to cold bagged blood.

Rachel was silent, a look of distaste clear on her face. "And now I'm like you?"

Lissianna took her hand so that both she and Bastien held one. "Yes," she said solemnly. "Etienne turned you to save your life. You are now a vampire."

Rachel's shoulders slumped. "But I don't even like blood pudding or rare steak. If it's even the slightest bit pink, I gag. I'll never be able to—"

"That can all be worked around," Lissianna assured her. "If necessary, you can continue to take your blood intravenously as you have been."

Rachel didn't look much impressed. "My dentist is

going to love this. The first time he does a set of X rays, he'll freak."

"That won't be a concern. You won't need to visit the dentist anymore," Bastien assured her.

"I won't?"

"No," Lissianna answered. "Or a doctor, either. You are now cavity-and illness-proof. The blood will see to that."

"No more flu shots or dentist drills?" Rachel asked.

Lissianna turned a triumphant smile on Etienne. "I knew you hadn't presented it properly. I bet you didn't tell her about the orgasms, either."

"I told her she'd live forever and never age. That should hold more sway than dentist or doctor visits," Etienne said irritably.

"Maybe to someone who's never had to suffer them," Rachel said distractedly. Then she asked, "Orgasms?"

"Well, that's my cue to leave." Greg picked up his glass and turned to the door. "When women start talking sex . . ."

Bastien patted Rachel's hand and stood as well. "Yes, this part is best left to the women, I should think."

"Hmm." Lucern grunted in agreement, but he really looked as if he would rather stay and take notes. He got reluctantly to his feet and headed for the door, approaching Etienne at the same time as Bastien. As if it were a shared thought—which it probably was—

they each took him by an arm and dragged him to the door.

"Come along, little brother. You can show us the latest additions to your new game," Bastien said.

Etienne didn't protest. There was no use in doing so. Even being a vampire didn't help dealing with two overbearing brothers like Lucern and Bastien.

"Orgasms," Marguerite said as the door closed behind the men.

Rachel glanced at Etienne's mother. The woman— the much older woman, if she was really seven hundred and thirty-six years old—was smiling with wicked glee as she came to take Bastien's vacated seat. "You won't believe it."

Lissianna chuckled at her mother's enthusiasm, then explained, "Marguerite can explain better than I. I was born of vampires and never experienced a mortal sex life. But Mother started out human and was turned like yourself. According to her, the difference is mind-blowing."

"I'll say." Marguerite ran her tongue over her front teeth and made an appreciative sucking noise. "I fainted every time for the first year."

"Fainted?" Rachel gaped. "The whole first year?"

"Oh, my dear!" Marguerite patted her hand. "The difference just can't be explained. It's overwhelming. You connect with your partner and experience his pleasure as well as your own combined."

"So, it's like twice the pleasure?" Rachel asked.

Marguerite shook her head. "More like twenty times. Somehow the blood increases sensitivity. Your sense of smell will be ten times better than ever, you'll be able to hear more, see farther, and you'll be extra sensitive to touch."

"Sex, twenty times better?" Rachel tried to wrap her mind around the idea but just couldn't. Perhaps it would have helped to have had more experience to draw on. Rachel hadn't expended a lot of time or effort on her social life the last few years. She had been engaged at University, but after catching her fiancé in bed with her roommate, she had concentrated most of her attention on work.

"Being more experienced wouldn't help, dear," Marguerite said sympathetically. "You'll understand once you've experienced what I'm talking about."

Rachel stared at the woman, uncertain, then cleared her throat and asked, "Did you just read my mind?"

"I'm afraid so." Marguerite bit her lip. "I *am* sorry. It's a bad habit. I'll try not to intrude on your thoughts in future."

Rachel shrugged. She'd just have to guard her thoughts. And she was more interested in other things at the moment. "Can I read minds now too?"

"Not yet. You'll have to learn to do it. There are many things you will have to learn."

"Like what?" she asked curiously.

Marguerite pondered. Rachel suspected she was trying to decide what wouldn't overwhelm her. Finally, the older woman said, "You'll find you're much stronger than you used to be. Quicker, both in body and mind. You'll be able to see better in the dark too."

"Like nocturnal predators," Rachel said.

"Yes. Your eyes will shine when light hits them in the dark, like those of a night animal."

Rachel raised her hand self-consciously toward her face and glanced from Marguerite to Lissianna. They both had silver-blue eyes. Etienne did too. "Are my eyes like yours now?" She hadn't really noticed when she'd looked in the mirror upstairs.

"More a silver-green color, dear," Marguerite judged. "The original color was green?"

"Yes." Now Rachel was curious to see.

She'd barely had the thought when Lissianna stood and moved to a purse resting on the bar. The blonde dug through it briefly, then turned back, a compact in her hand. Opening the compact, the young woman walked over. "I'm two hundred and two years old," she said, handing Rachel the mirror.

Rachel managed an embarrassed smile at having the unasked question answered, reminding herself she'd have to watch her thoughts around this family. Then she peered into the mirror to examine her eyes.

"Wow," she breathed. The concern over guarding her thoughts was quickly forgotten. Then she frowned. "This will be interesting to explain to my family."

Glancing up, she was just in time to catch the exchange of glances between mother and daughter. "What?"

Lissianna shook her head, but her smile was a little strained. "Claim they're contacts."

"Good thinking," Marguerite said. But the words were suspiciously hearty, and she got to her feet. "Now you should rest. You're tired."

Oddly enough, the moment the other woman said the words, Rachel *did* feel tired. She also had the inkling that reading minds might not be the only thing they could do.

"You can control minds," she accused.

"It's a useful trick that helped in the old days of hunting," Marguerite said calmly.

At least she didn't lie, Rachel thought with resignation. Then another thought struck her. "Was Etienne controlling my mind earlier?" She didn't specify those passionate moments in the bedroom, but she didn't have to. Marguerite could read her thoughts, after all.

"Luckily enough, Etienne is unable to either read your thoughts or control you," Marguerite said.

"Why is that lucky?" Rachel asked. She thought it was, but why did Marguerite?

"Because good life mates can't read or control each other. Otherwise, it wouldn't be a partnership. It would be a master and a puppet."

The comment was slightly confusing to Rachel, since she had just met them all and wasn't anyone's life mate, but another question came to mind. She asked, "How old is Etienne?"

"Three hundred and twelve."

"Three hundred and twelve," Rachel echoed. Her distress returned. The man was three hundred and twelve years old. She'd tried to jump an old man. He was a serious geriatric.

"Do not fret," Marguerite said. This time her voice was soft, whisper soft. Almost as if she hadn't spoken at all but breathed the words. Or merely thought them. "Ease yourself. Things will be less distressing after you rest."

"Yes." The word slipped from Rachel's mouth of its own accord. Not that Rachel much cared. The only thought in her mind was that she was weary and needed rest.

"Come," Marguerite said, getting to her feet. Rachel did as she was told.

"Brilliant!" Bastien grinned and slapped Etienne on the back as Etienne shut the program down. "This one will be an even bigger hit than the first." Lucern and Greg nodded.

"That good is it?"

All four men turned to the door in surprise at the sound of Lissianna's voice. Greg smiled at the sight of her and moved to her side, his arm slipping around her in welcome. He pressed a kiss to her forehead.

"All done explaining the delights of vampire sex to Rachel?"

"Hmm." She smiled and kissed him back, then turned to her brother. "She's enthralled, Etienne. We may have increased your chances."

"Ha ha." Etienne turned off the computer and stood. "Where is Mother?"

"She took Rachel upstairs to put her to bed."

Etienne laughed. "Tucking her in like a child?"

"She *is* a child," Lucern commented, leading the way out of Etienne's basement. "She's barely twenty-five."

"Nearly thirty," Etienne corrected.

"Still a child," Lucern said with a shrug.

"Everyone's a child to you, Lucern," Lissianna joked.

"Not everyone. Just everyone under four hundred."

"You mean everyone but you, Mother, Bastien, and maybe a hundred of the more ancient vamps in the world," Etienne said with disgust. At three hundred and twelve he was growing tired of being called a child. He even sometimes yearned to be human, to have a normal lifespan and family. But that feeling always passed.

"Well, what are we going to do about your friend Pokey?" Greg asked as they returned to the living room.

"Pudge," Etienne corrected.

"Your mother said his name was Pokey."

"She seems to have a mental block when it comes to his name."

"I've been thinking about it," Bastien spoke up. Everyone listened. When Lucern had chosen to pursue writing and other creative pursuits upon their father's death, rather than run the family businesses, it was Bastien who had taken on the mantle. They all respected him for it, and for the effort he went to on everyone's behalf. "As we discussed, since the hospital officials and police already think Pudge carried Rachel away with him, it would be expedient if we could persuade her to claim such. They would arrest him and put him away for kidnapping. Etienne must convince her to do this."

"A sound idea," Lucern commented. Arching an eyebrow at Etienne he asked, "Do you think you can?"

"I can try," Etienne decided. Then he smiled. "I'll have plenty of time to convince her while she's here."

"If she agrees to stay," Lissianna pointed out.

"She will."

"She isn't a stray dog, Etienne," Marguerite said dryly, entering the room. "You can't just keep her as you like."

"No, she isn't a stray dog," he agreed. "But she *is* one of us now."

"So?" Lissianna said. "Her being one of us doesn't mean you can keep her chained up. She'll most likely want to return to her own life."

"But she'll need to feed," he protested.

"Yes, she will," Bastien agreed. "And certainly we will make our blood bank open to her, if she needs it."

Etienne's head snapped in his brother's direction. "If she needs it? Of course she'll need it."

"Not necessarily," Greg commented. "She works in a hospital. She can probably take care of herself."

Etienne said nothing but felt his mouth tighten with displeasure. He didn't at all like the idea of losing her, and briefly struggled with the reasons behind it. He was thoroughly confused by his passion, for he hardly knew the woman and shouldn't feel so strongly about this—but he did. He'd like to think it had nothing to do with his body's passionate response to her when she had kissed him, or the pleasure he had felt when she'd crawled on top of him.

His gaze drifted to the door and the stairs visible beyond as his family continued to talk. Rachel would be asleep in his bed at that moment; his mother would have seen to that. It was for the best. Her body had suffered a good deal of trauma of late—a mortal wound, the turning, healing. And mentally she had been through the ringer as well. It couldn't be an easy thing to accept that your whole life had changed so abruptly.

Etienne frowned. His own life had taken a sudden unexpected turn along with hers, and he was feeling rather traumatized himself. Suddenly, he was faced with the care and concern of another being. The closest he'd felt to this was the protective nature of an older brother when Lissianna had been a child, but that hadn't been nearly as strong. He felt a connection to the woman sleeping in his bed, one he couldn't define or really understand. Perhaps it was because he had turned her, and that had created a bond he hadn't been warned of. Regardless, he felt his life was now interlaced with hers on many levels.

On the other hand, perhaps he simply needed to look into more of a social life. It couldn't be good for him to have gone celibate for so long.

"How long has it been?"

"Two or three decades," Etienne answered before he could catch himself. Then he glared. "It's rude to read other people's thoughts, Mother."

She merely smiled sweetly at him. Marguerite had a bond with each of her children, perhaps from birth. She had always been able to read their minds and such—a talent not reciprocal to her children. Each of them could read the thoughts of humans—or usually they could, Etienne corrected himself, recalling that Rachel's mind seemed sealed against him. They could also read each other's thoughts when they weren't guarded, which they usually were. But none of them could read Marguerite's.

"It's getting late and I have things to do," the woman announced, getting to her feet. "Besides, we should leave Etienne to consider how to convince Rachel to go along with the plan. We can meet to discuss this matter further tomorrow night."

Much to Etienne's relief, everyone else concurred. He saw them out, closed and locked the door, then made his way upstairs to his room, unable to prevent himself.

His houseguest slept with the innocence of a babe. As she lay there curled up under his blankets in his bed, there was absolutely nothing about her to suggest the mischievous, even lusty woman who hid beneath. Etienne smiled slightly at his recollection. Rachel was a firecracker, as her red hair suggested, and Etienne was very much enjoying the show. He could hardly wait for sunset to come and a new night to begin.

Chapter Seven

The glowing red numbers of the digital clock on the bedside table read 12:06. Still deep night. She hadn't slept very long this time. Despite her dislike of the night shift, being on it for so long had affected her sleeping patterns, and Rachel knew right away she wasn't going to get back to sleep. Normally she'd be well into her work shift by this hour . . . and wishing she worked during the day.

Sitting up, she slid her feet to the floor and reached for the clothes lying across the foot of the bed. She had a vague recollection of Marguerite promising to collect more for her, and distinctly recalled murmuring something of an agreement to that, but she couldn't imagine why she'd agreed. She had no intention of staying here another day. She was going home.

While she had no idea what life held in store now, Bastien's explanations the night before had convinced her life had definitely changed.

Funny, while she was willing to admit that she had changed, she didn't feel any different. She still loved her family, and her goals and ambitions were the same. She wasn't really sure how she felt about being a vampire, but suspected she was going to have trouble. It was one thing to fantasize about never aging and living forever—though from what they had said, it wasn't necessarily *forever*-forever—but it was quite another thing to be faced with it.

Rachel had spent the night dreaming the world was moving around her at an accelerated pace. In her dream, faceless people had been milling about. They were born, grew up, and aged while she stood still, the Argeneaus at her back, none of them ever changing; watching those around them crumble into dust. And there were always others being born to take their places and die as well.

Pushing away the bleak dream and the concerns it brought to light, Rachel finished dressing. She left the room to find that, as it had been the first time she'd woken, the house was silent and still. Much to her relief, a light had been left on in the hallway though, making it easy to navigate the stairs. There was no one on the ground floor when she reached it—apparently Etienne's family had gone home. Working on instinct, she walked to the kitchen, not surprised to see the line of light beneath the door to the basement.

Rachel opened the door and headed down, determined to find her host. She was leaving. Now. Her footsteps slowed as she reached the bottom of the stairs, though, and recollections of her previous encounters with the man struck. Her earlier behavior left her squirming inside. How could she face him? She briefly considered leaving but couldn't move herself to be that rude. The man *had* saved her life, after all. Rachel wasn't yet sure she cared much for *how* he had saved her life, but save her he had. She owed it to him to at least offer thanks and let him know she was going.

Having convinced herself she could not in good conscience just flee, Rachel forced herself to continue on. The door was unlocked, and as she swung it open, Rachel noted that it was constructed wholly of metal and at least six inches thick. It made her think of a bank vault. High-tech security, she thought with distraction, then noticed Etienne sitting at the desk. He was rolling his wheeled chair between monitors, making adjustments then rolling back. He wasn't sleeping in the coffin tonight.

Her gaze shifted to that long box and she frowned at it, wondering if she would have to sleep in one as well. The idea wasn't appealing. Rachel had a touch of claustrophobia.

"Oh, you're up."

She glanced at her host. He swung his chair around to face her and was smiling brightly. He seemed to smile a lot, she noticed. He was obviously a happy kind of guy. But then, why not? He was wealthy, good-looking, forever young, and apparently with few cares to burden him. Realizing that she was simply standing there staring, Rachel forced herself to smile and move forward. "What are you doing?"

"Working." He turned back to his monitors and tapped a keyboard, changing the image. Rachel's eyes widened incredulously as she recognized the screen he brought up.

"Blood Lust?" she asked softly. Her eyes widened as the image finished forming. The title was made up of red letters which dripped away like blood. "Blood Lust Two!" she exclaimed. "I love the first version. I didn't know the second was out."

"It isn't. Yet."

"Yet?" Her gaze fixed to the monitor as the title page gave way to the production company logo; then her eyes shot to Etienne. "You aren't saying you're the creator?"

He nodded, his lips splitting in another grin.

"Wow." She looked back at the monitor. "I had heard it was a Torontonian who designed it, but . . ." But she was rather shocked to find it was a vampire. The game was about vampires: bad ones and a lone female hunter out to destroy them.

"I've pretty much finished Blood Lust Two, except for the final battle," he answered. "I was just about to test play it for flaws or tweaks. Care to join me?"

Rachel hesitated, but not for long. She'd thank him and leave later. The opportunity to play an unreleased prototype to the second version of her favorite game was just too tempting.

"Well, if you designed Blood Lust, I suppose you can't be all bad," she said half-teasing. Settling in the chair he rolled across the room, she watched him sit back in his own again.

"Gee, thanks." He sounded amused. Working his keyboard, he brought up the game.

"So, is this how Pokey figured out you were a vampire?" Rachel asked. His fingers danced across the keyboard. He was very fast. She was impressed. She herself was a hunt-and-pecker when it came to typing.

"Not exactly," he answered. "Though it might have given him some help. What really gave me away was the coffin, my habit of staying out of daylight, and the fact that I never seemed to eat."

Rachel stared at him blankly, then asked in confusion, "But how did he know all that?"

Etienne shrugged, concentrating on what he was doing. "Pudge is a techie. I think he was jealous of my success. He kind of fixated on me and tried to get me to hire him, but I prefer working alone." He grimaced. "The fellow hounded me for over a year. He even offered to work for free. When I still refused, he started following me about, breaking into the house when I was away and so on. I think he was trying to gather information, but I'm pretty sure what he learned isn't at all what he expected." His words were a dry understatement. "It was apparently enough to convince him that he had to kill me and finish me off the traditional way."

He was referring to Pudge's attempt to cut off his head, Rachel supposed. "Isn't staking the traditional way to kill a vampire?"

"Staking and cutting off the head," Etienne agreed. "I suppose he decided the stake wasn't really necessary."

"Jeez." Rachel grimaced. What would have happened had she not jumped between Etienne and the ax-wielding Pudge? In her mind, she visualized the man holding Etienne's dangling head from one hand, and she was glad she had prevented that. "This Pudge is a bit sick."

"Yes. I think he needs mental help," Etienne agreed. "Actually, I know he does."

"How? I mean, aside from the fact that he's tried to kill you countless times?" she asked in wry tones.

"I can't get into his mind to wipe his memory clean or control his actions." When Rachel's gaze narrowed with sudden suspicion, he added, "No, I can't read your mind or control your behavior either, but in your case I'm sure it has nothing to do with insanity."

Despite herself, Rachel smiled at his teasing tone. "So, there are some people you just can't read?" When he nodded, she suggested, "Then perhaps he's just like me, one of those people."

Etienne shook his head. "I explained it wrong. I *can* get into his mind, but it's such a painful procedure." He looked away and shrugged. "His thoughts are confused and murky. Fragmented is probably the best description. I couldn't make enough sense of his thoughts to do anything with them. Whereas with you, I simply can't read your thoughts."

"Hmm." Rachel considered, not sure she believed him. "Your mother doesn't seem to have any problem."

"Don't remind me." He sounded irritated.

"Why is it that she can and you can't?" Rachel asked, though she wasn't sure that was the case. It would be less embarrassing to believe her earlier behavior was due to his mind control. Unfortunately, she couldn't convince herself.

Etienne didn't answer. "Here we go," he said, drawing her attention to the game screen. "Level one."

Rachel watched the opening sequence in fascination, a smile of anticipation curving her lips. She was a secret video-game junkie and her work hours made a social life somewhat difficult, and so she had been known to waste hours playing them. The fact that Etienne was the creator of her favorite game raised him in her estimation. Gorgeous *and* brilliant? He was looking better by the moment, and he had looked pretty darned good at the start. Even as a corpse.

They played. Etienne was a stern taskmaster. There were no cheat codes allowed, and he wouldn't even give hints on what was coming next. He also insisted they couldn't use the sissy Easy level; they started and played on Expert, working as a team to hunt out and stake various meany vamps.

Rachel decided not to analyze the fact that the game was all about wiping out an evil vampire cadre. However, she couldn't help but wince every time she succeeded at dusting one of the villains. At last, Etienne noticed, and explained that these were "rogue vampires," not good ones like themselves. These guys liked to eat the old-fashioned way and took life doing it. She relaxed a bit then and really got into the game—to the point that when Etienne moved away for a minute, she hardly noticed until he set a mug by her hand.

Suddenly aware that she was thirsty, Rachel reached blindly for the mug and gulped down its contents. She then promptly spit it back. "Ewwww!" The tinny taste of cold, thick blood coated her tongue.

"Sorry." Etienne didn't sound very sorry. He was chuckling as he took the mug and grabbed a box of Kleenex off the end of his desk. She cleaned up the blood that had not made it back into the mug. "It's an acquired taste. I should have warned you."

Rachel grimaced and wiped her mouth. "I don't think I'm likely to acquire it anytime soon."

"Hmm." He looked troubled and drank from his own mug. Then, setting it aside, he said, "Well, if necessary we can feed you intravenously."

Rachel heaved out a defeated breath. "That sounds . . . wimpy."

He shrugged. "Inconvenient but manageable. Lissianna had to do it until recently."

"Your sister?" Rachel was surprised. Lissianna had seemed a strong woman, not at all squeamish like Rachel was feeling.

Etienne nodded. "She's suffered hemophobia from childhood. The sight and smell of blood made her faint. The only way she could feed was biting or taking blood intravenously."

"Biting? Wouldn't she taste it that way?"

"No. If you do it right, the teeth soak the blood in. It never touches your tongue."

"Then why didn't she just bite bags, like you did today?"

"The sight made her faint too," he reminded. "And she can hardly go around stabbing her teeth blindly into blood bags. She might make a heck of a mess if her aim is off. Then, too, there is the smell," he added. "The moment your teeth sink into a blood bag, the scent wafts up. It's a particular smell, bagged blood. For the rest of us, it's not a problem, but it is for Lissianna."

"I see," Rachel murmured, then became aware that he was frowning at her.

"How are you feeling?" he asked.

Rachel considered. They'd been playing Blood Lust II for hours, and she couldn't even recall the last time she'd eaten. She didn't think she had since before Pudge attacked her. "I'm hungry."

He nodded slowly. "I thought so. You look pale. Nothing will satisfy that hunger but blood."

Rachel grimaced. "Don't you guys eat any *food*?"

"*We*." He emphasized the word, reminding her that she was one of them now. "We certainly can and do eat food, especially while young. Children have to eat normal food as well as ingest blood to help muscle and bone grow. Those who don't are usually easy to tell—they're often stunted and emaciated. But after reaching adulthood, it isn't as necessary. After a hundred years or so, most grow tired of the hassle and sometimes even the taste, and they simply rely on blood with the occasional meal to help maintain muscle mass. Although Bastien is sure it isn't necessary."

Rachel considered, then cleared her throat. "Well, that means I have roughly seventy years before I get tired of eating."

Etienne managed a crooked smile. "I'll order something delivered from the deli."

"Deli?" Rachel frowned and glanced at her wrist-watch—which of course wasn't there. "What time is it?"

"A little after ten A.M."

"After ten?" she almost screeched. They'd played the night through and into morning. She supposed the saying was true that time flew when you were having fun. Still, it was hard to believe that they'd wasted the whole night.

"What would you like?" Etienne asked as he began to punch numbers into the phone on his desk.

Rachel thought, then asked for a Reuben, chips, and a Coke. She was *really* hungry, a feeling that was growing by the minute now that she was aware of it.

They played more Blood Lust II as they waited for the food to be delivered, but Rachel was distracted. She was relieved when the doorbell finally chimed, announcing the arrival of her order. Etienne excused himself and went to answer. Rachel knew he expected her to wait below in his office, but she just couldn't. Pausing the game, she followed him upstairs. She stepped into the kitchen just as he entered from the hallway, a deli bag in hand.

Rachel managed to control herself as he found her a plate and set out her food, but then she fell on the sandwich and chips with a ravenous hunger that was almost embarrassing. She didn't stop eating until she had consumed every last crumb and drunk every last drop of pop; then she sat back and frowned. Her stomach was full to bursting, yet her brain was still claiming she was hungry.

"You need blood," Etienne told her gently, seeming to realize her craving. "Bastien said you'd need a lot of it for a while. Your body is still changing."

"I thought I was done."

"Mostly done," he corrected. "There are still a couple of things left."

"Like what?" she asked curiously. She wondered if he would mention orgasms.

"Your senses will sharpen. Your ability to smell is already improved, but it will grow keener. And your eyesight, of course. You'll be able to to see in the dark."

"Your mother mentioned that," Rachel admitted. It didn't sound too bad. It was certainly better than facial lumps and bumps.

"Come." He stood. "We'll fix you up with an intravenous."

"I hate needles," Rachel complained, but she got reluctantly to her feet. "I mean I *really* hate them. I practically have a phobia."

"You need more blood. You won't feel better until you get some," Etienne lectured. He led the way up the hall.

Rachel stuck out her tongue at his back, but she knew he was right—she needed more blood. Her body was positively clamoring for it in a way that was almost painful. It was becoming obvious that her plans to leave were scotched unless she could bring herself to down bags of cold blood, but the very idea made her shudder.

"Can't I just bite someone?" she asked. For some reason, the idea held more appeal than a cold Baggie—although not much more. "Of course, it would have to be someone I don't like."

Etienne glanced back, mouth open, but paused when he caught her eyeing his neck. "Hey! I created Blood Lust, remember? Your favorite video game."

"Yes, but you're also the one who turned me in the first place," she reminded him.

Apparently, Etienne didn't catch that she was teasing. Guilt crossed his face, and he looked apologetic. "I am sorry about that, but I couldn't let you die."

It was simply no fun at all to tease someone so guilt-ridden. He obviously felt bad about the whole ordeal. Shrugging, Rachel moved past him and started up the stairs. "I'll get over it. I suppose this really is better than dead, right?"

Etienne's heavy sigh made Rachel pause and turn back. She didn't like him all grim and unhappy like this. She hadn't really meant to make him feel bad. Jollying him out of it seemed the best way to fix things, so she smiled brightly and said, "So . . . since you don't want me to bite you, maybe I can go find my boss and bite him. He's the one who put me on the night shift for three years."

Etienne looked uncertain. "It's daylight."

Rachel arched her eyebrows. "I thought you said we could go out in the daylight?"

"We can, but then you'll need more blood to repair the damage sunlight does to you. Besides, biting really *is* something we try to avoid at all costs."

"You know," Rachel said with mild disgust, "sometimes you seem lacking in a sense of humor." She turned to continue up the stairs. "I was kidding about the biting bit. If I can't stomach biting a Baggie, I certainly wouldn't do much better with a live person. Sheesh."

"Oh. I thought you might be joking, but I wasn't sure."

Rachel laughed, not believing him for a minute. It didn't really matter, though; she had only been teasing him in an effort to distract herself from the idea of having to go through the intravenous deal again.

It had always amazed Rachel's family that she could work in the medical field yet still act like a baby when it came to shots and such. She'd grown better over the years. For instance, she no longer cried like a baby as it was done. Still, shots were a stressful ordeal for her. But she had too much pride to show fear to Etienne, so she suffered his hooking her up in silence and merely closed her eyes, hoping he would think her weary and not cowardly.

"Well . . ."

She opened her eyes and glanced at Etienne curiously. He had finished with the IV and now stood uncertainly by the bed, looking as if he weren't sure what to do next. Noting his gaze was fixed on her lips, she had the brief thought he was debating kissing her; then he gave himself a slight shake and moved away, muttering, "I'll be in my office. Wake me if you need anything."

Rachel grimaced at the idea of his sleeping in that small dark box meant for the dead, but merely murmured good night and watched him leave.

The moment she was alone, she closed her eyes to avoid looking at the intravenous. Her mind wandered, immediately beginning to pull out images and sensations from earlier. She recalled in detail those passionate moments here on the bed with Etienne, every little sensation, every indrawn breath, but when the point came where Marguerite entered the room, Rachel's mind rebelliously made up its own scenario. Instead of being interrupted, the door stayed closed and Rachel found what her hand had been seeking. In her mind, Etienne was well endowed, as he had claimed. He was also as hard and smooth as a time-tempered stone, and . . .

Etienne sighed and shifted in his coffin, his mind full of images: He was back in his room. Rachel lay atop him, her breasts revealed to his hungry gaze, her hand slipping inside his slacks to curl warm and firm around his erection. He groaned, jerking in her hold, his body responding with eagerness. When her hand slid the length of him, he had to stop her or embarrass himself.

Growling deep in his throat, he bucked and shifted, rolling her onto her back in the bed, then rolling over her to take control of the situation. The abrupt shift startled Rachel into a gasp and made the top she wore gape open, revealing even more of her pale breasts. Taking advantage, Etienne dropped his head to lick the smooth, salty-sweet skin as he'd longed to do earlier.

Rachel bit her lip, biting back a moan and squirming, struggling to free the hands he held captured in his own. He knew she wanted to touch him back, wanted to caress him as well, but he didn't have the control at the moment to allow that—and he wanted her as excited and hungry for him as he was for her. Shifting, he took both of her hands in one of his, then reached down to remove his belt.

"I could help with that," Rachel offered, arching restlessly beneath him. He fumbled one-handed with the chore, merely smiling and shaking his head. At last he succeeded in removing the item of clothing, then wrapped it around her trapped hands, slid the end through the buckle, and pulled it tight.

"What are you doing?" Rachel gasped as he tied the belt to his headboard. "I don't—"

He silenced her protest with a kiss.

Rachel arched on the bed, her mind a jumble of confusion. Somehow her fantasy was barreling out of control. Things had been fine in this dream until Etienne turned the tables on her and rolled her onto her back, but now the fantasy was taking a path she had never expected—and she seemed helpless to stop it. Of course, Rachel wasn't sure she wanted to stop it, but the very fact that it was happening was bewildering. She was positive that she was alone in bed, dreaming, but she could feel Etienne against her in the darkness, could smell the musky cologne he wore, could taste the essence of him as his tongue thrust into her mouth. Bemused, she decided to just go with it. Allowing her mouth to widen, her own tongue slid out to join and tangle with his, and she tugged uselessly at the belt around her wrists in a vain effort to free herself to hold and touch him too.

She was gasping when his mouth left hers, panting with excitement but disappointed that he had broken the kiss . . . until his mouth traveled down her throat to the swell of her breast. Somehow the shirt she wore had come open, leaving her naked to his pleasure. Fortunately, his pleasure was her own. She cried out and arched back as he caressed and suckled first one breast, then the other. When he moved lower, his lips trailing down her belly, Rachel moaned and shuddered, very aware that his fingers were leading the way, trailing down over her hipbone, then down her outer leg and up her thigh.

Her legs seemed unsure what to do, and Rachel shifted restlessly beneath his caress. First her thighs pressed together, then they opened slightly, then they simply quivered and twitched beneath Etienne's fingers. Rachel wasn't much of a singer, but she suspected she hit a high C when his caress reached her center. She jerked, moaned, and twisted her head on the bed, especially when his mouth replaced his fingers.

She did very little thinking after that. The only cogent thought Rachel managed was that Etienne was damned good—but then, he'd had three hundred years of practice. Well, it showed. Rachel had never experienced anything like it. Etienne had said earlier that her senses weren't fully developed, but she was definitely experiencing something intense. Her pleasure was perhaps not twenty times what it had once been at its peak, but it was at least two- or threefold. It was almost scary. Almost.

The ringing of the phone woke Etienne. His eyes shot open, his mind and body immediately alert. Although his body appeared to have been already alert, if the erection he sported was anything to go by. Forcing himself to ignore the clamoring of his body, he pushed his coffin lid open and sat up. In the next moment, he crossed the room to snatch the phone.

"Hello?" he barked, unable to hide his annoyance.

Silence. Etienne listened for a moment, eyes narrowing as the dead air stretched, malevolent and angry. Then he guessed, "Pudge?"

A click as the line went dead was his answer. Etienne set the phone back with a troubled frown. The techie hadn't called since Etienne had told him in no uncertain terms he wasn't going to be hired; then the killing attempts had started. Yet Etienne was sure that had just been Pudge. He didn't know why the fellow had called, but he suspected it wasn't good.

He turned back to survey his coffin with irritation. The idea of getting back in wasn't appealing. His dream had wound him up. He was now too restless to sleep—at least alone in a dark, confining coffin. It suddenly didn't seem the cozy, comforting spot where he could think and plan, it just seemed cold and dark. And lonely.

Sighing, Etienne left his office and headed upstairs. He would check on Rachel and change her blood bag, then perhaps work for a while. He didn't think he'd get back to sleep anytime soon.

His guest was sound asleep when he reached her. She was also scowling. It was an expression he had seen on her face several times while awake, but he had never expected to see it while she was sleeping. What did it mean? He moved to the side of the bed rather than to the refrigerator. The scowl was one of dissatisfaction, perhaps, for the bed was a tangled mess of sheets and blankets, half kicked aside, half twisted around her body. Rachel was obviously just as restless as he. Then he noticed that her hands rested above her head—in much the same position he had restrained them in his dream. The dream that had seemed so real.

Realization struck. Doubt immediately followed,

however, and Etienne decided to test his hypothesis. Closing his eyes, he reached out with his mind . . . and immediately retracted his thoughts when, instead of the blank wall he usually encountered, he glimpsed Rachel's thoughts. It seemed her mind, which was firmly closed to him when she was awake, was wide open when she slept. Which meant the dream or fantasy he'd experienced had probably been a shared moment. Either he had been pulled into Rachel's dreams, or she had been pulled into his.

It didn't really matter who had started the episode, Etienne supposed. The most important fact was that, despite everything, Rachel was still attracted to him. There was no mistaking her little moans or her response to him—at least in dreams—as anything like repulsion or disgust. That was good. He was certainly attracted to her. It gave Etienne hope. Perhaps he wouldn't have to spend eternity without a life mate. Perhaps things would work out. It would take some time to find out for sure, however, and to get that time he would have to convince Rachel to remain here with him.

He supposed he could do the normal mortal dating thing: take her out, wine and dine her, seduce her. But there were complications. Pudge was one. Then, there was that she had to learn to live her life differently. Controlling her body's responses was one of the more important lessons she needed to master.

Walking to the refrigerator, Etienne fetched fresh

blood, then moved to replace the nearly empty bag on the IV stand. Once that was accomplished, he peered down at Rachel again, finding himself reaching out to brush a tress of red hair away from her face and smiling when she sighed in her sleep and turned into his touch. He would find a way to make her stay with him. He wanted to protect her, though she didn't seem the kind who would take well to coddling.

After straightening the blankets and tugging them up to cover her, he quietly left the room. He had to marshal his thoughts and come up with a convincing argument to make her stay for a couple of weeks. And he had to work on convincing her to fall in with the family's suggestion she claim Pudge had kidnapped her. Pudge was still very much a threat, and Rachel still had a lot to learn.

Chapter Eight

It was already dark out when Rachel woke up. She was used to that however, though usually only in late fall and winter when night came early. One of the things she had always hated about working nights was in the winter, coming home at seven in the morning and having to sleep away the few daylight hours available. Oddly enough, this time, sleeping so long didn't seem to bother her. She woke up refreshed and eager to start her day—or evening, as was the case.

With little choice when it came to wardrobe, Rachel re-donned the tight jeans and T-shirt Marguerite had retrieved for her, then raided Etienne's wardrobe for a long-sleeved dress shirt. Drawing it on over her, she tied the loose ends of the open shirt at her waist, then spent a moment in the bathroom, brushing her teeth and hair. She considered slapping on some of the face powder and lipstick Marguerite had also been thoughtful enough to bring, but in truth she didn't need it. Her skin glowed with good health and her lips were redder than usual. It appeared there were other benefits to being a vampire—she would save a fortune on cosmetics.

Grinning, Rachel left the bedroom and jogged downstairs. Wandering to the kitchen, she didn't find Etienne there so she continued on down to the basement. The office was dim, with just the glow of screen savers on the monitors. She could see that the room was empty, though, except for the closed coffin. Etienne obviously hadn't woken up yet.

Rachel's gaze slid to the desk and the phone there. It was the only one she'd seen in the house, and she wanted to make a quick call to her family, just to let them know she was all right. She didn't like the idea of them worrying about her.

She took a step toward the phone, then caught herself. Making the phone call would wake Etienne, and if it did . . . Well, she wasn't sure what his reaction would be. He should awake soon, anyway. She could ask him then to use the phone. She backed silently out of the room and returned upstairs.

Debating what to do next, Rachel decided to explore. She wandered aimlessly from room to room on the ground floor, appreciating the eclectic modern style but not stopping until she came to the library.

She'd always been a bookworm. Pausing to survey the shelves and the books available, one caught her interest. She settled in one of the overstuffed chairs, tucked her feet up under her, and began to read. That was how Etienne found her.

"I thought you were still sleeping," Rachel said as she closed her book and stood to replace it on its shelf.

"No. I went to get you some more clothes. I thought you might like a change."

"Oh. That was kind of you." She looked at the discomfort on his face, then the bag he carried, then back. "How exactly is it that you and your mother are getting into my apartment? Can vampires manipulate locks with their minds or something?"

Etienne grinned. "No. We've been using your keys. They were in your purse."

"Ah," Rachel murmured. "My purse is here. That's good to know." She would need it when she decided she was ready to leave.

"I put it up in your room before I went out this afternoon."

"You mean your room," Rachel corrected Etienne, then tilted her head inquiringly. "Which reminds me, am I going to have to sleep in a coffin after the change is finished?"

"No." He shook his head. "We don't really need them anymore. Homes in the old days were drafty, and it was hard to keep out light. Then too, there were servants and such to be concerned with. Nowadays, a good set of blackout blinds, a lock, and an alarm system are enough to do the trick."

"Oh, good." Rachel moved to his side and took the bag he'd packed for her. "I guess I'll go change my top at least. That way you can have yours back."

"Fine." He waited until she was in the hall before he asked, "Rachel?"

She turned back. "Yes?"

"Come back when you're ready. We need to talk."

Rachel was silent for a moment, then she nodded and walked upstairs. The serious expression on his face made her nervous. What did he want to discuss? Rachel suspected it was something she wasn't going to like. Perhaps there were more drawbacks to this whole business that hadn't yet been mentioned.

Deciding it wasn't something she was likely to guess at—and that even if she did, she wouldn't know if she was right until they talked—Rachel hurried to her room and set the bag on the bed. Sorting through what he'd brought back, she found an array of her rather limited wardrobe. Dress slacks and blouses made up the majority of it, all work clothes. With a practically nonexistent social life, she hadn't needed much else besides a robe and fluffy slippers.

Rachel chose one of the tops and changed into it, but she didn't bother to change out of the jeans. They had stretched with wear and, while still tight, were becoming comfortable again. Rachel supposed they hadn't been all that tight to begin with, and had simply seemed so because she had become used to loose dress pants over the years. After a quick check of herself in the bathroom mirror, she took a deep breath, straightened her shoulders, and headed downstairs.

Rachel tried to mentally prepare herself for whatever unpleasantness Etienne might wish to talk about, but since she wasn't sure what it was, she couldn't really do much.

Etienne paced the library, his mind racing, trying to line up his arguments. He figured that once he convinced Rachel to stay, he would have the time necessary to work on the Pudge matter. Despite her protest, he didn't think it should be too difficult to convince her to claim the man had kidnapped her—it was in her own best interest too.

Etienne decided it would be best to start by sympathizing with her. Rachel would be concerned about her job and the possibility of losing it. She would be worried about her family, her friends, and their fears and worry over her. She might even have a boyfriend out there, anxious about her well-being.

The thought caught Etienne by surprise. Until that moment, he hadn't even considered that there might be a rival for her affections. It didn't make him very happy to consider it now, but it was definitely something he needed to know.

After explaining that he understood her concerns,

Etienne would then point out that, while these were all valid concerns, the main concern was Rachel's health and well-being—as well as that of his people. He would point out that her immediate return to work and home might threaten her welfare. First, there was Pudge. The man would know she was one of them now if she returned healthy, and that would make her a possible target. Then there was her inexperience and lack of control. Should her teeth pop out, or her hunger overcome her while at work, her change would be revealed, threatening both her and his family. Worse, unable to control minds yet, Rachel wouldn't even have a chance to repair the damage she would cause. And then there was the blood issue. Not being able to feed herself was a major problem.

"Here I am."

Etienne turned from the window and looked at Rachel. She had kept on the jeans, but had changed her top to a green blouse that brought out the color of her eyes. She looked gorgeous. Breathtaking. Every argument Etienne had lined up in his head now marched gaily out of it, leaving him rather lost.

"You wanted to talk?" Rachel prompted, moving farther into the room as he merely stood staring at her.

"Yes. Talk," Etienne agreed, but that was as much as he could manage. He felt like someone had pole-axed him.

Why? It wasn't like it was the first time he'd seen the woman. He'd been aware of her beauty from the first. Perhaps the attraction was from the uncertainty on her face and the way her eyes held mild anxiety. Or the way she caught her lower lip with her teeth to worry it. Then again, it might be the fact that, instead of the covered T-shirt, she was now wearing a blouse with the top two or three buttons undone. That exposed cleavage he had licked in his dreams—or their shared dream.

"Didn't you want to talk?"

Etienne gave himself a mental shake. "Yes. Yes, I . . . Look, I know you're probably upset not to be able to contact your family and friends and boyfr—Do you have a boyfriend?" he interrupted himself.

"Not at the moment," Rachel said.

"Oh, good." He grinned.

Her eyebrows rose. "Why is that good?"

"Why?" Etienne was stumped for a moment, then settled for, "Well, it's one less worry, right?"

She nodded slowly, looking perplexed.

"Well, anyway." He cleared his throat. "I know you're upset about this, but—"

"But I have to learn to feed before I can leave here," she interrupted.

"You do?" he asked with surprise. Then he corrected, "I mean, you realize that?"

"Of course. It wouldn't do for my teeth to pop out at work, or for me to take a bite out of a family member, coworker, or our priest."

"No. No, that wouldn't be good," he agreed, grinning with relief. She was being very sensible.

"So we should probably get down to the business of teaching me to feed."

"Yes." He nodded but just stood there, staring at her until she arched her eyebrows.

"Where should we do it? The kitchen?" she asked.

"Yes, of course." Etienne forced himself to move forward, but his mind was racing. She seemed determined to conquer this problem, which was good, but he'd rather she didn't resolve it too quickly. He wanted to keep her in his home for a while.

There were ways to delay her managing to ingest blood, but it meant he'd have to put in a call to Bastien. "Why don't you sit down and relax a while?" he suggested, pausing at the door. "We have to wait on an order of blood to be delivered anyway."

"I thought you had lots," she said with surprise.

"No," Etienne lied. "We used the last of my supply last night. I had to change your bag several times."

"Oh." Rachel sighed. "Okay. I'll read a while."

Smiling, Etienne left her to it and hurried out of the room.

"Oh, God!" Rachel spat the blood back into the mug and pushed it away with disgust. "How do you drink this stuff? It's disgusting! Gross! It smells like skunk! Are you sure it hasn't gone bad?"

Etienne tried not to look guilty. The blood hadn't *gone* bad. It was bad blood. It was basically reject blood—a combination of the thick clotty blood of cigarette smokers, the skunky corpuscles of pot smokers, and a trace of the blood of patients on Valium. It was nourishing enough and wouldn't really hurt her, but it was vile to consume and had the unpleasant side effects of wooziness and nausea.

Not knowing what he was giving her, Rachel was of course putting her physical response down to a psychological aversion to the idea of drinking blood. Etienne didn't correct her misconception. He was also insisting she be able to consume it from a glass rather than a bag, telling her she had to be prepared for all occasions before she would be ready to leave and rejoin the world. During the last two days, since the reject blood had been delivered, Rachel had tried three times a day to consume the bad mix, only to spit it back up. After each attempt, they either played his latest game or talked, or simply sat reading together in the library.

Other than the unpleasant attempts with the blood, it had been a nice couple of days. Unfortunately, to keep her from being suspicious, Etienne had been forced to drink the bad blood too. He wasn't sure how he had managed without gagging.

"Well, I suppose that's enough for today," he said empathetically. "You gave it a good go. Maybe tomorrow—"

"Tomorrow is going to be just like today," Rachel predicted gloomily. "I'll never get used to this stuff."

Etienne was searching his mind for some way to cheer and encourage her—and maybe even distract her so that he could avoid finishing the mug he had poured for himself—when the doorbell rang.

He wasn't surprised to find his mother on the doorstep. He *was* surprised when the first words out of her mouth weren't a greeting.

"Where is Rachel?" she asked.

"Right here."

Etienne glanced over his shoulder to see Rachel approaching. "Is something wrong?" she asked, looking anxious.

"No, no. I just thought you might be getting a little housebound and would want to get out," Marguerite said lightly. She ran her eyes over the outfit Rachel wore. "That will do, dear. Would you like to come play?"

"I don't think—" Etienne began.

Rachel stepped to his side and interrupted. "Where exactly?" she asked.

"To Lissianna's wedding shower, dear. Our side of the family only. It will give you the chance to meet other young women like yourself."

Etienne felt his hopes for the evening dissolve into a pang of loneliness.

"What's this?" Rachel asked with suspicion. Lissianna's friend Mirabeau held out a plate containing what looked very like a slice of cake.

"German seven-layer chocolate cake, dear," Marguerite answered.

"*Real* cake?" Rachel asked. She accepted the plate and murmured a thank-you to Mirabeau.

"Of course." Etienne's mother chuckled. "What were you expecting?"

"I don't know," Rachel admitted with a wry twist of her lips. "Black Forest blood cake?"

Marguerite and the women around her burst into gales of laughter. "Isn't she adorable?" Etienne's mother asked when it died down. Rachel blushed, for there was general agreement voiced.

She'd had a surprisingly good time at the shower so far. Marguerite had taken her to a special salon to purchase a gift for Lissianna, insisting on paying for it herself when Rachel realized that she hadn't brought her purse. Actually, despite Etienne's claim that he'd put it up in the room she was using, she had yet to see it. But then Rachel hadn't really looked; she hadn't needed it for anything since being turned. She had decided she would have to look around when she returned to the house, because she wanted to repay Marguerite right away. The woman had been incredibly sweet, and Rachel didn't want to take advantage of her kindness.

"What woman could live without chocolate?"

Rachel glanced to the speaker—Jeanne Louise, a woman as beautiful in her way as Lissianna and Marguerite, though she looked nothing like them. Her face was rounder, her lips a little thinner, her eyes more exotic and her hair a midnight black. She was a cousin to Lissianna and niece to Marguerite, and while Rachel liked all three women, Jeanne Louise was someone with whom Rachel was pretty sure she could be best friends. The woman worked for Argeneau Industries in their labs, and had regaled her with stories of the work she did. She'd been rather vague until realizing Rachel had no problem following what she was saying; then excited to find someone who had a working knowledge of experimental techniques and jargon, the other woman went into depth, fascinating Rachel with the tests she was performing. It seemed Argeneau Industries was as interested in medical research as anyone else.

The two women had only stopped talking once the games started, which were, much to Rachel's amazement, the usual at wedding showers. At that point, it had all seemed so pedestrian she might have forgotten the guests were vampires. Rachel sat silent for a while, simply noting the different looks and personalities in the room. The guests were all different: short women, tall women, beautiful women, homely women. As for personalities, there were a couple of sophisticated types who seemed to drawl their words and look down their noses; girl-next-door types who were sweet and kind; a few smart-girl types who looked slightly uncomfortable and spoke softly; and there was even a vampy vamp in a skintight black outfit who teased

Lissianna unendingly about the wedding night to come. It was your basic mix, just like your everyday shower.

Forgetting that Marguerite could read her mind, Rachel had been startled when the woman suddenly leaned close and murmured, "Of course it is, dear. We're normal people, just as you are."

"Except that you're all several hundred years old and likely to get a lot older," she'd pointed out.

"So will you," Marguerite reminded her with amusement. "But we're all still just people. Think of us like cars. We have extra rust protection that will make us last longer, but we're still just cars in the end—with the same worries and concerns as cars without rust proofing. Besides," she'd added, "there are a couple of girls here who are under a hundred. Jeanne Louise is only ninety-two."

Rachel had turned to look at the beautiful lab technician and shaken her head. "She's the sexiest ninety-two I've ever seen."

Jeanne Louise had overheard the comment and laughed.

"Besides, Black Forest blood cake doesn't sound very appetizing at all," she was saying now.

Drawn back to the conversation at hand, Rachel sliced off a piece. "No, it doesn't. I don't know how you manage to stomach ingesting blood. Etienne says it's an acquired taste, but I seem to be having trouble.

If it weren't for the pain and weakness when I don't get it, I'd give up."

She forked herself some cake and started to chew, then paused when Jeanne Louise and Marguerite exchanged a glance. Rachel didn't know if it was her improving instincts or not, but she was positive the women were conversing mentally. About her. Eyebrows raised in question, she asked, "What?"

"Nothing, dear." Marguerite patted her arm and smiled. "Enjoy your cake. And here, have some tea."

Rachel accepted the tea, and she ate and drank in silence for a moment, simply listening to the talk around her. Then she asked Marguerite, "How long did it take you to adjust to ingesting blood?"

This time she didn't mistake the glance Jeanne Louise and Marguerite exchanged. They *were* talking silently about her. Then Etienne's mother smiled and said, "I adjusted relatively quickly, dear. Right away, really. But it was different, then. There were no blood banks. We had to eat 'off the hoof,' as we used to say."

Rachel didn't even try to hide her horror. "Off the hoof?"

"Well . . ." Marguerite smiled and shrugged. "You call corpses crispy critters and such to help disassociate yourself from the unpleasantness of them being dead. We, much in the same way, had phrases and such to distance ourselves emotionally from having to feed off otherwise perfectly lovely people."

"Oh." Rachel nodded. She then ate in silence, her

mind consumed with the thought that people like her family and friends were now her main food source. How icky was that? It was definitely one of the negatives to this deal. She was almost relieved that biting was not allowed any longer. Biting people might be easier and make for fewer dishes, but at least the packaging allowed her to pretend she wasn't eating people. She supposed it was like the difference between buying meat in the grocery store and slaughtering your own cow.

Lissianna opened her gifts after the food was done. She got some lovely things and seemed to really like the cream-colored negligee Rachel had chosen for her.

Beverages were then served—the beverages Rachel had expected all along. Long-stemmed wine goblets full of blood were produced. Rachel took hers but merely held it, not wanting to gag or otherwise embarrass herself in front of these people as she circulated. They were all lovely women, and all too kind to comment on the way her teeth kept popping in and out every time she caught a whiff of blood. The tinny scent didn't appeal to her, but her teeth certainly seemed to like it. Obviously she needed to work on that problem. Etienne had insisted it wasn't as important as learning to actually consume the blood, but Rachel found it rather embarrassing today and decided to talk to him when she returned home that night.

That thought caught her by surprise and made her pause. Home? She'd meant Etienne's home, which wasn't her home. She was becoming far too comfortable there. Perhaps even too comfortable with Etienne himself. The man had saved her life in return for her saving his but, as far as she could tell, that was the only relationship they had. He certainly hadn't shown her anything but friendship and kindness.

Well, that first night he had . . . but then it had been her who attacked him. And, much to her disappointment, he hadn't acted interested in her since. At least while she was awake. In her dreams, the man came to her every night and tortured her. Erotic kisses and caresses he gave, and all that left her wound up and unsatisfied because they always ended abruptly before Rachel could find satisfaction. It seemed she hadn't quite got the hang of wet dreams yet. She knew they didn't leave Sylvia frustrated and wanting, so she was obviously doing something wrong. Her mind shied from completion for some reason.

"It was a pleasure meeting you, Rachel. I hope we see you at the wedding. Are you going?" Jeanne Louise asked.

Rachel tore herself from her thoughts and glanced around in surprise. Everyone was gathering their things and preparing to leave. It seemed the shower was over.

"She's certainly invited," Lissianna announced as she joined them. "And I *hope* she'll attend."

163

"It depends on whether we have that other matter cleared up," Marguerite said. Looking thoughtful, she added, "Although, if we were to change her looks somewhat and call her R. J. instead of Rachel, there shouldn't be any trouble with Greg's family recognizing her from the news footage." She nodded. "Yes, we might manage it."

"Good," Lissianna said firmly. She hugged Rachel. "I'd like you to be there. I think we'll be grand friends. Like sisters."

Rachel smiled, but she didn't miss the exchange of glances between Marguerite and Lissianna. She really had to make Etienne teach her the mind-reading business. She felt sure the silent conversations going on here were much more important than the verbal ones.

"Damn!" Rachel slammed the mug of blood down and glared at it furiously. She just couldn't stomach the stuff. She'd managed to work herself up to being able to gulp down a couple swallows, but the taste was so vile and the smell so putrid that her mind and stomach rebelled.

"You're doing better," Etienne assured her. "Soon you'll be able to manage it without a problem."

Rachel glared at him, then stood and paced to the kitchen window to glare out at the starlit night sky. She hadn't been out of the house in the two days since the shower, and it felt like that was weeks ago. She was starting to go stir-crazy, locked up in this house all day and night with nothing to do but read and try to consume blood. She was sick of it. She needed fresh air. She could also use some damned exercise. Her nightly erotic dreams had continued, but still without any satisfaction. Every time, just before Rachel got to the point she wanted, the dream stopped abruptly. She was wound as tightly as a clock.

"I have to get out of here," she announced, turning to glare at Etienne, as if her edginess was his fault. "I need fresh air and exercise and . . . I just need to get out of here. Now."

Etienne was silent for a moment. At first he looked reluctant, but then he nodded. "I have an idea. Wait here. I'll be right back."

Scowling, Rachel watched him hurry from the room. She very much feared he would take her for a nice moonlight walk, something sedate and stately. She didn't want sedate and stately. She needed hot, sweaty exercise to work off the sexual tension that was cramping her body. If anyone had suggested it to her before she'd been turned, Rachel would never have believed that life as a vampire could be so damned boring.

Chapter Nine

"This is great! Just what I needed."

Etienne smiled at Rachel's excitement, leading her to an open table where they were seated. His idea was obviously inspired. He didn't usually go to the Night Club—a private club solely for vampires, open from sunset to sunrise—but he had understood Rachel's desires. He was in dire need himself. After several nights of shared dreams interrupted each time by a repeat of that first phone call, he was ready to burst.

Etienne now had no doubt that Pudge was making those nightly calls, but he didn't know what to do. He considered just leaving the phone off the hook but worried about family being able to contact him if there was an emergency. Thus, every night he had left the phone on the hook, gone to sleep, and joined

Rachel in some of the most erotic dreams he'd ever had—only to be interrupted at that crucial junction. If her frustration level was as high as his, only a visit to the Night Club would help relieve it.

At least he hoped this visit would work, for both their sakes. He had to work off some tension or he was likely to jump Rachel soon—something he didn't want to do until he had a better idea how she felt about him. Relationships were difficult when one couldn't read the other's mind. Etienne had never been one to control a woman and make her want him, but if he found a woman attractive and read her mind to find that she was equally interested, in the past he had been able to approach the situation with more confidence. With Rachel, he was feeling his way around a minefield.

Of course, he knew she was attracted to him, but he wasn't sure how much of that was just gratitude for saving her life. He wanted more than gratitude from this woman. He had decided they would do very well together as life mates, so that was what he was working toward. But he had never done that before, so he felt rather like he was stumbling around in the dark. Etienne had never felt at quite such a disadvantage before. He'd never had so much on the line. He didn't like it.

"Wow! This is a happening place!"

Etienne smiled as Rachel bounced enthusiastically in her seat, tapped her fingers and feet to the music, and glanced around. It was obvious that she wanted—perhaps even needed—to dance. He opened his mouth to suggest just that, but then his gaze shifted over the dance floor and took in the hip-bumping and wild gyrations of the dancers. He'd been something of a dandy in his day, had kept up with the popular dances of the time, right up until he had become bored with the interchangeable women he was bedding, but when he had grown tired of that, he had cut back on the social life bit by bit until it had died altogether. He now didn't have a clue what the people on the dance floor were doing. It looked like half of them were having some sort of seizure.

"Yo! Cousin!"

Etienne glanced around at that exclamation, an affectionate grin curving his lips as he spotted his cousin Thomas. Rising he hugged the younger man and slapped his back.

"I can't believe you're here, man!" Thomas said. "Talk about a shocker! What's it been? A century?"

"Not that long," Etienne answered dryly.

"Nearly," Thomas insisted. Then he glanced at Rachel with interest. "You must be Rachel. Jeanne was talking about you. I'm her brother Thomas. You can call me Tom."

Rachel smiled and accepted his hand. "You must mean Jeanne Louise. I really enjoyed talking to her at Lissianna's shower. She's your sister?" Her eyes took in Thomas's stylish hair and his tight black T-shirt and leather pants, with amusement, Etienne hoped. "Let me guess; you're her *younger* brother? Twenty-eight or twenty-nine to her ninety-two?"

"Wrong." He grinned. "I'm older. Two hundred and six. Mom wants to have another baby, but she has to wait another ten years or so."

"Oh, yes." Rachel made a face. "I forgot about the hundred-year rule."

Thomas chuckled, then glanced over Rachel much the same way she had looked at him—only his attention was on the way her hands and feet, nearly her whole body, were moving to the music. She was pretty much dancing in place. "You're gonna be dancing on a table in a minute if someone doesn't intercede," he teased lightly. "You look like a woman who needs to groove."

Rachel laughed. "How very astute of you to notice."

"What can I say? I'm an astute dude," he teased. Taking her hand, he said, "Come on, I'll be your knight in leather pants and take you to the dance floor."

Etienne grimaced as Rachel went off with his cousin. She hadn't even looked his way. He shouldn't have hesitated over dancing, he told himself with irritation. He should have taken her straight out there. It was what they both needed.

"You snooze, you lose, cousin." Those laughing words reminded Etienne that he was in a vampire haven where several of the more powerful vampires could read his thoughts. Including his cousin. He had

obviously become too used to his own company, where guarding his thoughts wasn't necessary.

Irritated with himself, Etienne firmly slammed his mind closed to keep others from probing his thoughts. Then he settled back in his seat, watching with irritation as Thomas and Rachel began to have their own seizures on the dance floor.

"So, how are you getting along with Cousin Etienne?"

Rachel smiled and shrugged. "Fine. He's a nice guy."

"Oh, man!" Thomas grabbed his chest as if she'd stabbed him. "Nice? That's the kiss of death."

Rachel laughed at his dramatics, even more amused when he arched one eyebrow several times and said, "That makes it obvious my cousin isn't making moves. He needs a poke, I think. Come on, let's poke him."

Much to Rachel's confusion, Thomas's idea of poking Etienne was to pull her into his arms and begin dancing in a slow style to the hiphop beat around them.

"Er . . . Thomas, have you noticed this is a fast song?" Rachel had to yell to be heard over the music.

His hands slid down her back to rest on her behind. "Yeah. Etienne's noticed too," he yelled back, drawing her closer still and laughing. "Here he comes! Definitely poked! You can thank me later, dudette—I'll be your knight in shiny leather any day." He gave her a slap on the behind, then unhanded her as Etienne appeared. With an innocent expression, he yelled, "Cutting in?"

Etienne's answer was a smoldering look that made Rachel incredulous. Had she wondered if he was interested in her? The jealousy and anger on his face seemed to suggest that he was. Yet he hadn't acted anything but friendly when they were alone.

She didn't get the chance to ponder the matter further. Etienne ignored the fast-paced music just as Thomas had, and pulled her into his arms. She hadn't thought it possible, but he actually held her closer than his cousin, and whereas Thomas's hands had rested lightly on her rump, Etienne took a firm grip, steering her around the dance floor. Rachel was plastered against his front, intimately aware of every bump and curve in the man's physique in a way that was breathtaking. After only a couple of moments, she was feeling hot, breathless, and in desperate need of a drink.

Much to her relief, when she suggested it to Etienne, he concurred at once. He escorted her back to their table. Thomas had apparently decided to join them. He was seated there and grinned at them widely when they arrived.

Etienne scowled at the younger vampire as he pulled out Rachel's chair—a gesture she hadn't experienced in her whole life of modern dating. He said, "Behave. I'll be right back."

Rachel watched him leave with surprise. He disappeared into a door marked with the international symbol for a man. The bathroom.

"Drinks, people?"

Rachel peered uncertainly at the waitress smiling at her. Then her gaze drifted helplessly to Thomas. "I'm not sure what they have," she admitted, feeling a little lost. It being a vampire bar, she presumed they served blood here. But did they serve other drinks?

"Allow me," he suggested. Rachel would have been relieved by the offer, except for the way the man was grinning. "Two Sweet Ecstasies and a Virgin Mary."

"What's a Virgin Mary?" Rachel asked suspiciously as the waitress walked away. She supposed that the Sweet Ecstasies were for the men and the Virgin Mary for her. Thomas's answer corrected her misconception.

"Blood, Worcestershire and Tabasco sauce with a squeeze of lemon. I like hot and spicy," he said with a grin.

"Oh," Rachel said faintly. The drink sounded disgusting. She was almost afraid to ask what was in the Sweet Ecstasy.

"Sometimes it's better not to know." Thomas leaned forward so that he wouldn't have to yell. He had obviously read her thoughts. It was rather annoying not to be able to have a thought of your own without people listening all the time. Rachel was much more comfortable with just Etienne, who claimed not to be able to read her mind. If he was lying and really could, at least he was polite enough not to comment.

"It doesn't matter," she answered Thomas. "I should have warned you not to bother if all they serve here is blood. I haven't quite mastered the technique of ingesting it yet." She shuddered at the very thought.

Thomas considered her for a moment. Rachel suspected he was sifting her brain for what might be the problem, then he nodded. "Don't worry about it. My sister-in-law had the same problem. We found a fix. I'll show you when the waitress brings the drinks."

Rachel felt a moment's hope that he really might have a solution; then her thoughts turned to wondering what was in the Sweet Ecstasies he had apparently ordered.

"They have all sorts of drinks here," Thomas said, obviously reading her thoughts again. "Some are mixed drinks like the Virgin Mary, which is straight blood with something added, and others are specialty bloods. Like Sweet Tooth."

"Sweet Tooth?" Rachel asked.

"Mmm." He nodded. "The blood of diabetics. Aunt Marguerite really likes those," he added before continuing. "Then there is high iron or high potassium blood. Oh, and High Times. That's a drink made from the blood of pot smokers."

"No way!" Rachel gaped at him.

"Sure. Get the buzz without the damage to the lungs that smoking causes." He chuckled at her expression.

Rachel stared at him for a moment in disbelief, then asked, "So, do they have one with a high alcohol content?"

"Oh, yeah. It's called Wino Reds. Etienne's dad was big on that drink. *Real* big."

The way he said it made Rachel ask, "An alcoholic?"

"Yeah." He nodded solemnly. "We have alcoholics and druggies just like the regular population. We just have to consume it through blood."

"Alcoholic vampires," Rachel muttered, hardly able to believe it.

"I'll tell you a secret." Thomas leaned across the table again so that their heads almost met. "They were all worried about Lissi following in her father's footsteps for a while."

"No." Rachel sat back in shock. "Etienne's sister?"

"Yes." He nodded solemnly. "She was a hemophobic from childhood on."

"Yes. Etienne mentioned that. So, was she drinking to get over it, or—"

"No. She didn't drink. At least not the way you mean. Lissianna had to live at home and take her blood intravenously for the first couple hundred years. It was so bad she couldn't even hook herself up. Marguerite had to control her mind and put her to sleep to do it. But then, when old Claude died—"

"Claude?" Rachel interrupted.

"Marguerite's husband. He drank too much Wino

Reds, passed out with a lit cigarette in his hand, and burned to death."

"So fire can kill us?" Rachel asked.

"Yeah. Fire. Having your head cut off and destroying or stopping the heart too," he informed her. After a moment, to be sure she didn't have any more questions, he returned to the story. "When Claude died so suddenly, Lissianna was really shook up. You know, death happens so rarely to us that it shakes everyone up. Anyway, she decided she needed to be more independent. She needed to 'live her life,' she said. So she took social work at the university, got a job in a local shelter, and moved out on her own."

"How did she feed if she—"

"That was the problem. We're not allowed to bite as a rule, but in some instances—emergencies, for instance—it's allowed. And because of her hemophobia, Lissianna was allowed." He glanced toward the men's room door, but there was no sign of Etienne. Thomas turned back and continued. "The concern was her choice of victim. She chose clients of the shelter. They were close at hand and easy to prey on. The problem was, a lot of them were alcoholics or druggies. Lissi tried to avoid those, but sometimes . . ." He shrugged.

"Her family worried, obviously," Rachel murmured.

Thomas nodded. "About a year ago, Marguerite decided enough was enough and kidnapped a human psychologist to treat her hemophobia."

"Kidnapped?" Rachel gasped.

Thomas laughed. "It's all right. Lissianna freed him . . . eventually. The psychologist was Gregory Hewitt."

"Her fiancé?" Rachel shook her head.

"Telling family secrets, Thomas?"

Rachel and Thomas started guiltily as Etienne dropped into the seat next to her.

"Well, she's practically a member of the family, isn't she?" Thomas answered defensively.

Rachel glanced from one man to the other as they stared at each other. There were undercurrents here she didn't understand, and she had no idea what Thomas meant. Was she now considered a member of the family because she was a vampire? They had obviously taken her under their wing to train and assist with the change, but did she now have a new family? One that would long outlive the family she had been born into?

"Here we go!" The arrival of the waitress brought an end to the uncomfortable moment. "Who gets the Virgin Mary?"

"That would be me." Thomas accepted the drink with a charming smile.

"That means these are for you two." The waitress set the remaining two glasses before Etienne and Rachel.

"What is this?" Etienne asked Thomas as soon as she left.

"Oh, hang on." Thomas leapt up and hurried after

the waitress, returning a moment later with two straws. He moved to Rachel's side and dropped them in her drink, then picked up the glass and smiled at her. "Okay, open that pretty mouth of yours."

Rachel hesitated, then opened her mouth, slightly embarrassed to do so because her teeth extended as usual.

"Nothing to be embarrassed about," Thomas assured her as he affixed the straws to the ends of her teeth. "This should do the trick. Now just relax. Your teeth will do all the work."

Rachel remained still even after he removed his hands from her mouth and moved back to his own seat. She didn't think anything was happening until Thomas smiled and said, "It's working."

"So it is," Etienne commented, drawing Rachel's gaze. He sounded less than happy at the realization, and pounded down half his drink in one agitated gulp.

"You see?" Thomas said with a grin. "I told you there was a way around it. It's amazing how much power those teeth have, hmm?"

Rachel risked tipping her head down to peer into the glass. She managed to do so without dislodging the straws and was amazed to see that it was indeed working; her glass was already half empty. It only took a couple of minutes for her teeth to suck up the last of the drink. The moment it was done, she unhooked the straws and leaned over to give Thomas a hug.

"Thank you, Tom. I've been trying to drink, but the taste is just horrid. Now I won't have to worry." She sat back in her seat and grinned at Etienne. "Now we can move on to teaching me to control my teeth and stuff."

"Hmm." Again, Etienne didn't seem happy, but Rachel couldn't think why. He knocked back the last of his drink, set his glass down, and stood. "Let's dance."

It wasn't really a request. He took her hand and tugged her to her feet. Rachel nearly had to run to keep up with him as he rushed her onto the dance floor. This time, there was slow music playing. Etienne took her in his arms, held her close, and began to move about. He started by holding her at an almost respectable distance, but with each song he urged her closer and closer until their bodies met everywhere. Rachel went willingly enough, her body melting into his and a little sigh escaping her. She let her head rest on his shoulder. She murmured in pleasure as his hands roamed her body, caressing and pressing her closer at the same time.

Rachel felt incredibly . . . incredible. Little currents of pleasure coursed through her everywhere Etienne touched, followed by little shivers of excitement. When his hand slid up into her hair to tug gently, she let her head tilt back, her eyes open sleepily watching his lips descend on hers. What started out as a languid kiss soon deepened into an exciting search for pleasure. Before she knew it, they had stopped even pretending to dance and were simply standing on the dance floor necking like teenagers.

"I want you," Etienne growled, breaking the kiss to trail his lips down her throat.

"Thank God," she breathed with relief. She was sure she would die if he didn't make love to her soon.

"Now."

"Now?" Her eyes opened to find him peering around in irritation.

"Yes. Now. But not here." Keeping one arm around her, he ushered her quickly off the dance floor. Rachel thought he would return them to their table at least long enough to make their excuses to Thomas, but it seemed he couldn't wait even for that. Instead, he steered her straight out of the club and to his parked car. He saw her into the passenger seat, hurried around to the driver's side, and climbed in to start the engine. That was as far as he got. The moment the car revved to life, Etienne turned and drew her across the seat and back into his arms.

Rachel went willingly, nearly crawling into his lap, her mouth open and ready when he lowered his head to claim it. She had never felt this excited in her life. Everywhere he touched, every inch of skin his breath brushed was suddenly on fire. Passion lodged itself heavy and wet between her legs.

"I need you," Rachel gasped when he broke their kiss.

Etienne's answer was something of a grunt. He

tugged at her blouse, freeing it from her jeans. She definitely wasn't the only one experienced at undressing people—Rachel's top suddenly gaped open and he quickly and efficiently unsnapped the front snap of her bra.

"Oh." She moaned as her breasts sprang loose and he caught them in his hands. Rachel sighed another little moan of pleasure-pain as he alternately caressed and suckled her nipples. When she felt his hands at her waist, she reached down to help him, but their bodies were too close, the space too cramped.

Cursing, Etienne set her back in the passenger seat and shifted the car into gear. "Home." That was all he said and all he had to say.

Rachel bit her lip and grabbed the dashboard as they lurched out of the parking lot. She briefly considered fastening her seat belt, but Etienne was driving so swiftly she felt sure they would arrive before her shaky hands accomplished the task.

They were both out of the car before the engine finished shutting off. Etienne met her at the front of the car, caught her hand, and made a run for his front door. He managed to unlock and open it, drag her in, and slam the door closed before pulling her into his arms again. Rachel was suddenly slammed up against the hallway wall, Etienne's mouth and hands seemingly everywhere at once. They tugged at each other's clothes.

"I can't wait to get you upstairs," he said apologetically as her slacks slid down her legs.

"Don't," Rachel said. She didn't have it in her to wait either. She wanted him, needed him right there, right then.

It was all the permission Etienne needed. He ripped her panties off with one quick tug, caught her behind the thighs, lifted her, then settled her back down onto him. He slid into her and they both groaned as he filled her completely. Thanks to those erotic nightly dreams, it seemed like they had been working toward this for weeks.

Etienne paused, then stepped sideways. Suddenly afraid that she was dreaming again, and that the dream would stop now as it usually did, Rachel dug her fingernails into Etienne's shoulders and urged him on.

"More," she pleaded.

Etienne set her down on something—she thought it must be the hall table—and began to move inside her. Withdrawing, he pounded back into her, only to withdraw again.

Rachel hadn't realized she was a screamer. She'd never been a screamer before. But not only did Rachel scream when she found her pleasure, she screamed, then sank her teeth into Etienne's neck, drawing blood from his body into hers as her body rippled and pulsed around his. It was the best sex of her life.

* * *

"Hello."

Rachel blinked sleepily and peered with confusion at the man leaning over her. *Etienne*. She recognized him, of course, but the change in position threw her off. The last thing she recalled was her body exploding and shattering in the most powerful orgasm she'd ever experienced. Now Rachel was somehow on her back on a soft surface—in the bedroom, she realized with confusion. How had they got here?

"You fainted," Etienne told her gently. "I hope I wasn't too rough."

"Rough? No," Rachel reassured him, then blushed as understanding slid through her. "Your mother warned me this might happen."

Marguerite had also claimed that the pleasure would be twenty times anything Rachel had ever experienced. Rachel wasn't sure it had been twenty times the pleasure, but that had been at least ten times stronger, and she wasn't even fully changed yet.

"You bit me," Etienne murmured, feathering his fingers over one of her still erect nipples.

"I'm sorry," Rachel said. Her voice was husky, and she shivered in response to his caress.

"Don't be. I liked it." He allowed his hand to drift across her belly. "I liked that you were that excited. I like everything about you."

"Oh, good." Rachel moaned and closed her eyes. Her body arched as his hand dipped between her legs. Catching her lower lip with her teeth, she shifted and squirmed restlessly beneath his intimate caress, then popped her eyes back open and reached for him. "I think I need you again."

"I *know* I need you again," he growled back. Her hand slid the length of him. Etienne shifted over her and nudged her legs apart only to stop. His expression suddenly went stiff, as if a thought had electrified him. His eyes narrowed. "What were those drinks?"

"Drinks?" Rachel asked in confusion, her legs shifting restlessly beneath him. She didn't want to talk, didn't even want foreplay, only wanted to—

"Yes. The drinks Thomas ordered for us," he explained.

"Oh." She sighed, wondering why it mattered. "Umm, Sweet Tooths? No, that's the drink Marguerite likes. It was Sweet something, Sweet . . . Sweet . . ."

"Sweet Ecstasies?"

"That's it! Yes. Sweet Ecstasies." Rachel smiled, hoping he'd get back to business. But much to her dismay, instead of doing that, Etienne groaned and lowered himself against her. "What? What is it? Was there something wrong with those drinks?"

"Wrong? Not exactly. Think vampire Viagra or the mythical spanish fly."

"Really?" Rachel asked curiously. The idea didn't upset her too much. She had been suffering so much sexual tension over the past few days, a little more hardly seemed worth getting upset about. Besides, it had moved them to release their sexual tension. She just wished he'd do a little more releasing.

Etienne was three hundred years old, however, and apparently had loads more control. He seemed to be in a chatty mood now too.

"Yes, really," he answered. "Only worse. Those drinks were chock full of oxytocin, dopamine, norepinephrine, phenylethylamine and God knows what else."

Rachel was impressed that he could even say those names, let alone remember them. She recognized them all. Most were hormones involved in sexual excitement, although Oxytocin was called the cuddle chemical and was released by mothers to help bond with babies. There was some supposition it was released between couples as well, but that had yet to be proven. Still, she was very impressed. She'd be more impressed if the erection cuddled against her were inside her, but she was impressed nonetheless.

"How long does it last?" Rachel asked, wondering if it was wearing off him already.

"Hours," Etienne groaned. "I'm sorry. I'll beat Thomas silly the next time I see him. I should have checked on the drinks before we drank. He's always been the prankster in the family, and—"

"Etienne," Rachel interrupted.

"Yes?" He looked rather wary, as if he might be worried she was going to blast him for what his cousin had done.

Rachel removed the fingers she had clawed into his back and caressed his cheek. "If you don't want me, I'll understand. I'll probably die, but I'll understand. I—"

"Of course I want you," he interrupted quickly. "I've wanted you for days."

"Good." She smiled brilliantly as relief coursed through her. "I really want you too—chemicals or no chemicals. So, why not stop blathering on about Thomas and just—" It was as far as she got. Etienne silenced her with a kiss and thrust into her.

Rachel would have sighed with relief, but she was too busy groaning with pleasure. She was on fire with a need that only he could answer, and he was most definitely finally answering it. Yet it still wasn't enough. She wanted to feel . . . Her thoughts died as he suddenly shifted, moving onto his knees between her legs while they were still joined and scooping her up into a sitting position on his lap. Her legs wrapped naturally around his hips.

Their bodies slid against each other, and Rachel shuddered with pleasure. They were now meeting and touching everywhere. Her breasts scraped across his chest; her arms closed around his shoulders and she nestled her face in his neck, pressing kisses to the skin there, then nipping at the tender flesh as her excitement grew. Rachel had never been a biter, but she now wanted to sink her teeth deep into him.

She gasped and cried out as he beat her to it. It was

a quick bite, probably drawing little blood, but Rachel took it as permission and sank her own teeth into his neck. She used that as an anchor as their passion reached fever pitch and exploded around them. Rachel felt herself grow faint, sensed the world darkening around her, but held on with her teeth and felt the rush of energy and excitement through her. It was like a drug. It *was* a drug. She felt herself being supercharged, then overwhelmed, and released her hold on his neck with a moan as her body shuddered and quivered around him.

Darkness again crowded in.

Chapter Ten

Etienne was up and gone when she woke. Rachel yawned and stretched in bed, smiling happily. She felt great. A little hungry maybe, but otherwise great. She was sure last night had been better than any erotic dream. Sylvia must really have a sad sex life if she thought any dream could beat out reality.

Etienne had made love to her all night long. Their lovemaking had continued on into the morning, and it had been noon before they'd collapsed together, exhausted and finally satisfied.

Rachel grinned at the drapes over the bed, then sat up and tossed the tangled sheets aside. The man was an automaton. He had more energy than anyone she'd ever met, and three hundred years of skill to back it up. Etienne had done things to her that made her shiver and blush to think of. Shivering and blushing, she hurried into the bathroom and straight to the shower.

She probably could have used a cold shower at that point—which was hard to believe after the marathon session of lovemaking—but it was true. She chose a warm one, however, and stood under the shower nozzle, enjoying the pounding of the water on her head and back for several moments before shampooing her hair. Her body was still trembling and sensitive. Rachel wasn't sure if it was the Sweet Ecstasy still affecting her, or simply her memories of the pleasure Etienne had given her, but every scrape of the washcloth over her wet flesh made her shudder and long for him again. The man really was like a drug. A good drug.

Out of the shower, Rachel dried herself off, dressed, and ran a brush through her hair. She paused to make a face at herself in the bathroom mirror, then hurried out of the room in search of Etienne. She had a deep need to see him again, just to be close to him. To maybe cuddle him, maybe more.

Rachel grinned at her wayward thoughts as she jogged downstairs. The silent house didn't surprise or worry her, and she headed directly for the basement knowing she would find Etienne there. He was no doubt working at his computer.

He was in his office, but while he was seated at his desk, the computers were all shut down. He was talking on the phone. Rachel walked up behind him and rested her hands tentatively on his shoulders as he spoke into the handpiece. When he immediately reached up with his free hand to cover one of hers, she smiled and relaxed, realizing only then that she had not been completely sure of his welcome. Etienne had claimed he'd wanted her for days, but that didn't mean much. He might have simply been saying that. He might also have lost interest in her now that their passion was satisfied. It hadn't happened.

"Great! I'll watch for him then," Etienne said and hung up the phone. The moment it clicked into place, he stood and turned to pull her into his arms for a welcoming kiss. He growled, "Good morning, beautiful. How are you feeling?"

Rachel flushed and kissed the tip of his nose. "Famished."

Etienne chuckled. "You're insatiable."

"Yes, I am. But I meant hungry-famished."

"Ah." He released a small sigh and hugged her, then took her hand and led her out of his office. "Yes, so am I. Unfortunately, we're out of blood. I was just asking Bastien to send over some more. It should get here soon, but in the meantime . . ." He paused as they stepped into the kitchen, his eyes shooting to the window in the back door and searching the darkness outside.

"What is it?" Rachel asked curiously. Stepping to his side, she peered out into the large yard behind the house. She'd looked out at it both in daylight and at night, and it was lovely at both times, with a large fountain, a rock garden, and lots of trees.

"I thought I saw someone out there," he murmured, then gave her hand a squeeze. "Wait here. I just want to take a quick look around."

He was out the door before Rachel could comment. She held the door open so that she could see everything, and watched him walk out into the yard. She had intended on looking around to see if she could see anyone lurking about, but her gaze got caught on his behind and seemed to want to stay there. She decided not to fight it. He had better night vision than she did, anyway. And really it was a nice view. A very nice view. Rachel had never realized how attractive a man's butt could be. She just wanted to grab it and squeeze it and . . .

"Must be the effects of that drink," she muttered and gave her head a shake. But her gaze returned to his behind again the moment she glanced his way, and Rachel decided she might be best to join him rather than stand with her tongue hanging out. Letting the door slide closed behind her, she walked silently to him.

"Did you see anything?" she asked in a whisper, a tad distracted by his scent. He smelled really good. Yummy. Rachel had noticed that he smelled good the few times she'd had her face in his neck and had inhaled the scent of him, but now she could smell him almost as well just standing next to him. Her senses must be strengthening, she realized, and found herself pleased. Perhaps she would be able to control her teeth soon. And even drink blood. That straw trick Thomas had shown her worked nicely. But she would rather be able to drink it straight out of a glass like the rest of them. Until she did, Rachel would feel like the child drinking tea with half the cup filled with milk.

"No. I might have been mistaken. It could have just been a shadow."

"Hmm." Rachel sniffed the air and stepped closer to him, her gaze slipping to his neck. He really did smell delicious. Good enough to eat, even. For some reason, at the moment he reminded her of a great big porterhouse steak, nice and rare.

Off the hoof. Marguerite's words came into her head, and Rachel's eyes widened in horror.

"What is it? Do you see something?" Etienne asked when she stepped abruptly away.

"No," Rachel said, guilt overwhelming her. "No. We should go inside now, don't you think? It's rather cold out here." It *was* unseasonably cold, and neither of them was wearing a jacket. Not that she'd noticed the cold until it was a handy excuse.

"Are you cold?"

"No," she admitted, then tilted her head. "Why am I not freezing? I should be freezing. It's a cold night out here, Etienne."

"Your body's more efficient than it used to be. You

don't have to worry about cold or frostbite or anything anymore," he explained. "Still, we should go in. You'll use up more blood staying warm and will need to feed that much sooner—and I know you're already hungry."

"Desperately hungry," Rachel agreed. Her gaze found his neck, and she looked away with discomfort.

"Well, the delivery guy should be here soon with breakfast," he said reassuringly. He walked back to the door. "It will probably be Thomas. He often runs errands like that."

"Oh. That's nice of him," Rachel commented. She paused as Etienne grabbed the door handle and turned it, then turned it back. "What is it?"

"Uh . . . Rachel, did you unlock the door or just let it close?"

"*You* unlocked the door. I just let it close behind me. Why? What's wrong?"

Etienne grimaced. "The door locks automatically unless you flip the lever thing. We're locked out."

"What?" She stepped up to his side and turned the door handle, but to her horror the door stayed closed. "We can't be locked out, Etienne."

"I'm afraid we are." He sounded more amused than upset.

Rachel wasn't amused. She was already famished to the point that he was looking like a tasty treat, and if the cold made her need blood more urgently . . .

Turning a stern look on him, she ordered, "Climb in a window."

He shook his head. "Sorry. High-tech security system. It'll go off if I try anything like that."

"Well, can't you bypass it or something?"

"Sure I could, but why wreck my system to save myself a couple of minutes in the cold? Whoever delivers the blood will have a cell phone. I can call Bastien and have him bring my extra set of house keys. We'll only be out here a couple of minutes, I promise. And it's a nice clear night. I can show you my garden up close. You've only seen it from the house till now. I have some lovely night-blooming—"

"Etienne," Rachel began with irritation, then held her tongue. She was suddenly reluctant to admit that he was looking like breakfast. Her previous revulsion at biting people had been eased quite a bit by their love bites. Now was as good a time as any to find out whether she could control herself. She didn't want to bite one of her co-workers one night when she was feeling peckish.

"What is it?" Etienne prompted when she remained silent.

"Nothing," she said at last. "Show me your garden."

Smiling, Etienne took her hand. He led her back out into the yard and around the fountain to the main garden. It was a huge backyard. Rachel could only think that he obviously lived on the outskirts of Toronto. She couldn't be sure, however, since the yard was surrounded by a huge privacy fence that made it impossible to see out. Reminding herself to ask him later, she followed through the garden as he pointed out and named various plants.

It was a lovely garden, obviously made to be viewed at night, which she supposed made sense. There were lights here and there that she supposed were for highlighting, but none of them were on. Their path was lit only by moonlight. Rachel didn't have any trouble seeing, however. She guessed that meant her eyesight was improving, as Marguerite had said it would. She might have been more excited, but she was too hungry. Her body was actually beginning to cramp with her need to feed. Since Etienne didn't appear to be suffering the same, Rachel supposed she was still needing more blood due to the change.

"Why are you looking at me like I'm a big roast pig with an apple in its mouth?"

Rachel dragged her eyes away from his luscious neck and forced a smile. "Because you look so delicious," she said lightly. Without thinking, she moved closer and ran her hands up his chest, catching them around his neck to urge him down to kiss her.

Etienne came easily, lowering his lips with eager passion. Rachel sighed into his mouth with relief that it was so easy, then broke the kiss and began to trail her lips over his cheek to his ear. She nibbled lightly and teased, "You smell good enough to eat."

Etienne chuckled at her words, but his laughter

died quickly and he stiffened in her arms. She'd begun to nibble along his neck. "Er, Rachel honey? I think you might be confusing bloodlust with lust. Its not a good idea for you to—aaah!"

His warning died as she found him through his jeans and squeezed. His breath immediately picked up and he was almost panting in her ear as she fondled him. "Well, maybe a little nibble wouldn't hurt."

Rachel laughed huskily and licked his neck. She really didn't have any idea what she was doing, was just following her instincts—and she instinctually wanted to lick his neck. Actually, Rachel wanted to lick everywhere. Etienne was like a big lollipop, or perhaps a Tootsie Pop. She wanted to know how many licks it took to get to the center of this Tootsie Pop, but knew she would bite long before she ever found out.

Rachel licked his neck again, her tongue running over the vein, sensing it with a natural ability that startled her. She wanted so badly to bite him. She was starving, cramping with hunger. She supposed it wasn't unlike a drug addict jonesing for a fix. She needed it bad, but it seemed rude to just bite him, and she couldn't quite bring herself to do it. She had bitten him several times last night, but always in the throes of passion. Rachel was feeling pretty passionate about him right then, but not enough to make it right. She had to fix that.

Releasing her hold on him, she slid her hands up

over his chest, grasped his collar, and tugged his shirt open. Etienne just grinned as the buttons snapped off. Rachel was a little less sangfroid. She hadn't expected that, thought perhaps one button might pop and then she'd have to undo the others manually, but it appeared she was gaining some of the strength that was to be hers.

Her surprise only slowed her down for a moment. With his chest suddenly revealed, glowing almost silver in the moonlight, she heard an almost animal growl purr from her throat and let her hands slide over that exposed flesh. His skin was cool and smooth, soft as velvet but with the hardness of steel. Sighing in pleasure, she leaned forward to press her lips to the skin over his heart. The beat beneath was strong. He was vital and strong, and she wanted him.

Tipping her head back, Rachel slid a hand into his hair and drew down his face. She covered his lips with hers, rubbing them softly at first, then opening her mouth to catch and nip at his bottom lip with her teeth. She drew on it until it slipped from her teeth with a small plop that made them both chuckle. Then that was apparently enough play for Etienne. Gathering her in his arms, he covered her lips with his. There was no gentle rubbing, no teasing kiss. He covered her mouth, then opened his and thrust his tongue out to separate her lips. Rachel opened to him without hesitation and slid her own tongue forward to meet his, a moan half-smothered as their tongues tangled and slid against each other.

An answering moan from Etienne made Rachel smile, breaking the kiss somewhat. She let her lips drift away over his chin and down along his throat, inhaling the scent of him, but not stopping to be tempted by the promise of his jugular. She coasted her lips down his chest, pausing at first one nipple to nip and suckle and flick at it with her tongue, then to the other to do the same. Her nails ran firmly over his back as she did, so that he definitely felt it, but she drew no blood.

When Etienne groaned and arched and caught at her arms to attempt to draw her back, presumably to kiss her, Rachel laughed teasingly and simply dropped into a crouch. It put her at waist level. Tipping her head back, she smiled up at him wickedly and reached for the snap of his jeans. Etienne sucked in a startled breath as she undid them, then seemed to hold it as she drew down the zipper.

Rachel let her smile widen, then reached inside to pull out his member. She knew she had made a mistake the moment she leaned forward to take him in her mouth. The scent and taste of him made the urge to bite almost irresistible. Rachel could actually feel the blood pulsing and throbbing beneath the fragile skin covering his hard shaft.

Dear God, it would be like biting a sausage, she thought faintly. The juices would squirt thick and sweet into her mouth, then slide down her throat and feed the craving that made her body ache so. The thought was oddly erotic. It was also rather horrifying. Rachel couldn't believe she was kneeling before a man, contemplating taking a chomp on the manhood that had given her so much pleasure the night before. Jeez, it seemed obvious she wasn't ready to go back to work yet. If she was contemplating this, no one would be safe from her hunger.

"Rachel?"

She lifted her eyes the length of his body and met his uncertain gaze, realizing she had gone still with him in her mouth. Giving herself a mental shake, she raised a hand to hold the base of his manhood and allowed her mouth to slide the length of his member, then back again. She could do this. She could resist. She had to, Rachel told herself firmly. She had to prove to herself that she could resist anything, that she would be safe around her co-workers, that even with temptation this close—in her mouth, in fact—she could prevail. A groan from Etienne encouraging her, Rachel slid her mouth along his length again, her tongue working his flesh with an interest that seemed focused on the bulging vein it followed. Just a little bite, her mind tempted. A nip, really. She pushed the thought aside and drew him nearly out of her mouth again, slowly becoming aware of his responses. Rachel had experienced the sensation several times with him already, their passion merging, heightening for both of them into overwhelming waves of excitement and desire. This time was different, however. Her mind, preoccupied as it was with the need to feed, was not aroused, and so she was now experiencing only his passion and pleasure. It flooded her mind as if it were her own, filling every corner with the sensations he was experiencing, sensations of almost unbearable pleasure.

The feel of her own warm, moist mouth sliding the length of him was a pleasure she would never have experienced as a mere human. The scrape of her teeth over the tip of him made them both moan, and Rachel squeezed her thighs together as a new ache settled there. It was such pleasure-pain, she repeated the action several times until she was sure neither of them could stand it again without shattering.

Aware that these thoughts reflected Etienne's state as well as her own, and unwilling to end the pleasure so soon, Rachel changed the rhythm of her caresses. Etienne's disappointment touched her like his pleasure, and she smiled despite it. Sliding her free hand up his jean-encased thighs, she tightened the hold she had on the base of his manhood and twirled her tongue over his flesh.

"Rachel." It was a plea for release, but she was feeling heartless. She was hungry—both for blood and pleasure. She wanted to make this an experience he wouldn't ever forget, and since she was experiencing it with him, knowing exactly how it felt and affected him, she could.

Every woman should enjoy such mind-melding, she thought vaguely. They would never again doubt their ability to pleasure a man, or fumble about counting on him to verbalize what he liked or didn't. They would simply know, and do what felt good. They would also share in the enjoyment of the experience in a way not normally possible.

"God, Rachel."

She ignored his pleading. She was feeling what he was feeling, and knew he was again ready to burst. So was she, so this time Rachel didn't change technique or rhythm. This time her hungers would not be denied.

He cried out and exploded into her mouth a heartbeat before her own body climaxed. Rachel's mind suffused with his pleasure and her own; then her newer instincts took over and she sank her canines into the vein her tongue had been toying with. She felt Etienne's startled reaction, then felt her own pleasure hit him as blood flowed through her teeth. The two sensations blended together, flowing back and forth between them from one mind to the other, seeming to strengthen each time it was exchanged until nothing could seem to hold on to it.

When Etienne began to sway before her, Rachel allowed her teeth to retract, freeing him. Then she sat back weakly as he dropped to his knees before her.

Her mind was struggling to accept the pleasure overwhelming her and was now suffused with weakness. Was it her own?

Etienne encompassed her in his arms, but his hold was light, barely there. When he spoke, his words were slurred and so faint that she couldn't grasp what he said. Then he began to tumble backward. Rachel tried to catch and help him stay upright, but she didn't seem to have the strength. She was sliding into the warm liquid darkness that had overwhelmed her after each lovemaking session with him.

This time was different, however. The other times, Rachel had been the only one overwhelmed, while Etienne—stronger and more used to the experience after three hundred years—had been her anchor. This time, he seemed to be slipping into that darkness with her. The realization gave her a sudden fright. Rachel wasn't sure if the alarm was her own or Etienne's, but as she slipped into unconsciousness, she knew that something was very wrong.

Rachel woke slowly, unsure what had disturbed her. She lay still for several moments, her cheek resting on something cool and hard. Her eyes were closed. She felt incredibly weak—drained, really—and didn't understand why. The memories of what had occurred in the garden swept through her mind and she smiled where she lay. That smile was quickly followed by a frown. She shouldn't be so weak. She had taken some

201

of Etienne's blood and should be stronger for it, not weak. Shouldn't she?

"Etienne?"

That far off shout roused her from her languid state, and Rachel opened her eyes to see the shapes and shadows of the garden. She was lying with her head resting on Etienne's chest amid the blooming night flowers. Moving slowly, she managed to raise herself enough to look over the plants that lined the path and glance toward the house. There was nothing to see; the house appeared as still and empty as it had when they'd first been locked out.

Sighing, Rachel allowed herself to drop back onto the cold ground again. She was both shocked and a bit frightened at the weakness she was suffering. With a turn of her head, she was able to peer at the pale outline of Etienne. He lay in the dewy grass beside her, his body gleaming in the moonlight. Rachel patted his chest weakly, but there was no response.

She felt concern claim her. "Etienne?" She nudged him with a little more force. "Etienne?"

"Etienne!" That male voice was an echo to her own. It sounded closer this time, but still muffled, as if heard through ear muffs or at a great distance. "Rachel? Dammit, you two—answer me! I can sense your presence, but it's too weak to follow."

Despite that claim, the voice was drawing closer. Rachel barely had the chance to peer down at her clothes and make sure they were in order before she heard the back door of the house slam. Rachel forced herself to sit up again as Bastien strode into view.

"There you two are." He hurried toward them. "I was worried sick when Tom said there was no answer and the door was locked. I rushed over with Etienne's extra keys and— What the hell happened to the two of you?" he asked with alarm as he got close enough to see Etienne prostrate beside her. Then his gaze found his brother's body and his eyebrows flew up. "Oh."

Rachel glanced at Etienne, flushing when she noted that his pants were still undone, his flaccid penis hanging out bearing a pair of unmistakable teethmarks.

"Oh, dear. You bit him, huh?"

Humiliated, not to mention too weak to stay upright, Rachel dropped to the ground with a moan. She let her arm flop over her face.

"Thomas, bring the blood!"

Rachel let her arm drop back in alarm. It was bad enough that Bastien was a witness to this moment, but to have Thomas there, too . . . Her panic eased a bit when she noticed Bastien kneeling beside Etienne and straightening his clothes.

"How are you feeling? Pretty bad, huh?"

Rachel glanced at Bastien, surprised by his solicitous tone. "Yes. I don't understand why, though."

"You must have ingested too much blood," he explained. He scowled at his unconscious brother. "Etienne shouldn't have let you. He knows better."

"He was, er, preoccupied at the time," Rachel admitted with another blush. She cleared her throat. "Why is it I shouldn't have—"

"You keep a certain number of nanos inside you, the perfect amount for your body. It replaces those that die when necessary, and kills off extra ones should they develop. A sudden influx of extra nanos from another vampire takes time for your body to process. In the meantime, those nanos consume blood, using it up at an accelerated rate. It's bad enough for such a thing to happen when you are well fed and full, but Etienne told me you've been underfeeding because you can't stand the taste of blood. And then too, neither of you had any available to you this morning—which is why Thomas came."

As if on cue, Etienne's cousin came sauntering into view carrying a medical cooler. His gaze dropped over Etienne's unconscious form, then over Rachel's disheveled and weak state, but he merely smiled. "Hi, Dudette. Looks like I came in the nick of time."

He opened the cooler and withdrew two bags of blood, handing one to Bastien, then taking the time to retrieve two straws from his pocket and stab them into the second bag. "I didn't think Etienne would have any straws, and I knew you'd want them so I picked some up at the corner store on the way over earlier," he explained as he held out the doctored bag.

Rachel accepted it with a grateful smile and quickly affixed the straws to her teeth. The liquid in the bag began to disappear at once, and she sighed with relief as her weakness and pain began to recede.

"Another bag, Thomas." Bastien exchanged the already empty bag he had slammed into Etienne's teeth for a fresh one. He urged Etienne's mouth open again and popped the second pint into the teeth, too. Glancing from his brother to Rachel with concern, he asked, "How much did you take?"

Rachel gave an embarrassed shrug. She had no idea.

"Bit him, huh?" Thomas asked sympathetically. "It's a common occurrence with newbies."

Bastien grunted what might have been agreement, but Rachel wasn't paying attention; she was watching with a sinking feeling as Thomas peered at his cousin. He frowned and asked, "Where did you bite him? I don't see the marks."

"Get her another bag of blood, Thomas," Bastien ordered, patting Rachel's knee. She flushed and squirmed where she sat. Her mouth was firmly closed. She wasn't going to admit where she'd bit him. Not in this lifetime.

"Sure." Thomas took the empty bag from Rachel, pulled the straws free, grabbed a fresh bag, and fixed it up as he had the first, then handed it over with a smile, his question apparently forgotten. Rachel wasn't fooled, however. She had caught the exchange of glances and was sure the two men had communicated with their minds. She just hoped Bastien had admonished him to let the subject go. A decidedly amused light filled the man's eyes.

Sighing miserably, Rachel slid the straws over her canines and allowed her teeth to do the work of ingesting the blood she sadly lacked.

Much to her surprise, Thomas patted her shoulder. "Not to worry, little one. This is all my fault, not yours."

Rachel had a grim moment as she recalled these men could not only communicate with their minds, they could read thoughts. Bastien probably hadn't had to give away the location of the bite; *she* had probably done so herself without meaning to. Then she caught the man's words and peered at him curiously. How could he possibly claim it was his fault? Before she could unhook the straws from her teeth and ask, a moan from Etienne drew her attention.

"Relax," Bastien ordered as Etienne's eyes popped open. He began to struggle to sit up. "You need a little more blood before you get physical."

Etienne relaxed back on the ground, his eyes shifting until they landed on Rachel; then his hand slid across his stomach to touch her knee reassuringly. She supposed, or at least hoped, that this was a silent message that he wasn't upset. She felt better for it.

"This is becoming a bad habit, Etienne."

Rachel and Etienne both glanced at Bastien in confusion as he popped yet another pint into his brother's mouth.

"This is what? The third time I've had to save you lately?"

Etienne managed a curse around the bag in his mouth, which Rachel found rather impressive. She didn't think she could speak intelligibly while ingesting—but then she supposed that Etienne had a couple hundred years' practice. She wondered, however, if it wasn't considered rude to speak while eating. *She* had been raised to believe that it was. For humans, at least.

"You are one of our people now, Rachel," Bastien pointed out quietly. When she remained quiet, he turned to glance at Etienne. "So, you thought you saw Pudge out here earlier."

This time, Etienne pulled the bag from his mouth before saying, "Stop reading my mind, Bastien. It's rude."

"The thought was just lying about on the edges of your mind," his brother said with a shrug. "Although it seems rather silly to be indulging in . . . er, anything if you thought Pudge was lurking about. He could have jumped the two of you while you were distracted."

"I must have been seeing things," Etienne groused. "I checked the yard and there was no sign of him. Then we let the door close and were locked out. We were waiting for Thomas to arrive so that he could call you and get you to bring my extra keys."

"And you decided to share body heat and fluids

while waiting," Thomas guessed. He laughed, earning a glare from Etienne. The younger man shrugged, giving Rachel an apologetic glance. "Sorry, Dudette. Couldn't resist that one."

"Have you had enough blood to get back into the house to finish recovering?" Bastien asked abruptly.

"Yeah, yeah." Etienne handed him the last empty bag and sat up, then got to his feet with Bastien's help.

Rachel accepted the hand Thomas offered and got to her feet as well. Some of the embarrassment and discomfort she suffered slipped away when Etienne claimed her hand and held it on the walk back to the door. This had been a new experience for her, but it would seem she was in for a lot of those. Life had definitely taken a twist.

"So?" Bastien asked as they stepped into the kitchen. "Have you talked to Rachel about—"

"No," Etienne interrupted.

"Well, are you—"

"I will," Etienne interrupted again. "Soon."

Bastien sighed but apparently decided to let the subject, whatever it was, drop. Clapping a hand on Thomas's shoulder, he turned him to the door, announcing, "You'll need more blood. You'll probably use this up quickly, repairing the damage you've done to each other. I'll send Thomas back with more later. Try not to kill each other in the meantime."

Etienne's answer was a grunt.

His two relatives left the kitchen and started up the

hall. When the front door closed behind them, some of the tension left his shoulders and he grabbed another bag of blood from the cooler Thomas had set on the table.

"So," Rachel said quietly as she accepted the bag. "What is it exactly that you were supposed to talk to me about?"

Etienne stared at Rachel. He supposed it really would be a good thing to talk and try to convince her that it was in her best interests to claim Pudge had kidnapped her. But he was reluctant to spoil the rapport they had shared since Night Club—the bond they were building so new and fragile, Etienne was hesitant to possibly ruin it with an argument. Distracting her with something that would bring them even closer together seemed the better option.

"You don't like the night," he said abruptly, and could tell by her expression that he had startled her.

"I don't dislike it. It's just . . ." She frowned, then shrugged. "I don't like working at night while everyone is sleeping. I'd rather sleep, then work during the day like everyone else."

"Why?"

"Well . . ." She scowled at him, obviously annoyed. "It's not so bad on work nights," she said finally. "But I can't stay up on work nights and keep normal hours on my nights off, so I'm up all night then and there's nothing to do but sit around twiddling my thumbs or playing video games by myself. Everyone I know but my co-workers on the night shift work normal hours. There's nothing to do."

"Nothing to do?" He gaped at her, then shook his head. "I'm afraid you need an education, my dear."

Rachel took in Etienne's certainty with doubt. She'd worked the night shift for three years now and doubted there was much he could teach her. She'd searched desperately for things to do on her evenings off, and while she could always hit the malls or a movie early in the evening, it was the wee hours—11 to 7, when she would usually be working and was awake as could be—she had trouble filling. Other than the bars that closed at 2 A.M., and Rachel wasn't really a bar person anyway, there wasn't much to do but wander around her apartment lonely and bored.

"Go get changed," Etienne ordered. "Dark pants and top. And a jacket—it's chilly out." When Rachel merely stared at him, he waved her away. "Go on. Get changed."

Giving another shrug, she tossed her last blood bag into the garbage and left the kitchen. Change, he said. She would change. But Rachel didn't believe for a minute that he was going to teach her anything about the night that she didn't already know.

Chapter Eleven

"I've never been on the beach at night," Rachel admitted with a sigh. She leaned back in the sand as the warm breeze brushed her arms. This was the second evening Etienne had taken her out to show her the night. Their first jaunt had been a night walk in the woods. They'd walked hand in hand, listening to the sounds of animals and catching glimpses of them. Surprisingly enough, Rachel hadn't had any trouble navigating the uneven path beaten into the dirt. It seemed her senses were really improving—she had been able to see almost as well at night as in daylight.

Etienne's eyes shone silver in the night, or perhaps they simply reflected the moonlight, so she asked if her own eyes were glowing. Etienne smiled and nodded, and Rachel contemplated that. She was now a nocturnal animal. She was a vampire. A hunter.

Rather than alarming her as the idea had once done, the thought gave Rachel an odd surge of confidence. As a woman in the modern world, working at night, she was rather used to being threatened by any number of perverted sickos out there. She had spent most of her life darting from her vehicle to wherever she was going, ever alert for trouble. Now she was experiencing the first tastes of her new strength and abilities.

Her vision wasn't the only thing improved. Last night they had climbed and run and played in the woods, and she had learned that her body was stronger and faster than ever. Much stronger. Inhumanly strong, though she wasn't sure how the nanos managed that. She hadn't bothered to try to figure it out. She was enjoying it too much to care.

"It's a nice night. Want to go for a swim?"

Rachel glanced over the deserted beach and the water reflecting the moonlight. It *was* a nice night. While yesterday was unseasonably chill, tonight was warm as a summer evening should be, and a moonlight swim sounded enticing. But they hadn't brought any swimsuits.

She smiled to herself and peered up the beach again. They had it all to themselves, which would have been impossible during the day. The few policemen who patrolled at night were watching for underaged partiers who had already arrived and been sent away by Etienne. Really, she supposed, a swimsuit wasn't absolutely necessary. Etienne had already seen her naked. Several times.

Rather than answer his question verbally, Rachel tossed a wicked grin Etienne's way. Reaching for the hem of her T-shirt with both hands, she raised it up and over her head.

"Beautiful," Etienne murmured as her breasts were bared.

His suddenly serious expression made Rachel laugh, and she tossed her T-shirt in his lap as she got to her feet. She hadn't bothered with a bra tonight. Actually, she didn't wear them much at all anymore. There was no need. Her breasts were firm and perky, as they had never been, the nanos keeping them that way. She was going to save a ton of money in the future.

Standing before him, Rachel unsnapped her jeans and shimmied out of them. She felt herself blush as she did so, but he *had* seen her naked before, and besides, she was aware that her body was now flawless. It was really rather freeing. Well, mostly. Someday she could actually envision managing undressing without blushing.

A featherlight caress up her calf made her glance down. Etienne was looking heatedly up at her, trailing his fingers lightly along the sensitive skin of her inner leg. If she gave him the chance, Rachel knew they would be rolling around on the sand within minutes, growling like animals—but he was the one who had mentioned a swim, and now she really wanted one. She danced lightly out of his reach and, leaving him seated upon the blanket holding their picnic basket, Rachel turned away to jog lightly to the water's edge.

Her first step into the water was a bit of a shock. While the night was warm, the water was cold. It closed around her foot, but she barely let that slow her down. Rachel continued determinedly forward for several steps until the water reached her waist, then raised her hands and dived under the rounded waves. She swam underwater for what seemed an impossible time, surprised by the fact that she could. When she finally surfaced, it wasn't out of a need for air so much as a curiosity as to how far she'd swum.

Deciding she had a lot more questions to ask Bastien about the effects of nanos, Rachel swiveled in the water. She stopped treading water and nearly sank under the surface upon seeing how far she was from shore, but she then caught herself. Stronger and faster didn't begin to describe her new state. Rachel hadn't been swimming very hard, but she had propelled herself an incredible distance.

A dark shape broke the surface of the lake on her right, and Rachel smiled as Etienne appeared. His hair was slicked close to his head, his eyes again aglow in the moonlight. He swam closer.

"You look beautiful," he said solemnly.

Rachel glanced down at herself. Her breasts were

half-revealed above the water, and the silver moon-light gave her skin a pearlescent sheen. Etienne shifted closer, reaching out to catch her hand and draw her forward. As her breasts brushed his chest, he rolled onto his back, taking her with him so that she draped half over his floating chest with her lower body in the water beside him. He began to paddle his feet, propelling them back toward land.

Rachel slid her arms around his waist and went with him, kicking halfheartedly to aid. At last, Etienne stopped and stood. The water reached to just above her breasts as Rachel also stood, but she barely noticed before he pulled her into his arms. She went willingly and lifted her face as he claimed her lips. Rachel first let her legs brush his under the water, then wrapped them around his hips as she twined her arms around his neck. She arched against him, her body stretching and lengthening with awareness. She was conscious of several sensations: the night air now slightly chill on her damp skin; the water itself, warm and silky around her now that she had adjusted to the temperature; his body hot everywhere it touched hers; her passion feverish as it built inside her.

They had made love several times now, each time more explosive and better than the last, so the rush of excitement Rachel felt was overpowering. She had felt like this before—this hunger for him, this pleasure in him, this desire—but this encounter would be even better. Their minds opened to each other, and his desires joined hers. The first rush was almost unbearable as it attacked her nerves, making Rachel swoon.

She heard the half-growl, half-purr that erupted from Etienne's throat as she slid her hands into his hair and scraped her nails across his scalp. She responded with one of her own as the sensations echoed inside her. The feeling was so enjoyable, she did it again, then again, before finally sliding her hands down his neck and running her nails over his upper back and shoulders. Rachel had never known that such a simple action could be so erotic, but her own back muscles rippled in sympathy and desire.

Etienne's hands were wandering over her body at the same time—caressing her back, following the curve of her hip, cupping her bottom then squeezing briefly, before smoothing along her legs. The combination of their caresses and pleasures quickly had Rachel trembling. Etienne had stripped off his clothes on the beach, and she could feel his erection, hard and excited, where it was trapped between their bodies. Rachel tightened her legs around him and shifted herself upward. Rubbing against him, she stilled and groaned deep in her throat as his urge to climax swamped her mind.

Recalling every time they had made love, and the way she had fainted after each, Rachel wanted desperately to break their kiss and suggest they move back to the blanket—but it seemed too much effort, and breaking the kiss seemed impossible. It was as if she needed it to breathe.

"Rachel." Her name was a growl in her head, for Etienne was still kissing her and not speaking. It took her a moment to realize he was speaking mentally; that with their minds fevered and wide open, they needn't speak to communicate. *"I want you."*

Rachel sighed and tried to answer mentally that she wanted him too, but she wasn't sure he got the message. She had no idea if she had attained the ability yet. Still, she didn't repeat the thought aloud when he broke the kiss and propelled her backward through the water. Rachel felt sure he was taking her to the blanket, but he stopped while still in the water and urged her up to the surface. She floated on her back with her knees bent. He grasped her legs and shocked her by suddenly pulling them wide open.

Rachel nearly sank under the water in surprise, so she dropped her hands to keep herself afloat. In the end, she didn't have to paddle; her arms hit sand almost at once and she realized Etienne had moved them closer to shore—close enough that she could hold her upper body up out of the water. He shifted between her legs and bent his head to caress her hot flesh with his tongue.

Rachel jerked, her feet shooting upward and splashing water everywhere as he set to work. Her mind went through myriad emotions—shock, embarrassment, and the brief mad desire to scoot away from the delectation he offered all shot through her in rapid order, but then pleasure took over.

Moaning, she caught the soles of her feet on his shoulder blades and used them to pivot her hips. Her legs spread wider apart, opening farther to facilitate him. This was . . . Well, Rachel had never experienced such intense pleasure. She almost feared she might die of it—but it was a heck of a way to go, she decided as the throes of her first climax struck, echoed out to Etienne and then were reflected back even more intensely.

A soft chuckle drew her back to consciousness, and Etienne unhooked Rachel's legs from over his shoulders and crawled up her body. He settled on top of her where she lay on the damp sand. Obviously, he had moved her farther out of the water, which was probably a good thing. She would have drowned if he hadn't. She had fainted again, and even now she didn't have the strength to hold her head or anything else up. It was even an effort to force her eyes open, but she did and dazedly stared at him.

"How? Where did you learn . . . ? How?" she asked incoherently.

Etienne grinned and brushed a damp strand of hair off her face. "Do you remember the garden?"

Rachel's mind was still so befuddled that she had to actually think for a moment. Understanding dawned at last, and she distinctly recalled feeling what he was experiencing as she had licked, kissed, and caressed him. Obviously he had experienced the same thing tonight, allowing him to hit just the right spots with just the right pressure to send her over the moon. And probably himself with her, Rachel realized, recalling that she had shared his ecstasy.

"Oh," she breathed, and found herself grinning foolishly. The sex was definitely a plus about being a vampire. She was beginning to discover all sorts of pluses to this business. What had she made all the fuss about? "You're good."

Etienne grinned back. "Yes, I am. And so are you. We're a pretty good pair."

"Yeah." She sighed happily and stretched beneath him. The way she was arching forced her breasts up until they rested mere inches from his mouth, and Rachel grinned when she felt his sex begin to stiffen again. She already knew from experience that vampires had boundless stamina. Another plus. It was starting to look as if those pluses were boundless, too.

Catching her while she was still arched, Etienne scooped one hand under Rachel's back, then shifted to kneel in the sand and caught her under her knees. Lifting her into his arms, he got to his feet. Rachel laughed huskily and caught her hand around his neck as he carried her to their blanket. He took a moment to straighten the cloth with a foot, then dropped to his knees and laid her out. He started to stand, but Rachel tightened her hold on his neck, preventing him and trying to draw him down for a kiss.

Etienne allowed it, but only for a moment. Then he muttered, "Food," and swiveled to grab their picnic basket.

Rachel was hungry, but not for food. Not for blood either—which was rather surprising, since she had been hungry for blood almost nonstop since he had turned her. She wondered briefly if that meant she was nearly finished with the change but was distracted when Etienne began to pull items out of the basket.

"Strawberries?" she asked with surprise. He set a bowl of the ripe red fruit on the blanket.

"Yeah. Strawberries dipped in chocolate," he announced with a proud grin. "It's called fondue or something."

Rachel arched an eyebrow at the squeezable bottle of chocolate syrup he retrieved and set on the blanket beside the strawberries. When he closed the basket and pushed it away, she tried to hide her amusement. "I think fondue is warmed chocolate that *you dip the strawberries into.*"

Etienne shrugged. "Rachel, honey, I'm a guy. A three-hundred-year-old guy but still just a guy. This is fondue to me."

Rachel laughed.

Etienne picked up a strawberry and squirted some syrup on it, then popped it into his mouth. He grabbed and squirted chocolate sauce on a second, this one for her. Rachel laughed and opened her mouth for it, then shook her head as she chewed and swallowed. She commented, "I don't think I've ever seen you eat real food before."

He shrugged then grinned. "I don't very often. Only on special occasions. But I didn't think a picnic basket full of blood bags felt right."

Rachel grimaced. "No. Not nearly as romantic."

Etienne laughed at her expression then suggested, "Well, perhaps if we both drank it out of the same champagne glass."

Rachel arched her eyebrows, and they grinned at each other. Then Etienne shook his head and they both said, "Nah."

"Ah, well. Guess impressing you with my romantic nature is out of the question," he said good-naturedly. Pushing the strawberries and basket aside, he added, "Guess my sexual prowess will have to be enough." Rachel burst out laughing.

Etienne dropped to lay on top of her and covered her open mouth with his. Her laughter soon turned to moans of pleasure. Then Rachel shifted, and she managed to turn him onto his back. The only reason she managed was that she took him by surprise. Unwilling to give up the advantage, she quickly climbed on top of him. Bracing her hands on his chest, she grinned down at his startled expression. "You don't have a problem with me being on top, do you?"

His surprise slowly gave way to passion. He shook

his head. "But now that you're there, what do you plan to do?"

Rachel considered then suggested, "Ride you like a wild pony?"

Etienne's eyes widened incredulously. Giving a howl of mirth, he flipped her onto her back, caught her hands, and raised them over her head, holding them both there with one of his own. Arching one eyebrow at her wickedly he said, "I should have brought my handcuffs."

"Handcuffs?" Rachel squealed. "That sounds kinky."

"Hmm." Etienne dropped his head to catch her nipple in his mouth, and suckled delicately. Lifting his head, he informed her, "In a hundred years or so, when we get tired of straight sex, you'll appreciate my kinkiness."

Rachel shook her head, amused. Sighing as he bent his head to her breast again, she watched him lave her nipple with his tongue then nip lightly at it. Arching, moaning, and squirming as he did, suddenly his words registered in her mind. *In a hundred years or so, when we get tired of straight sex, you'll appreciate my kinkiness.*

Did he really mean that? Did he expect her to be in his life in a hundred years? Was this more than an affair? They hadn't been together long, and she knew it was too soon to ask his intentions—if there ever really was an appropriate moment in this day and age for such—but the thought nagged at her. Where were they headed? What was she to him besides the woman who had saved his life and whom he had saved, the woman his cousin had tricked him into sleeping with.

"What am I doing wrong?"

Rachel jerked back and met Etienne's gaze with confusion. "What?"

"Your mind is closed to me," he explained quietly. "Which means you aren't excited. I'm doing something wrong. What is it?"

Rachel managed a smile and shook her head. "Nothing. I was just thinking."

Before he could ask what about, she lifted her head and claimed his lips. She had no desire to let him know what she had been thinking. If he had intentions or hopes for their future, she didn't want to put him in a spot where he felt he had to announce them before he was ready. And if he didn't have any intentions, she'd really rather not spoil this by knowing. Life held no guarantees, even for vampires, it seemed.

They frolicked and made love on the beach until well past midnight, then decided to head home to feed. Etienne's home, Rachel corrected herself as she picked up the blanket and folded it. Etienne rinsed out the bowl and two champagne glasses at the shoreline. They had eaten the strawberries and every last drop of chocolate, at a couple of points using each other's bodies for plates. Then Etienne had produced champagne and two glasses. Rachel had been curious to know how the drink would affect her now that she was a vampire. She had never been much of a drinker; two drinks had always been enough to put her under the table. As it turned out, making love on the beach was a thirsty business, and she had managed to put away half the bottle Etienne produced without much effect.

Etienne finished replacing everything in the basket, picked it up, then straightened and held out his hand. "Let me take that."

Rachel handed over the blanket and watched him lay it atop the basket under the handles. She placed her hand in his when he held it out again, and they started up the beach toward the parking lot.

The path was narrow and they had to walk single file. Since he knew the way better, Rachel stepped behind Etienne, allowing him to take the lead. They were several feet onto the wooded trail when he stopped, turned sideways, and whispered, "Look."

Rachel stepped to his side and peered where he was pointing, then sucked in a breath. The air was full of brightly shining miniature lights.

"What are they?"

"Fireflies."

"Fireflies?" she asked with disbelief. She shook her head. These weren't like any she'd seen before. They were much brighter, like tiny stars, really. She couldn't believe these brilliant lights were insects. Etienne apparently recognized her incredulity.

"Your eyesight is different," he explained. "They'll appear a little different now than before the change."

"Oh." Her gaze locked on the tiny lights. Rachel was so enthralled, she hardly noticed Etienne slipping his hand around hers to clasp it. He tugged her gently sideways to lean into him, and they simply watched in silence for several moments. At last Rachel sighed and said, "It's beautiful."

"Yes," Etienne agreed. He gave her hand a squeeze and bent to press a kiss to her forehead.

Rachel glanced up at him with surprise, but he was already looking back at the fireflies. She stared at him silently, wondering what he'd meant. He had kissed her in passion, made love to her even, but this kiss had felt different. It had been affectionate, perhaps even a loving caress. It was the first sign that he might feel something besides desire for her, and she found herself cherishing the idea. Her own feelings were confused and slightly muddled, but she knew they went beyond desire. Rachel liked Etienne Argeneau. She also respected and was learning to trust him. She was starting to think things could get serious, at least on her part. But she wasn't sure what his feelings were on the matter, and frankly, that left her nervous.

"We should go," Etienne murmured. "The sun will be making an appearance soon, and I didn't bring any blood."

Rachel nodded and straightened, then fell into step

behind him. They continued along the wooded path. This time she didn't even bother to try not to stare at his behind as they walked. The man had a butt you could bounce coins off.

Chapter Twelve

"Well, I think that's the one."

Rachel stared at herself in the mirror, surprise clear in her expression as Marguerite plucked at some of the blond curls and drew them forward to frame her face. She couldn't believe the difference a wig could make. Rachel hardly recognized herself, and was quite sure that no one else would.

"Yes, this will do nicely," Marguerite decided with a satisfied sigh. She smiled at Rachel in the mirror. "Now you can go to Lissianna's wedding . . . and so can Etienne."

Rachel managed not to wince. Much to her dismay, she had learned today that Etienne, who was supposed to be one of the ushers, had skipped the dress rehearsal the night before because he hadn't wished to leave Rachel "alone and unprotected." She hadn't even known that he had skipped it until Marguerite arrived today, full of determination to take her shopping. She'd also said: come hell or high water, Etienne was going to be at his sister's wedding even if they had to disguise Rachel as a goat to get her there. The older woman had quickly followed that up with a reassurance that she was quite sure disguising Rachel as a goat would not be necessary; she had simply been making a point.

Rachel herself had been too busy glaring at Etienne to appreciate the woman's soothing words. Now, she stared at herself in the mirror and happily agreed that being disguised as a goat wouldn't be necessary.

"Well, it's makeup and nails next, and then we're done," Marguerite announced. With a pleased sigh, she glanced at the woman who had been fitting Rachel with wigs. "Where is Vicki?"

"Waiting in her room," the woman answered. "I'll escort you back."

"Good, good." Marguerite moved so Rachel could rise.

Following the girl, Rachel wasn't terribly surprised when Etienne's mother fell into step. She would no doubt oversee the makeup session as diligently as the wig selection. Marguerite was definitely a take-charge kind of gal, Rachel decided as she was led into a small room in cream tones.

To be honest, Marguerite had been in charge from

the moment they left Etienne's house. She had taken Rachel to her favorite clothing store first. It hadn't taken Rachel long to figure out why the designer was Marguerite's favorite. The shop owner had fawned over her as if she were royalty. The woman was also a vampire—Rachel had recognized it right away. She wasn't exactly sure how; she had just somehow been able to sense it, and supposed it was another instinct no one had bothered to mention to her. It was no doubt a handy skill to have. After all, feeding off other vampires could be quite debilitating, as she had found out.

Rachel had remained silent and agreeable as she was dressed in gown after expensive gown and paraded out for Marguerite's inspection. Etienne's mother had insisted on footing the bill for the excursion, saying that it was her pleasure. Besides, she was sure Rachel wouldn't wish to attend something as boring as a wedding were it not necessary for Etienne to go.

Rachel had tried to argue the issue until it was pointed out that she could hardly use her bank card or credit card as either would lead the police directly to her—and she hadn't yet gained control of her teeth, so being found wasn't an option just yet. Promising herself that she would repay the woman once her life was returned to normal, Rachel had acquiesced. And since the woman was paying for it all—even if only temporarily—she felt Marguerite should have the major say in what she wore.

Fortunately, the gown Etienne's mother chose was Rachel's favorite. Created of dark blue lace over a long satin underdress, it was off-the-shoulder, featuring a fitted bodice and long tight sleeves of lace. Rachel felt absolutely beautiful in it, despite the fact that the skirt was a touch long. There were shoes made of the same material. Fortunately, the heel was just high enough that the gown was no longer too long.

"Here you are." The wig girl stopped and opened a door, then held it for Rachel and Marguerite. Rachel led the way into the room. A young woman was seated at a table filled with cosmetics, obviously waiting for them. She jumped up at their entrance and rushed forward to greet them, and ushered Rachel and Marguerite to sit at the makeup table. After ensuring neither of them wished refreshments, the girl asked what they wanted, and Marguerite explained about the wedding, the color of the dress, and so on. Within moments the girl was working on Rachel's face, murmuring over the purity and healthy color of her skin.

Rachel didn't say anything in response to the girl's compliments, rather distracted as she was by gaping at her face. She had noticed that makeup wasn't as necessary anymore, but hadn't really taken a close look. Now, in the magnified mirror the girl held out, Rachel simply stared at herself. Her skin was as smooth and soft as a baby's bottom. She marveled as the girl worked on her face, answering questions rather absently and agreeing with most of the woman's suggestions.

Marguerite suggested a beauty mark be applied to aid in disguising her, and Rachel found herself suddenly sporting one above her lip on the left side. The small addition, combined with Vicki's artistry and the wig, really made a difference. By the time they were done, even Rachel thought she looked exotic. She couldn't stop looking at herself as they moved to another mirrored room where both her nails and Marguerite's were shaped and painted.

"Well, that was fun," Marguerite said as they got back into her limo.

"Yes," Rachel agreed. She felt pampered and pretty, but also a touch guilty that she hadn't paid for any of it. "Thank you."

"You are more than welcome, my dear. And please stop feeling guilty. It was my pleasure to do all this."

The woman put the whammy on her as she gave the order. The guilt Rachel had been experiencing melted away, so she knew it. However, she decided not to resent the woman's slipping into her brain, instead deciding to enjoy it. Guilt was really no fun at all.

"Here we are."

Rachel glanced out the window of the limo as it

came to a halt in front of a house. A huge house. Not Etienne's.

"Where are we?" she asked in surprise.

"My home, dear," Marguerite answered. The driver got out from behind the wheel and walked around to open the door for them. "Etienne is going to meet us here to ride to the church. That way I can decide what jewelry you should wear."

"Oh." Rachel followed her out of the car. What kind of jewelry would a vampire own?

Etienne tugged at his tie, then promptly straightened it again, only to tug irritably at it once more. He hated wearing ties. He hated tuxes, too. Why had he agreed to be in this wedding party? He was more a jeans and T-shirt kind of guy, which was why he enjoyed working with computers. He didn't have to wear business clothes to work. He only had to dress up for meetings with the company that produced and distributed his games.

Etienne readjusted his tie and sighed as he paced his mother's salon. He supposed ties were better than the cravats he'd been forced to wear when younger. That fashion craze had been one huge pain. Most of the clothes in the early eighteenth century had been rather foppish, although they had shown his muscular legs to good advantage.

He grinned at that slightly egotistical thought as the tap of high-heeled footsteps in the hall made him glance toward the door. Probably his mother. Marguerite had always been quick at getting ready for such occasions. He wasn't sure if it was hundreds of years of practice, or simply that it took very little work to make her beautiful, but she had been quick at the task for as long as he could recall.

But it wasn't his mother. It was the most incredible blonde Etienne had seen in his life. It took a moment for him to register that it was Rachel in a wig. She floated into the room, a vision in blue lace and silk.

"Your mother sent me down to tell you Lissianna's almost ready. She also said it's getting late, and you and Bastien should go pick up Greg and Lucern and get them to the church."

"That's a good idea." Bastien entered the room. Rachel turned and offered a smile to the man. He smiled back, a tinge of surprise on his face as he took her in. "You look lovely, Rachel. Just as lovely as a blonde as you are as a redhead."

"Thank you." She blushed prettily, then moved around him and left the room, leaving Etienne to stare after her. Suave devil that he was, he hadn't said a word about her appearance. That was when Etienne realized that, for all his centuries of knowledge, he was a first-class idiot.

"Nice move there, Etienne," Bastien said, grinning. "I can see the old silver tongue is working hard."

Grunting, Etienne flopped into a chair.

Bastien merely laughed harder at his disconsolate

expression. Walking over, he clapped him on the shoulder. "Come on. Lucern probably has his hands full with a nervous Greg about now. We should go help him pack the groom in the car and get him to the church."

Etienne heaved himself to his feet. Following his dark-haired brother out of the room to the front door, he glanced about, hoping he might spot Rachel again and perhaps get to give her the compliment he should have—but of course she was nowhere to be seen. He'd missed his chance. And if there was one thing Etienne had learned in his three-hundred-plus years, it was that life rarely gave you second chances.

"They make a cute couple, but it isn't him she wants."

Etienne stopped glaring at the dance floor where Bastien was, in his opinion, holding Rachel far too close, and turned to scowl at his cousin. Thomas had paused beside him and was watching the couple dance too. Etienne glowered at him for his trouble and turned back to watch, trying to ignore the jealousy and resentment rising within him.

The wedding had gone without a hitch. The meal was over and the reception was in full swing, yet Etienne hadn't been able to share a single word with Rachel yet. He really wanted to correct his earlier flub and tell her she looked beautiful . . . among other things. Unfortunately, as one of the ushers, Etienne had been forced to sit at the head table with the rest of the wedding party. Rachel had been placed at Jeanne Louise and Thomas's table. He'd felt bad about that at first, but she'd seemed to enjoy herself—at least, every time he'd looked her way Rachel had been laughing at something, so he assumed she'd had a good time. He himself had been bored to tears and impatient to rejoin her. Unfortunately, Bastien had been quicker, and had reached Rachel first. He'd immediately scooped her up and onto the dance floor—which Etienne felt was kind of a crappy thing for a brother to do.

"They're just dancing, Etienne," Thomas said. He sounded vastly amused.

He didn't appreciate Thomas poking inside his head, but then Etienne was already a bit cheesed off at his cousin. Getting to enjoy Rachel's company during the meal was one reason, but he knew his jealousy was ridiculous, so he ignored it and said, "I have a bone to pick with you, cousin."

"Uh-oh." Thomas couldn't even dim his grin. He obviously wasn't too concerned. "What have I done now?"

"Sweet Ecstasies?" he asked, scowling. "What kind of setup was that?"

"Well, it was obvious what you two needed," his cousin said unapologetically. "And it worked, didn't it?"

When Etienne remained silent, Thomas laughed and clapped him on the back. "You're welcome. I'm sure you would have managed it without the drinks eventually. You're just a little rusty, so I decided to give you a little push."

"Well, what if she hadn't wanted—"

"Not a chance, dude. I read her thoughts. Dudette was way hot for you." He shook his head. "Even I—despite being the reprobate that I am—was almost moved to blush at the thoughts she was having."

"Really?" Etienne asked.

"Oh, yeah." He grinned widely, then arched an eyebrow. "But why the flak now? You didn't say anything when I delivered the blood to your house. Is there trouble in paradise already?"

"No." Etienne glanced toward Rachel, his eyes devouring her body in its blue gown with both heat and knowledge. Then he turned to his cousin again and added, "I would have ragged you about it the day you brought the blood and we were locked out, but I wasn't really in any shape."

"No, I guess you weren't," Thomas agreed. "You were pretty drained. In more ways than one." He burst out laughing, then walked away, leaving Etienne with a scowl.

"You should cut in."

Etienne turned to find his mother, a soft smile playing about her lips. He temporarily ignored the advice and commented, "You look happy."

"I am," she agreed. "The first of my babies is married and settling down. *Finally.*"

Etienne chuckled at the emphasis. He'd heard humans complain about their children taking forever to marry and settle down. They didn't have a clue.

"So, are you going to cut in or not?" Marguerite asked. "She wants you to."

"Does she?"

Marguerite concentrated for a moment, a smile curving her lips, then she nodded and said softly, "Oh yes, son. Rachel enjoyed dinner and is having a nice time but would definitely rather be in your arms. She'd rather dance with you. Bastien knows it too, and his ego is suffering for it. You should go save him."

Etienne let his gaze drift out to Rachel again, nodding. "Thank you." Without another word, he crossed the dance floor to the slowly moving couple.

"Brother." Bastien greeted Etienne solemnly as he reached their side, then he released Rachel, gave her a polite, courtly bow, and left the dance floor.

"Hi," Rachel said softly.

"Hi." Etienne opened his arms in invitation and released a breath when she stepped into his embrace. It was where she belonged. He could feel it. In three hundred years no other woman had felt so right. He'd made the right choice in turning Rachel. She was meant for him.

"You look absolutely breathtaking," he murmured by her ear. "I've never seen a more beautiful woman in all my days."

He caught her blush out of the corner of his eye,

then she cuddled closer against him and said, "I find that hard to believe, Etienne. You've seen a lot of women."

"But none of them were as lovely to me," he assured her solemnly. "Even as a blonde."

Rachel stopped dancing and peered into his face as if doubting him. Smiling softly, she simply said, "Thank you." Then she grinned and added, "You're pretty hot yourself."

"You think so?" Etienne asked.

"Oh, yes," Rachel assured him. "You're very handsome. Sexy as hell, really. You have wicked eyes, a mischievous smile, and you're very intelligent. I've always had a weakness for intelligent men, Etienne."

"Yeah?" He grinned. "You like smart guys, huh?"

"Mmm." She nodded, amusement curving her lips. "Intelligence turns me on."

"Yeah?" Etienne raised his eyebrows and smiled mischievously. "Onomatopoeia."

Rachel blinked.

"Enkephalin."

Rachel's bewilderment grew. What was Etienne doing? Thanks to her medical background, she knew that Enkephalin was a substance similar to morphine that could be found in the brain and was thought to help control pain response. But she had no clue why he spouted it. Before she could ask, he added, "Oxymoron."

238

"Er . . . what are you doing?" she asked.

"Spouting big words to impress you with my intelligence." Grinning, he asked, "Are you turned on yet?"

Rachel was so taken aback, a loud burst of laughter slipped from her lips, drawing the attention of those around them.

Etienne smiled and nodded at the other dancers, then turned back to her. He gave a sniff and feigned a scowl. "You aren't supposed to laugh at a guy when he's trying to woo you."

"Is that what you're doing?" she asked.

"Yes. Is it working?"

Rachel chuckled and leaned her head against his shoulder. "I'm not sure. Maybe. Why don't you try a couple more big words?

"More, huh?" He wrapped his arms tighter around her. "Hmm . . . let's see. Ginormous. Dunnock."

"What's that?" Rachel lifted her head to ask. It was the first word she hadn't known.

"A hedge sparrow."

"Ah."

"Shall I continue?" he asked.

"Please don't."

Both Rachel and Etienne straightened in surprise at that dry request from Lucern. The dark-haired man was standing beside them on the dance floor, his solemn face pained. "I've been sent to inform you that Uncle Lucian wants a word with Rachel."

Aware of the way Etienne stiffened, Rachel glanced at him curiously. "You have an uncle?"

"Yes." He released a pent-up breath of resignation. "And he's a nasty old cur too."

"That he may be, but he's also the head of the clan," Lucern commented. "And he wants to talk to Rachel."

"And what he wants, he gets?" she guessed.

"I'm afraid so," Etienne said apologetically. His arm went protectively around her.

Rachel smiled reassuringly. "It will be fine, Etienne. I'm very good with people."

"Uncle Lucian isn't people," he said in grim tones. But, removing his arm, he took her by the elbow instead and led her across the dance floor. Lucern immediately fell into step on her other side.

Rachel smiled at the show of loyalty. She felt very protected as she was led to the head of their clan. Yet she was sure she didn't really need it. Rachel hadn't been kidding when she said she was good with people. She was quite confident that she could handle this nasty old cur just fine . . . and she continued thinking it right up until she was led to a table where a good-looking blond sat next to Etienne's mother.

It was the tense and anxious expression on Marguerite's face that finally shook Rachel's confidence. She had never seen it, and it didn't seem a good thing. Straightening her shoulders, Rachel forced a polite smile for the man she presumed was Etienne's uncle.

Lucian Argeneau was a very handsome man. He

was easily the handsomest man in attendance at the wedding. With his ice-blond hair and chiseled features, he would have fulfilled anyone's image of a Greek God. But, as he surveyed her, his expression was arctic, without a hint of any of the softer human emotions. If this man had ever felt anything like caring or love, those feelings had died or been killed off ages ago. The eyes he turned on Rachel were as empty as black pits.

She met his gaze and waited for him to offer a polite greeting, but there was none forthcoming. It didn't take but a moment to understand why. The man was reading her mind. That was a polite way to phrase it. In truth, he was raking her mind, searching every thought and feeling with a ruthlessness and lack of concern for her feelings that left her breathless. She could actually feel him in there, poking about and sifting through her thoughts. And he didn't care.

"You haven't spoken to her yet." Lucian Argeneau's first words were addressed to Etienne, though he didn't take his gaze off Rachel.

"No." Etienne made the confession just as coldly.

"You didn't want to anger her," the man went on. "You've been trying to woo her to your side in the *hope* that she would concede to your wishes."

Rachel gave a start, her gaze shooting to Etienne only to see his expression closed. He wasn't denying the accusation, however, and she felt all her enjoyment in the evening leak out of her like air from a balloon. Had all their laughter and passion been nothing more than a means to an end?

"You're one of us now."

Rachel jerked her eyes back to Lucian. That comment was meant for her, and she acknowledged it with a grim nod. "Yes, I am."

"If you want to stay one of us, you'll do what's best for the clan," she was informed.

"Really?" Rachel asked archly. "Is this reversible, then?"

"Death is the only release."

"Is that a threat?" she asked.

"It's a statement of fact," he said simply. "You've been given a gift. If you appreciate that, you'll act accordingly."

"Or?" she queried, her eyes narrowed.

"Or you'll be treated like a threat."

"Removed?"

"If necessary." There was no shame or apology in that statement. It was a simple fact, stated the same way he might say the sun would rise in the morning. The words were all the scarier because of that.

"I see," Rachel said slowly, then asked, "And what is it I'm to do?"

Marguerite suddenly put a hand on Lucian's arm, and though Rachel couldn't hear it, she knew that a silent conversation took place. Whatever Etienne's mother said must have been persuasive. Lucian Argeneau nodded once, then announced, "Etienne will tell you. And if you know what's good for you, you'll listen."

"There you are!"

Rachel gave a start when that cheerful cry intruded. It was followed by the arrival of a slender blonde who appeared at Lucian Argeneau's side and began to pet his shoulder and arm as if he were a cat. Rachel couldn't help noticing that while the woman was petting Lucian, she was the one purring.

"Lissianna," the blonde said, "you really should have told us what handsome men you have in your family. Your brothers are beautiful, and your cousin is absolutely scrumptious."

Rachel was surprised to hear Lucian Argeneau referred to as a cousin until she remembered that all the older relatives had been relegated to such connections to hide their ages from Greg's side of the family. There would have been too many questions had Marguerite been introduced as mother and Lucian as uncle. As far as the Hewitt clan was concerned, the Argeneaus were made up of the younger generation with absolutely no surviving older relatives.

Rachel wasn't terribly surprised that several of the single women in Greg's family were fawning over the Argeneau men in a way that was almost painfully embarrassing to witness.

"I grew up surrounded by them, Deeanna. I hardly notice their looks anymore. I only notice them now when they act like coldhearted bastards."

Rachel glanced over her shoulder to see Lissianna and her new husband, as well as Bastien, had joined their small party and were all standing behind her. She hadn't heard them approach. Cold fury filled the bride's face. Lissianna wasn't happy with her uncle, and she had no problem showing it.

"Come," Etienne murmured, taking advantage of the distraction. He pulled Rachel away.

She followed in silence, her mind whirring. Etienne was wooing her to try to get her to do something. The thought kept flowing through her mind as he escorted her out of the reception hall. If there was one thing Rachel hated most in this world, it was being used.

She got into the car when Etienne unlocked the door. She did up her seat belt as he walked around the vehicle to get in, then sat in stony silence as he started the engine and began to drive.

They were headed to his house, of course, to discuss whatever it was he wanted her to do. Rachel knew this. She also knew that the conversation they would have upon reaching his home was going to be unpleasant, no doubt terribly painful. While she wasn't looking forward to it, Lucian Argeneau had made sure there was now no way to avoid it. That being the case, all Rachel could hope for was that she might escape the conversation with at least her pride. She doubted very much if her heart would survive.

* * *

Love Bites

Etienne cursed his uncle silently all the way home. The man had always been a hardass. The rest of the family had often questioned whether he even possessed a heart, but tonight had taken the cake. If Etienne stood any chance at all with Rachel anymore, he would be very surprised. Lucian had just made his life incredibly complicated.

Unfortunately, it was all his own fault, and Etienne knew it. If he had just broached the subject of Pudge with Rachel before the wedding, as he should have done, this wouldn't be a problem. But he hadn't and, now he not only had to try to convince her that claiming Pudge had kidnapped her was the smartest move, but he had to get past her anger to do it. And Rachel had a lot of anger at the moment. A lot. Tons. While he couldn't normally read her thoughts, high levels of passion apparently opened her to him like a book—and apparently not just sexual passion. Right at that moment, she was broadcasting her anger like an FM radio at top volume.

Etienne parked in his driveway and shut off the engine, then sat still for a moment while Rachel undid her seat belt. When he made no move to get out, she paused and waited with what might have seemed patience—if he weren't being blasted by her thoughts.

"I didn't sleep with you to convince you to do what we wanted," he said finally, since that seemed to be the fear she broadcasted most strongly.

"Then why *did* you sleep with me?"

He wasn't fooled by her calm tone. She didn't believe him and was still furious. Etienne was silent as he sought an answer to her question. Why had he slept with her? That had to be one of the stupidest questions a woman could ask. Or perhaps it wasn't with a normal man. One of them might have answered, Because you were willing, or simply, why not? But Etienne had long outgrown the stage where he would sleep with anything that moved. Sadly, sex had turned out like food over the ages—thrilling and exciting at first with its variety, but then more of a bother than anything. Or so he had thought until Rachel. Then his appetite had been revived and he had wondered, what bother?

Just the memory of the heated moments between them was enough to arouse him. Hell, he was sporting wood now at just the thought. But how did he explain all that in a way she would believe? He glanced down at his lap, then to Rachel, and inspiration struck. Reaching out, Etienne caught her hand, drew it across the car, and placed it firmly over his suit pants. "Because you do this to me."

Rachel snatched her hand away as if she'd been burned and scrambled out of the car.

"Okay, so maybe that wasn't the best argument," Etienne muttered. The car door slammed. Obviously, for all his three-hundred-plus years, he hadn't yet lived long enough to understand women.

Chapter Thirteen

"Rachel!" Etienne slammed the car door and hurried up the sidewalk to his front door.

"Don't even talk to me," she snarled.

Yep. She was pretty mad. Etienne caught up to her on his front porch and grabbed her arm to turn her toward him. "You didn't let me finish."

"Finish?" she echoed with disbelief. "What is there to finish? I got it. I gave you a boner. But you men get erections at the drop of a hat. I've heard some of my male co-workers talking. 'Close your eyes and they're all Marilyn Monroe, right?'" She slammed a fist into his front door. "Open this damned thing."

Deciding it might be better to finish the conversation inside, Etienne pulled out his keys and quickly unlocked the door. She immediately shoved it open.

"Rachel," he tried again as they went inside. "It isn't like that with me. It might have been at one time, but that was long ago. I— Where are you going?"

She started upstairs, not even bothering to answer him but breaking into a jog that had her on the upper landing in a heartbeat. Frustration welling up within him, Etienne hurried after her, chasing her along the hall to his bedroom.

"Look, there was a time when I would have slept with anything that moved," he admitted as he followed her. "But I'd been celibate for at least thirty years before you came into my life. Sex just wasn't exciting anymore. You changed all that for me."

"Glad I could be of service."

Etienne winced. The woman had a razor for a tongue when she was angry. He liked it. "Look, I . . . What are you doing?"

"What does it look like I'm doing?" she asked with feigned sweetness. She began shoving her clothes back into the bag his mother had used to transport them.

"It looks like you're packing."

"Got it in one. You're so clever. Care to throw out a couple of big words to impress me?"

Had he just thought he liked her sharp tongue? Etienne glared at her. "You aren't going anywhere. We have to resolve this. We also have to discuss Pudge."

"Ah ha!" She turned on him with cold satisfaction. "I just *knew* that was what it was all about. Pudge! You want me to lie and claim he kidnapped me."

"It's the best way to deal with the matter," he said solemnly.

Rachel snorted in derision. "You mean, it's the most expedient for you people. But he didn't kidnap me. He didn't even really try to kill me. I just got in the way."

"He's dangerous, Rachel."

"Oh, please. Your uncle just finished threatening me with extinction. He would terminate Pudge in a heart-beat."

"Yes, he would," Etienne agreed. "But my family prefers to use death as a last resort. And in this case it isn't necessary, for a simple lie would see Pudge alive and well but locked up and no longer a threat. Or would you prefer to see him dead?"

He felt a modicum of satisfaction at the guilt that crossed her face. He'd scored a point. Bravo for him.

"I can't lie, Etienne. I mean that literally. I'm a rotten liar. I kind of grimace and get this nervous giggle."

"You could at least try. You hold the man's life in your hands. You can lie and see him alive, or you can refuse and force his termination."

Rachel gaped. "Now I'm responsible for his life? Like it's my fault? Next you'll be blaming me for start-ing Armageddon."

"Well, if you live long enough you just might be the cause of it," he snapped.

"Oh!" She turned back to slam some more clothes

into her bag. "You're *so* charming. It's a wonder you *weren't* able to woo me into doing what you wanted."

"I never asked you to 'do what I wanted.' " Etienne ran a hand through his hair with frustration. "And this is exactly why. I didn't want to ruin what was happening between us."

That caught her attention, and Rachel stopped packing. She even turned to stare at him. "What?"

"I like you, Rachel. And I want you. Constantly," he added dryly. "I wasn't sleeping with you to get you to do what I wanted about Pudge. In fact, our . . . relationship is the reason I didn't push the Pudge issue. My family kept urging me to. Bastien even did it in front of you the day we were locked out in the garden, but I couldn't do it. I didn't *want* to. I kept putting it off. Unfortunately, I put it off long enough that Uncle Lucian caught wind of it, and now it *is* a serious issue."

Rachel shifted on her feet, her mind in an uproar. She distinctly recalled Bastien's asking Etienne if he'd talked to her about. . . . He'd never finished the statement; Etienne had interrupted, assuring the man that he would. But he hadn't. Not that day or the ones that followed. Perhaps he was telling the truth. She wanted with all her heart to believe he cared about her, but her mind was in such turmoil she didn't know what to think. She needed time away from him. His nearness had the unfortunate side effect of confusing her.

Etienne added to her confusion by pressing a gentle kiss to her lips. "I don't think I'll ever be able to resist you, Rachel. You stir my blood like no other woman has managed to do in three hundred years. You make me hunger. You're beautiful."

He drew her into his arms, and Rachel was helpless to resist. She would think in the morning, she promised herself as she kissed him back. Everything would be clearer in the morning.

Etienne was a beautiful man. Rachel had known that from the beginning, but lying there watching him sleep by the light spilling out of the bathroom, she took the time to look him over minutely.

Etienne had made love to her through most of the rest of the night. Rachel had fainted as usual, but with her thoughts troubled as they were, she hadn't slept long. She had never been able to sleep at such times. It was now ten in the morning and she was wide awake, her thoughts awhirl as she stared at her lover.

He claimed to like her and to be truly attracted to her. Rachel had no problem believing the former—she thought of herself as a likable sort. But attracted to her? Did he really find her beautiful and desirable? She sighed and rolled onto her back to stare at the shadows spilling across the ceiling. Rachel could look in the mirror and see that she looked better than ever thanks to the turning, but she didn't really feel attractive inside.

She'd been the tall girl during her school years, the gawky carrot top more prone to being teased than flattered and asked out on dates. Her fiancé Steven had been her first real boyfriend, and that hadn't been until University. With him, she'd finally felt pretty and wanted . . . until she'd caught him in bed with her roommate.

She hadn't had much success with dating since. Some of that could no doubt be blamed on the hours she worked, but not all of it. No, Rachel wasn't confident in her attractiveness. The last few weeks had been like some sort of dream come true, having a handsome, sexy man like Etienne paying attention to her. But dreams were hard to believe in, and it was far too easy to believe he had been wooing her to get what he wanted.

Etienne sighed and shifted in his sleep, drawing her attention. Her gaze drifted over his naked body, pausing at the sheet twisted around his waist. The man was a distraction even now. She needed time away. Heck, maybe she needed therapy.

Grimacing at the thought of how that would go, Rachel eased out of bed and began to gather her clothes. She'd go walk through his garden or something. It would mean consuming more blood later, but she could do that easily enough now that she could use straws.

She would rather go home. It was her safe haven from the world, where she had always done her thinking. She also would have liked to at least call her family, so that they wouldn't be left worrying—but she was reluctant to risk either just yet. Not until she'd resolved all this.

Rachel managed to collect her clothes and make it to the bathroom without waking Etienne. Once the door was closed, she relaxed a little and quickly dressed. She ran a brush through her hair, washed her face, and stared at her reflection in the mirror.

"Pudge kidnapped me," she said experimentally. Her lips immediately twitched into something between a grimace and a grin. A nervous giggle slipped from her throat.

Rachel's shoulders slumped. She'd always been a rotten liar. It was inconvenient at times, but mostly made life simpler. If you didn't lie, you never got caught. Honesty was the best policy. Those were phrases she'd had drummed into her head repeatedly as a child. Rachel had always believed them. But now, faced with the problem of Pudge, she couldn't help thinking that in this instance a lie would serve everyone much better. And that included Pudge.

Turning away from the mirror, Rachel moved to the door and eased it open. Her gaze shifted immediately to the bed. Etienne was still lying in the same position as when she'd left. Smiling at how adorable he looked lying there with his hair all ruffled, his chest bare, and the sheets tangled around his waist, she turned off the light and eased into the room, then tiptoed to the door to the hall.

She felt like a thief sneaking out of the room and

creeping to the landing, but she continued to tiptoe all the way down the stairs. She had just reached the door to the kitchen when she heard the soft screech of protesting wood. Pausing in the kitchen doorway, she peered around the room. It was a moment before she noticed movement at the window, then she froze like a deer in headlights. The window had been pushed up, and someone was even now climbing in. They had one leg in and were maneuvering the rest of their body behind.

Heat prickled up the back of her neck, adrenaline pumped through her, and Rachel did what came instinctively—she ducked out of sight into the first available hiding spot, the hall closet. She was easing the door closed before she realized what she was even doing. It wasn't until she felt relatively safe in her hiding place that her brain seemed to engage, and she realized that she, Rachel Garrett, now a vampiress extraordinaire, was hiding from a common thief.

Rachel felt the fear run out of her like water from a glass. What on earth was she doing? She was a vampire. She could handle this cretin. Heck, she'd give him a scare he'd never forget. Teach him a lesson he'd never forget, either, she thought with amusement. Starting to ease the door back open, she only had it a few inches when the burglar straightened and she saw his face. Rachel paused again as recognition struck her. Here was the man from the morgue, the khaki-clad maniac who had tried to hack off Etienne's head. *Pudge*.

That was enough to make her ease the door closed again. This was no regular burglar; this was a man who knew Etienne and his family. He knew about vampires, and how to kill them. And that was no doubt what he was here to do, she realized. Panic immediately set in on her again, and Rachel spent a moment trying to think what to do. Her plans to slip out for a solitary walk were definitely out. She had to get upstairs and warn Etienne. And she had to do so before Pudge got to him.

Too late for that, she realized as Pudge moved past. She'd have to follow him and take him by surprise.

Rachel heard the creak as he started up the stairs, and she knew it was safe to come out of her hiding place. The stairs curved up to the right, so it was safe to leave the closet. When she stepped out into the hall, it somehow seemed darker than it had moments ago. The sun was still shining brightly, however, its rays coming through the windows made dust motes dance in the air. She would have to avoid it.

Pushing all thoughts away as inconsequential, she started to follow Pudge, then paused and peered back into the closet for a weapon. The best she could come up with was a mop and a broom. Rachel considered ransacking the kitchen, where she would at least be able to find a sharp knife, but she feared she didn't have time. Besides, she had seen enough of Pudge to

know that he was armed to the teeth. The man had
been carrying a rifle, a holstered gun, a knife long
enough to almost be a sword, and various other articles. She figured nothing short of a bazooka would
even things out at this point.

Snatching the mop because it at least had a sturdy
wooden handle, compared to the flimsier thin alu-
minum handle of the broom, Rachel hurried through
the hall. She raced as quickly and quietly as she could
up the stairs.

The upstairs hall was empty when she reached it,
which was hardly reassuring. She wasn't sure if it
meant the man knew exactly which room was
Etienne's and had already entered, or if he was searching each room individually and was presently out of
sight. He might come out behind her and take her by
surprise.

Praying that he was in one of the other rooms and
would stay there long enough for her to get to Etienne,
Rachel screwed her courage to the sticking place and
scampered up the hall on tiptoes. At the door to
Etienne's room, she paused to glance back at the
empty hall, then quickly opened the door. She was
just in time to see Pudge raising a stake high over his
head. Rachel did the only thing she could think to do
at that point: she let loose the loudest, longest shriek
she had ever managed in her life and charged forward.

Pudge paused, shocked eyes jerking around to her

and her mop, then just as quickly back to Etienne, who started awake crying, "What? What is it?"

Much to her horror, Pudge then plunged the stake down.

The sound Rachel released was full of fury, and came from a place she didn't even know existed within her. It sounded to her ears like a primal growl, almost a roar, as she swung her mop at the back of the man's head. Unfortunately, he saw and managed to duck.

Rachel had used enough force that she over-balanced. By the time she regained herself and swung back, Pudge was launching himself at her in a football tackle. His head hit her in the abdomen and knocked the breath out of her, and she stumbled backward onto the carpet, where the wind was knocked out of her again. They both slammed into the floor.

Pudge was quicker to recover, and he had his long, wickedly sharp knife at Rachel's throat before she could even attempt to struggle free. "Freeze, lady, or I'll cut your head off," he gasped.

Rachel froze. She could survive a lot of injuries, but having her head cut off wasn't one of them.

They stared at each other, both panting a bit, when movement on the bed drew their attention. Etienne was down but not out for the count. In all the excite-ment, Pudge's aim had been off. Etienne was even now sitting up, the stake protruding from his chest a bare inch to the side of where his heart would be.

Rachel nearly sobbed with relief when he tugged the stake free.

Pudge was less impressed. He cursed, then barked, "You freeze too, Argeneau!"

Etienne hesitated, then sank back onto the bed, his eyes narrowed. It was a standoff.

"Well, hell," Rachel said as she realized Pudge had the upper hand. She really didn't feel she had made a very good showing. She supposed she needed training.

"What are you going to do now, Pudge?" Etienne asked. He was starting to look a little better, and Rachel supposed the nanos must be working like mad to make repairs. He'd need more blood to fuel them, though. Still, he looked pretty nonchalant for someone who'd been staked and whose girlfriend was presently under threat of having her head cut off. If she could call herself his girlfriend. Did sleeping with a man make you his girlfriend? Or was he just thinking of her as— Don't even go there, girlfriend, she warned herself. Now was not the time for that kind of analysis.

"If you cut her head off, you lose your shield," Etienne continued.

Pudge was silent, but his knife pressed tighter against Rachel's throat. Confusion and uncertainty struggled on his face.

"I've been very patient with you, Pudge—mostly because I've found your antics entertaining to date. But I find you're becoming tiresome. I suggest you leave and never return, or you shall force me to put an end to our little games. Permanently."

It was amazing to Rachel that her lover could sit there with a gaping chest wound, yet still sound so threatening. She glanced at Pudge to see if he were equally impressed, and was a tad relieved to note the sweat popping out on his forehead. She just wasn't sure if it would result in a good thing or a bad one.

"Up."

Rachel scrambled to her feet, very aware of the long knife at her throat. She considered trying some fancy footwork in an attempt to break free, but her attempt and failure to save Etienne had rather sapped her confidence. She was afraid she'd make a mess of it as she had earlier.

Once they were both upright, Pudge shifted behind her, using her as the shield Etienne had mentioned.

"Stay back," Pudge ordered. His voice started out firm but ended on a quavering note that bespoke his fear. Not that Rachel needed that. She could actually smell the fear pouring off him. She didn't know how she recognized the scent but supposed it was a new ability. Most predators had it—dogs could sense fear, as well as cats. She supposed the nanos increased the abilities most useful to their carriers, and this was pretty useful for a predator to have.

"Let her go," Etienne ordered.

"Stay back." Pudge began to sidle away, taking Rachel with him.

"You aren't taking her with you."

"Stay back, or I'll cut off her head," Pudge warned.

"Don't hurt her. It's your fault I had to turn her in the first place. She would have died from that ax wound you gave her if I hadn't turned her."

That made Pudge pause. Rachel held her breath as he looked down at her.

"You're the doctor from the hospital." He sounded surprised. She supposed she'd looked a little less healthy at the time, having just recovered from the flu. She'd been pale and limp-looking, she was sure. She noted the guilt cross his face and felt a moment's hope. He said, "I'm really sorry about axing you, but you shouldn't have jumped between us. I tried to tell you what he was."

"Let her go," Etienne repeated.

Rachel felt the hope die in her as Pudge stiffened. His expression turned grim as he pressed the knife tighter to her throat. Apparently his guilt only went so far. "I won't hurt her if you stay right where you are." He sounded a little more in control now. Rachel couldn't decide if that meant his confidence had increased or if Etienne's repeated warnings were making him comfortably sure of the fact that he had the upper hand.

"If you hurt her, I'll hunt you down and kill you with my bare hands."

Rachel's eyes shot to Etienne. He looked capable of doing it. Gone was the easy facade, the charming computer geek. Etienne looked every inch a dangerous predator.

They were all three silent for several minutes as they waited for Pudge to decide what to do next. Rachel didn't have a clue what he *could* do. He couldn't let her go, which rather restricted him. Her gaze slid to Etienne. The bleeding had stopped, but he was looking a little gray around the lips. A lot of the blood left in him was no doubt being used up to repair his wound, she supposed. From what they had told her about his state, she supposed he was in dire need of an infusion. His body would be cramping with his need, and he would be terribly weak and vulnerable.

The only plus was that Pudge wouldn't be aware of that, she decided.

"You'd better decide what you're going to do quickly. His body is nearly done repairing itself, and who knows how much strength he'll have then." Very little was Rachel's guess, but if Pudge was going by the movies, television or the big screen, he'd probably think otherwise. At least she hoped he would. Judging by the way Pudge's hands tightened on her, she guessed she was right.

Rachel couldn't see his face, but she sensed the bewilderment Pudge was feeling. He asked suspiciously, "Am I supposed to believe you're trying to be helpful?"

Rachel forced herself to relax and managed an unconcerned shrug without beheading herself. "Believe what you want. I was sneaking out when you broke in," she said truthfully. She had been sneaking out for a walk, but she didn't bother to mention that. When Etienne's sharp gaze filled with betrayal, she was almost sorry she couldn't. Rachel hated to upset him, but she made herself continue. "I've been forced to stay here since that night in the morgue. I wanted to let my family and friends know I was all right, but calling them was out of the question." Which was all true, she assured herself as she felt a nervous giggle rise in her throat. She *had* been forced to stay—at least until she learned how to control her teeth and such, and calling anyone *had* been out of the question. She didn't have to specify that it was herself forcing these decisions.

"So I played nice and waited until Etienne was asleep, then was about to leave through the kitchen when I heard you coming in," she continued. "You blew my plan."

Etienne was looking upset, but Rachel ignored him. She waited while Pudge digested her words.

"It that's true, why didn't you just leave?" Pudge asked with disbelief. "Why stay and save him?"

Rachel shrugged. "My conscience wouldn't allow it. I couldn't just let you slaughter him in his sleep after he saved my life from the mortal wound *you* inflicted." She emphasized his part, hoping to bring about a return of the guilt she had seen on his face earlier. When she saw it flicker in his eyes, Rachel decided to drive the screw a little deeper. "Thanks a lot for that, by the way. Being a bloodsucking demon was never high on my list of dreams and wishes, and I can't tell you how pleased I am that I'll be stuck on the night shift for eternity."

Pudge actually winced. "I'm sorry," he said regretfully, then paused and glanced to Etienne. "What do you suggest we do with him to get out of here?"

Rachel considered. She didn't believe for a minute that he now considered them on the same side. She supposed he was testing her. If she gave an answer he didn't like, she'd be in trouble. But then, she was probably in trouble anyway. He seemed to see himself as a modern day Van Helsing, dedicated to eradicating the world of the vampire blight, and she was very aware that put her on his list. Her only hope was to convince him that she was too stupid to realize, and that she believed they were now on the same side. To that end, she was extremely careful with her answer. "Well, I don't want to see him dead after he saved me. If you really want to kill him, you'll either have to try another day when I'm not here, or stake me now and take your chances with him—but I wouldn't if I were you. At normal strength he's fast, agile and stronger than ten men. Right now he's not as strong, but I am. With the two of us, the odds aren't in your favor," she added.

Pudge was listening, and her honesty in refusing to see Etienne dead seemed to convince him. Rachel barely let that sink in before adding, "Then too, he has a security system. There are probably several of his kind on their way here right now. So you don't have a lot of time."

Pudge obviously believed her. Panic flashed across his face.

"If you tie him up," she went on, "he'll just break his bonds and probably be on us before we're out of the house." Or at least he would be after consuming some blood, she thought.

"I suppose the best thing you can do is lock him in his office. He's made it proof against competitors of all races," she explained. Then to sweeten the pot, she added, "It would give you a chance to destroy his latest work too."

"I should have let you die." Etienne's cold words drew her eyes back to him. She would have mentally congratulated him on his acting abilities, but she wasn't sure it was an act. She had just admitted to having been sneaking out while he slept, and though she hoped it wasn't true, he might believe everything. No. He knew the truth about vampires, and that she knew better than to think that he was getting stronger right now. Surely he realized she was stretching the truth to save him.

On the other hand, Rachel thought suddenly, his anger might be based on another reason. What if he hadn't saved any of his work, hadn't backed it up against the possibility of losing it? He might lose it thanks to the suggestion she had just made. But her main concern had been to leave him alive somewhere where there was blood for him to ingest.

Jeez, if he hadn't been sensible enough to save his latest game, Etienne might really wish her dead. But better alive and angry than dead with an intact game.

Pudge shifted, switching the knife at her throat from one hand to the other. She wasn't sure why he'd done it until he swung the rifle from his shoulder to point it at Etienne.

"I know this can't stop you, but I bet it still hurts," he said. "And I know it will slow you down. So, do what you're told and I won't have to shoot you. We're going to your office."

Etienne felt mingled relief and horror course through him. There was blood in his fridge in his office. He could replenish and repair quickly with it once locked in. He could then get out and hunt Pudge down. His horror was because while this plan saved him, it left Rachel in jeopardy. He had no idea what the man would do with her once he had options, but he assumed it would be villainous. Rachel was ten times stronger than she used to be, but she wasn't invulnerable. Etienne feared she would try something risky after he was safely tucked away.

"Move!" Pudge added an exclamation mark by shooting him.

Etienne grunted and jerked backward where he sat

on the bed. The bullet had torn through muscle and bone. He saw Rachel begin to struggle, only to stop almost as abruptly in the next moment. He understood why when he noted the line of blood at her throat. The bastard had cut her—not deep enough to do serious injury, but he had cut her just the same.

Etienne felt rage course through him, enough to help him gain his feet. He wanted to fly across the room at the man, but he might be useless once he got there. Besides, there was a possibility Pudge might panic and cut her head off, removing her as a threat. Etienne couldn't allow that.

Rachel gritted her teeth but ground out, "I told you I wouldn't allow you to kill him. If you shoot him again, I'll risk losing my head to kill you."

"Shut up," Pudge hissed, but some of his confidence left him. Gesturing at Etienne with his rifle, he backed out of the door, dragging Rachel with him. "Out."

Etienne moved dutifully toward the door, trying not to look as weak as he felt. He was in serious need of blood now, thanks to the newest wound. His thinking processes were becoming muzzy as his body drew blood from the rest of his system. It took all his concentration to keep putting one foot in front of the other to lead the way through the house and down to the basement. Etienne kept trying to think of a way out of this situation as he moved, but nothing came to mind—nothing that wouldn't jeopardize Rachel further, at any rate.

"Wow!" Pudge was obviously impressed with Etienne's work station. Etienne paused in the middle of the room and turned to watch the man's eyes light up as they roamed over his equipment.

"Man, if I had a setup like this, I'd be the king of games, too," he said resentfully. Then his gaze landed on the coffin to the side of the door and something else entered his expression. It took Etienne several minutes to realize it was envy.

"Get in it," he ordered.

Etienne hesitated, then did as he was told as the man jerked his rifle upward. Rachel shifted with a warning growl. Pudge immediately lowered the gun and controlled her by causing another red line of beaded blood where the first had just finished healing.

"I'm going," Etienne snapped, promising himself he'd repay the man for those wounds soon.

"Close the lid," Pudge instructed once he was seated inside.

Etienne did as he was told, reclining in the coffin and reluctantly pulling the lid closed. Then he jerked inside the coffin at the sudden explosion of gunfire. At first he thought the idiot was shooting him through the coffin, but when there was no exploding wood and no tearing pain, he decided the fellow was shooting up the room. The boom of either a monitor or a computer exploding verified this, and Etienne grimaced at the scent of burning circuits and melting plastic.

Chapter Fourteen

Rachel bit her lip, but she remained still as Etienne's machinery exploded around her. Pudge was enthusiastic with his gun, and the knife at her throat was pressed too tight for her to do anything. She was relieved when he finally decided he'd done enough damage and backed them out of the room.

At the door, he stopped to examine the locking mechanism. She had rather hoped he would just close it, but he wasn't that stupid. He pulled it closed, then shot up the electrical panel. Any hope that Etienne would be able to fix the panel died when Pudge then ripped it and several wires out willy-nilly. Etienne truly was locked in there, Rachel thought with dismay, and just hoped that none of the destroyed equipment started a fire. Burning to death wouldn't be a pleasant way to go, and it was the way Etienne's father had died.

Yet he had blood in there, she assured herself, grateful that Pudge hadn't examined the desk drawers. And no doubt Bastien and Lucern would visit later. They would set Etienne free and then probably come after her. She just had to stay alive in the meantime. Which would have been easier if Pudge didn't know she was a vampire.

Keeping her head attached to her body would be a good start. She'd like to do more, however—like keeping him from cutting her again. The thin slices he had inflicted so far hadn't even come close to endangering her life, but they hurt like crazy. Apparently being turned didn't mean lessening sensitivity to pain. It even increased her sensitivity, she realized. After all, she was more sensitive to pleasure. Why not equally more sensitive to pain?

"Damn."

Rachel gave up considering at Pudge's curse. They had traversed the stairs and were now standing in the kitchen at the back door.

"I forgot I can't take you out in sunlight," Pudge explained.

Rachel brightened. She could survive a few moments of sunlight but was hardly willing to tell him that. "Well, you could just leave me here and—"

Her words died as he dragged her backward to the kitchen table. She wasn't sure what he was up to until he ripped the heavy maroon tablecloth off the table, sending the floral arrangement smashing to the floor.

"You don't think you're going to . . . You are." She blew her breath out with a sigh as he drew the cloth over her head. Now she had a knife at her throat and was blind. Jeez, it just got better and better. This was even more dangerous. If she stumbled, she might behead herself. Rachel considered telling Pudge that she could survive a little sunlight but feared she might need the knowledge later.

"We're going to move quickly." He urged her forward, presumably toward the door. "I don't want you bursting into flames now, so try to keep up."

"Do you think you could ease up with the knife?" she asked, but the question was drowned out by the click and squeak of the door. Then Pudge was rushing her forward. Aware that any misstep could cost her her life, Rachel frog-marched, keeping her feet up but moving as quickly as she could. Despite her best efforts, she stumbled, grunting as the knife sliced her throat. It managed a deeper cut this time before it was eased away. She heard what might have been an apology muffled by both the cloth over her head and the ringing in her ears; then he jerked her to a halt.

"Get in."

The knife was pulled away, and Rachel felt herself shoved forward and down. Something pressed against the front of her legs, and she tumbled forward. Grateful the knife was no longer threatening her, Rachel immediately began to try to drag the cloth off her head. She received a smack for her efforts.

"Don't. The sunlight," Pudge warned. Then Rachel felt something at her wrist and heard a snap. She pulled, frowning when she was restrained, then cursed as a manacle went on her other wrist.

"These are galvanized steel," Pudge announced. "Four inches thick. You could probably break them, but not without a racket. If you try, I'll shoot you from my seat. And not with a gun—with a stake-shooter through the heart."

"A stake-shooter?" Rachel muttered. She heard a door close, followed by silence. She was just wondering if it was safe to try to shrug the cloth off and chance a look around when she heard another door open. This one was to her right, toward the front of what must be a van, she decided. The floor beneath her rocked a little as Pudge entered the vehicle.

Rachel forced herself to relax and cursed herself for not listening more closely to what Etienne had tried to tell her. She had no idea what her capabilities as a vampire were, except that she was stronger and faster than a normal human and could suffer more damage without dying. From what she understood, short of being burned alive or having her head cut off, nothing could kill her. Though being staked would stop her heart and force the nanos into a stasis until the stake was removed.

It was great to know, of course, but Rachel had no

clue how strong she was exactly, or even how much faster she was. She had no idea if she could possibly break her bonds, and if she could, was she now fast enough that she could break out of the van before Pudge could grab his stake-gun—whatever that was—and shoot her down. The idea of trying was tempting, but the idea of being shot—despite the fact that he would probably miss her heart—was somewhat dampening. Rachel hated pain. She'd thought a shot was bad. How about a stake? She could be a terrible wuss when it came to pain; a big crybaby, really. She decided not to risk it.

The ride that followed was short. Rachel spent the time trying to devise a plan of escape. She had no idea why Pudge had taken her. He had needed a shield, or thought he did at first, but once Etienne was locked up, he hadn't anymore. She was rather surprised he hadn't taken the opportunity to stake her then.

Rachel supposed guilt might be the reason he hadn't yet, since his attack was the reason she'd been turned in the first place. But that left her to wonder what he intended to do with her if staking wasn't the plan. Nothing good was coming to mind. Escape seemed her best action. She just had to devise how.

Presumably he would take her somewhere, park, then come at her again with his knife. This time she feared she might have to risk the pain of being cut.

She wasn't looking forward to that, but she might suffer worse if she didn't.

The rumble of the van stopped. It was escape time. She felt her body tense as the van rocked. Pudge was getting out, she realized, then heard the door close. Rachel gave her manacles a testing tug, surprised when the creak of metal stretching reached her ears. She was about to give a serious tug when she heard the back doors open.

Cursing her own timidity, she stilled and waited, startled when the cloth was suddenly tugged from her head.

"There are no windows in this garage. You're safe from the sun," Pudge announced. As if he had purchased this garage and the house that was no doubt attached specifically to keep her safe.

Rachel was less than impressed. Her gaze was fixed on the weapon in his hands. His stake-gun appeared to be a crossbow with a wooden stake rather than an arrow. Not that it really mattered. According to Etienne an arrow, stake, or whatever, if lodged in the heart and left there long enough, could finish her off. So much for escape. At least for now.

"Come on." Pudge stepped back, careful to keep the weapon trained on her heart. He gestured with his free hand for her to get out of the van.

Rachel raised her eyebrows at the order and merely rattled the short chains that bound her to the wall of the van.

"Oh." Pudge hesitated a moment, then apparently decided he didn't want to get close enough to risk being overcome, and simply tossed her the keys.

Rachel managed to catch them between her arm and one breast, then picked them up and set to work on the locks. It was her first good look at the manacles, and the sight was daunting. He hadn't been kidding about them being four inches thick, yet they didn't feel as heavy as they should. Rachel supposed that was due to her increased strength. She really should have gone for it and tugged herself free, she told herself, unlocking first one wrist, then the other.

"Okay, come on," Pudge repeated. Recalling the way he had shot Etienne when he hadn't moved quickly enough, Rachel scrambled to the edge of the van and dropped off to stand on the concrete floor of the garage. She held out the keys to Pudge, but he shook his head.

"You'll need them to open the door." He gestured her to the left.

Rachel turned to survey the direction he pointed toward, spotting the house door at once. It was a one-car garage, and the van, left little more than a foot and a half of walking space. Rachel moved along the passenger side of the van, pausing when she spotted the wreath of garlic with a cross in the center that hung on the middle of the door.

"Sorry. Back off a bit." Pudge quickly stepped up to remove the paraphernalia.

She didn't inform him it was useless. Instead, she pondered how paranoid the man must be to put such things on his door.

"Okay." Taking the cross and garlic with him, he backed out of the way and gestured forward, informing her, "It's the wide silver key."

Rachel sorted until she found the only wide silver key, then stepped up to the door and inserted it in the lock. When the lock clicked open, she turned to arch an eyebrow at her captor.

"Go on," Pudge ordered, gesturing with his crossbow. Rachel opened the door and stepped into his kitchen, then stopped dead. She had never seen such a pigsty. The counters and sink were stacked with filthy dishes, and there wasn't an inch of stove, fridge, counter, cupboard, or floor that wasn't covered with food slops or just plain filth. On top of that was a coating of grease that bespoke a good deal of fried food being cooked.

"Move." A sharp poke in her back made Rachel take a quick step forward, then continue through the kitchen avoiding touching anything. It was bad enough that she had to step on the floor; her sneakers stuck to the linoleum with every step. It was disgusting. And the dining room was just as bad, she saw, as she stepped through its arch.

"Sit down."

"I'd rather not." Rachel gazed over the table with its stacks of dirty dishes. Unfortunately, food wasn't the only thing on the plates. There were more than a couple of bugs crawling across them, feasting happily on month-old pizza and such. As for the chairs themselves, they were blessedly free of plates, but were instead covered with several months' old newspapers, flyers and junk mail. "You know, Pudge, a housekeeper wouldn't be a bad thing."

"Sit!" He was apparently feeling rather confident now that they were inside. He got close enough to grab her by the shoulder and steer her into the nearest chair. Rachel winced as the edge of a crumpled flyer poked her in the butt, but she didn't say anything as he moved around the table and seated himself, positioning his crossbow on the table aimed at her chest.

They were both silent a moment, staring at each other, sizing each other up. But when the silence continued to draw out and Rachel began to feel uncomfortable, she raised her eyebrows. "So?"

"So?" Pudge frowned. "What?"

"Are you going to kill me now or what?" Rachel asked.

"No!" He looked startled at the very possibility. "No way. It's my fault you're a vampire chick. Or is it vampiress?" While he sat muttering and fretting, Rachel tried to figure out exactly where that left her. Judging by the awe in his tone, Pudge was much more impressed by a female vampire. He seemed to see her being a vampire as a cool thing, whereas Etienne being one meant he was someone to be obliterated. She wasn't sure why.

"So . . ."

Rachel glanced at Pudge's face, made curious by his almost excited look. Nothing prepared her for his question, however. "Are you hungry?"

Taken by surprise she might be, but his question was relevant. She didn't think she'd lost too much blood from the cuts to her throat, but she was hungry. Her gaze drifted to the refrigerator in the kitchen. Did he have any blood in there? It didn't seem likely, but if not, why did he ask if she was hungry? Then again, if he did have blood, she wasn't at all sure it would be safe to drink in this bacteria factory he called a home. She half-suspected it wouldn't be. Could anything in this place be safe to put near her mouth?

"You could bite me," Pudge offered, drawing her attention. He looked rather excited at the prospect. Rachel felt her appetite die a quick death.

"Thanks, but—" she began politely.

"Oh, come on. You have to be craving blood. You could even turn me if you wanted." His gaze dropped to her chest.

Rachel tried not to look repulsed. The idea of his existing in the world forever was a horrible one, almost as bad as biting him. She doubted he was much cleaner than his house. However, she didn't want to cheese the guy off. She hadn't figured out what he intended to do with her, but until she had the chance to escape, she figured it would be a good thing to humor him.

"No, thanks," she said politely in response to his offer. Letting her gaze drift toward the bit of living room she could see, she noticed wood blocking the balcony doors and the metal bars over them. The house was rather gloomy. Glancing around at the other windows, she noted they too were covered with wood and metal bars. Perhaps he hadn't always intended to kill Etienne.

"You know, you aren't bad-looking."

Rachel's attention slid back to her captor. She wasn't quite sure how to respond. From anyone else, the words might be a compliment. The way he said it spoke of disappointment. She understood that disappointment when he explained, "Well, you know. You're pretty enough, but not quite what I expected. In all the movies, the vamp chicks are . . ." He paused, apparently searching for the right word. "Hotter. You know. Black vinyl bustiers and high-heeled, thigh-high boots." His gaze was fixed on her chest, as if he were trying to work out whether she might be wearing a black vinyl bustier under her sweatshirt.

Rachel sighed and decided it was going to be a long day.

Etienne gave his office door a frustrated kick, then turned and paced to the refrigerator in his desk. He had already ingested four bags while examining the damage done to the door and seeing if he couldn't somehow fix it. It was looking like it would be an impossibility. Pudge had really done a number on it, and that combined with the high-tech security he had installed to keep his office theftproof were working against him. He also wished he'd been smart enough to turn on that high-tech security system Rachel had mentioned. Unfortunately, between trying to soothe Rachel's anger last night and making love to her, he'd forgotten to reactivate it after entry.

Etienne cursed his stupidity. He'd never really been worried about his home or his possessions, or even himself before. His work had been the only thing he had thought both valuable and vulnerable until now. He'd never been concerned about being attacked. The average house robber would have been in for an unpleasant surprise had he tried breaking into his home, especially it he had the temerity to attack him. Then too, the days of threat from vampire hunters were long over—or had been until Pudge. But Rachel was very valuable to Etienne, far more valuable than he had admitted to her. And thanks to his neglect, she was now in danger, and he was helpless.

Etienne had made his office into a sort of panic room—both human-and vampire-proof—since everything computer was surprisingly popular with vampires. Now Pudge had turned his high-tech panic room into a cage by ripping out his door panel. No one could get in or out without an acetylene torch to cut through the six-inch steel. Unfortunately, Etienne hadn't had the forethought to keep one in his office. He was stuck until Bastien and Lucern arrived. Hours from now. Hours during which anything could happen to Rachel.

Etienne glared at the thousands of dollars' worth of ruined equipment that used to make up his work station. If he could get some of it up and running again, he might be able to contact someone sooner. It was a longshot. Pudge had been thorough in his destruction. Still, it was better than sitting imagining all the horrible things that could happen to Rachel.

He grabbed another bag of blood from the fridge, noting absently that it was starting to grow warm. Apparently Pudge had managed to hit the fridge too. Still, it wasn't really a concern. He'd had enough blood already and didn't mind it a tad warm.

He set to work fiddling with his equipment.

"I am not biting Muffin." Rachel glared at Pudge as he dangled the small terrier before her. She couldn't even believe he would suggest it. The man was a sicko. Taking her earlier diplomatic silence as encouragement, Pudge had explained that he really wanted to be a vampire. He thought it would be cool to live forever and run the night with vamp chicks on his arm. He seemed to see himself as the star of his own B-grade vamp movie, his skinny, greasy geek persona being traded in for the debonair bad boy of the night.

As if being turned would somehow change his looks and personality too.

When Rachel had made a murmur she hoped he would take as encouragement rather than the derision it was, he had got quite animated, explaining that he had fantasized about this a lot since realizing Etienne was a vampire. One of his plans had been to finally kill Etienne, then scope the funeral, pick out a vamp chick—" 'cause you know, lots of 'em would probably attend his funeral"—then pick the one he liked best and bring her back to his pad. There she would go down on him and turn him by biting his—

Rachel had interrupted at that point to inform him that, if he expected or tried to force her to bite him there, he could think again. He'd tilted his head and said, "But I have the stake. I've got the power. You have to do what I say."

Rachel had narrowed her eyes on the little cockroach and calmly told him, "Yes. You have the stake and therefore the power—for now. But if you try to force me to bite you there, I'll bite it right off. Like blood chewing gum." She'd then forced an evil grin, hoping all the while that her face didn't reflect her nausea.

Judging by the way Pudge had paled and crossed his legs, Rachel assumed her warning was a suitable deterrent. He'd certainly stopped insisting she could bite and turn him, but he had also forced her to her feet and ordered her to lead the way to the basement.

At that point, Rachel had feared she might have gone too far and made herself useless, thus signing her own death warrant. However, he hadn't killed her. He had chained her to the walls of his basement. He really had been all set up to bring a "vamp chick" here to his home, and apparently hadn't expected her to be cooperative right away. Presumably, he thought he could change that with a little time. Perhaps he was counting on Stockholm syndrome or something to kick in and help with the matter.

Whatever the case, he'd ordered her to step up to the wall and snap the steel manacles around her ankles, thighs, waist, and neck. He'd approached carefully once she had, keeping the crossbow pointed at her chest, and affixed the ones around her shoulders and wrists. He'd then left her there and returned upstairs. Rachel had immediately set to work trying to escape her bonds, but these had been even thicker and stronger than the ones in the van, and he had affixed them to the wall so that she stood legs spread and arms out, which made it difficult to gain full strength.

She had still been struggling with them and cursing when the door to the upstairs had opened moments ago. He had returned below to dangle a small fluffy white terrier from its leash before her and sing out the word "dinner."

"I am not biting him," Rachel repeated now. Then, unable to watch the poor animal struggle and choke, she tugged uselessly at her manacles and snapped, "Put that poor animal down. You're choking him to death."

"But I have to feed you," he complained, but lowered the animal to the ground and wound his leash around the stair railing as he muttered, "How else are you going to learn to trust me?"

Rachel watched with interest as he muttered to himself. It seemed obvious to her that the man spent way too much time on his own. He was obviously quite used to doing so, as he mumbled, "It's just the neighbor's yappy dog. He's always taking a crap on my lawn, the little barker. I don't know why you can't just eat the damn thing and get it out of my hair. I—"

"I am not eating anyone's fluffy little house pet," Rachel interrupted his mind's meandering abruptly.

He glanced at her with interest. "How about a rat? I have them delivered every week for my snake, but—"

He paused when Rachel shuddered and shook her head. She was beyond commenting on this one. Eating rat? Dear God.

"Man, you're a fussy eater," he said with exasperation. "If I'd known you were going to be this much trouble—" His irritated words died as a chime sounded through the house.

Rachel glanced around, unsure what the sound was until Pudge moved to turn on a television that sat in the corner. An image of the front door of a house, presumably this one, immediately popped into view. Pudge was into hi-tech gizmos just like Etienne, Rachel realized as she peered at the potbellied behemoth in the beer T-shirt now leaning against the doorbell with one hand and pounding at the door with the other.

"My brother." Pudge sounded glum at first, then suddenly he brightened and turned to her. "You could feed on him. I don't really like him. And you wouldn't even have to turn him. He's a big bully pain in the butt anyway."

"I am not biting your brother," Rachel gasped, shocked at the very idea. Jeez, what did he think she was? His very own assassin sent to get rid of any creature who annoyed him? She had never bitten a real live person before and didn't intend to start now. Well, except for Etienne, of course, but that had been rather . . . er . . . intimate in nature. Different. She had no intention of starting to bite complete strangers.

"Well, you have to eat something." He was looking irritated again.

Rachel decided she had to put an end to this. "I'm not hungry. I'm not biting anyone. Or anything."

"Well, hell!" Apparently deciding not to deal with his brother if she wouldn't bite him, Pudge turned away from the TV screen and paced the room as his brother continued to ring and pound. Just when Rachel thought the racket was going to drive her bonkers, Pudge's bully brother gave up with one last kick at the door and moved out of camera shot.

Some of Pudge's tension left him when his brother gave up and went away. He stopped pacing and paused before what appeared to be a large metal coffin to sit on its lid, then stared at her with displeasure. Rachel was getting the feeling that she was a major disappointment as a vamp chick. Too bad she couldn't work up any regret over that, she thought, and finally took a look around the basement. She had only got a glance around on the way downstairs, and then she hadn't taken the time while she had been trying to free herself. Now she saw that it was a haven of cheesy vampire paraphernalia. Half of it appeared to be filled with weapons to kill vampires, the other half of things vampires might need: the coffin, a cape hanging from a hook, fake teeth on a counter, every book on vampires ever published. Rachel had an image in mind of him wearing the cape and fake fangs and pretending to be a vampire. She shook her head. The man really was cuckoo.

"So when will you get hungry? And what exactly will you eat, since you're so fussy?"

Rachel glanced back to her captor and decided to be honest in the hope that he would stop offering her his relatives and pets to feed on. "I'm a little hungry now, but I've never bitten anyone. I don't think I can."

He looked surprised at this admission. "Well then, how have you been feeding? You must have been feeding since Etienne turned you. That was more than two weeks ago. You—"

"Bagged blood," she interrupted.

"Bagged blood?" He looked shocked at the thought. "You mean cold bagged blood, like in the hospital?" When Rachel nodded, his face screwed up with disgust. "Ewwwww."

She rolled her eyes at his reaction. Apparently, he saw biting people as a better alternative to drinking blood like wine. Oh, he'd be a great vampire. One of those rogues Etienne had mentioned. She definitely wasn't ever biting him. Setting him loose on mankind would be a bad thing to do.

"Well, we're gonna change all that. You—" He paused in saying what she suspected was going to be something she didn't want to hear and glanced toward the television screen when the door chimes rang again. Rachel followed his irritated gaze to see a short, round little gray-haired lady there, shouting at the door as she pushed the doorbell and rapped her knuckles on the wood.

This time Pudge grabbed a remote and turned the volume up to hear what the woman was yelling. Her staccato words burst into the room full of indignant fury. "Open the door this instant, Norman Renberger. I know you're in there, and you have my Muffin! I saw you snatch him out of the backyard. You open the door this instant or I'm going right home to call the police."

"Shit," Pudge muttered and stood to stomp upstairs.

Rachel turned her attention back to the television, a little worried as she waited for Pudge to answer the door. He hadn't taken the dog with him and suspected this wasn't a good thing.

She saw the door open and Pudge smile an oily smile at the furious woman.

"Hello, Mrs. Craveshaw."

"Don't you hello me, Norman! Where is my Muffin?"

Rachel winced as Muffin heard his mistress's voice and began to bark. Pudge had left the stairway door open, and apparently the sound carried, for in the next moment Mrs. Craveshaw cried, "Muffin!" and shoved her way past Pudge into the house. She was immediately out of sight of the camera.

"Where is she? Where's my baby? Muffin? Muffin!" Now the voice wasn't coming from the television but from upstairs as the woman followed the sound of the barking. "Muffin!"

The voice had reached the top of the stairs and the woman filled the doorway. Her eyes lit up when she spotted Muffin leashed to the rail, barking like mad.

"Run! Call the police!" Rachel cried, but it was too late. The woman had eyes and ears only for her Muffin. She barreled down the stairs at breakneck speed, cursing at Pudge, who was following her. She had reached the bottom step and was trying to untangle the leash from the post when Pudge hit her over the head with the crossbow. The action launched the stake it was armed with. Rachel jerked and flinched to the side as it shot at her. Unfortunately, she had nowhere to go to escape the stake. Her manacles held her in place. She cried out in pain as the stake slammed into her heart.

Chapter Fifteen

"Welcome back."

Rachel winced at those words as she blinked her eyes open. For a moment she wasn't sure where she was, but then Pudge's face came into focus before her and her memory returned. Following his gaze to her chest, she grimaced at the sight of her shirt hanging open to reveal her bloodstained lace bra.

"I took the stake out," Pudge explained, his gaze roving the smooth skin with fascination. "You healed like crazy. First the bleeding stopped, then the hole closed, then even the scar went away. It was mag, man!"

Rachel turned her head wearily away from his excited face. Mag. But now she desperately needed more blood. She couldn't sustain and recover from a wound like that without using a lot of it. Her body was in an agony of want, cramping and crying out for the fluid of life. She could actually smell the blood inside the man standing before her, and thought she might even be able to hear it pulsing through his veins. If he moved closer, Rachel wouldn't trust herself not to simply take a bite out of him despite her best intentions. With her body screaming for it, she was definitely feeling capable of the feat.

Rachel gave her head a shake and mentally berated herself for even thinking that way. She wasn't some soulless bloodsucking demon who couldn't control herself. Etienne had assured her she wasn't. She could fight it. She just had to convince the incompetent little stake-happy geek to go rob a blood bank and bring her nourishment. She wasn't biting him.

A moan from across the room made Pudge glance behind him, then he moved away. Rachel was so relieved that he had taken his blood-filled scent away that she closed her eyes and didn't pay attention to what he was doing until he returned. The scent returned with him, stronger than it had been before.

"Here you go. I thought about just killing her but decided to save her for you. You need blood. Bite her. Give her the vampire kiss."

Rachel moaned and turned her head desperately away as Pudge pushed a pale and still woozy Mrs. Craveshaw at Rachel until she was practically beneath her nose. The woman had apparently been unconscious the whole time, which could only be a good thing, Rachel supposed. At least the woman hadn't witnessed her "mag" healing. The problem now was that the older woman had a cut on the top of her head from where Pudge had hit her. The blood had poured out into her hair and made a trail down her neck to soak in the shoulder of her flowered blouse. The scent was intoxicating, tempting, damning. She felt her control slipping, then glanced down at the woman's face when she whimpered. Mrs. Craveshaw wasn't looking at her; she was eyeing Pudge in a frightened manner that made it clear she thought he was quite mad. Who could blame her? Rachel thought wearily. There was no such thing as vampires.

"Come on, bite her," Pudge whined, sounding impatient.

Rachel merely closed her eyes and shook her head, turning her face to the side in an effort to escape the tempting scent. She'd die before killing another being and very much feared that if she did bite the woman, she wouldn't be able to stop until she'd drained her dry. She wouldn't risk it.

"Not hungry enough yet, huh?" Pudge sounded disappointed. "Well, I'll just keep her here until you are. *Oh!*"

That exclamation drew her wary gaze back. Much to her relief, Pudge was urging the woman back across the room. She could still smell the blood, but it was fainter, less tempting. But the bright expression on his face as he glanced back made her wary.

"I bet you're tired, huh?" Pudge said as he tied the woman up. "I hadn't thought of that, but it's daytime and all that, and you're probably suffering that vampire weariness where you can hardly stay awake and you're really weak and stuff."

Rachel didn't bother to correct him. She didn't think it would be good for him to know any more than he already did about vampires.

"Come on." Moving back to her, he quickly undid the manacles around her neck, shoulders, and waist, then bent to undo the ones around her thighs and ankles too. Rachel stared down at his head as he worked, thinking mournfully that if she weren't so weak, this would be her opportunity to escape. But her body was seriously lacking in strength, her muscles rubbery with weakness. She wasn't even sure she could hold herself up much more than a moment, let alone knock the little jerk on his butt and make a run for it.

"You can sleep in my coffin," Pudge announced, straightening to quickly undo her wrists. He was obviously aware of her weakness, or she didn't think he'd have left his crossbow behind, but apparently he was putting it down to it being daytime rather than the blood loss due to the injury. But she hadn't bled out a lot, and he didn't know that the blood would have been used up to repair the damage.

"Originally, I intended to kidnap Etienne and keep

him prisoner here," he said chattily as he helped her to the large coffin she had noted earlier. "I thought that way I could make him give me all his computer ideas and maybe, you know, bring around the people I don't like for him to bite. There are a lot of people I don't like. I could have kept him quite a while. But then I realized he was too strong to risk that."

He tugged up the lid of the metal coffin and pushed it all the way open to reveal a red satin lining. Rachel stared into the huge space with bewilderment. It looked like two or three people could easily fit inside.

"I had it made special," Pudge told her. "I wanted it big enough for me and my vamp babes when I got turned."

Rachel shook her head at this information. Her thinking was growing muzzy with the need for blood, but she realized that this guy was beyond help, over the edge.

"In you go," Pudge instructed.

Rachel was exhausted and really wanted to lay down, but there was no way she was getting willingly into that coffin. She'd rather sleep on the concrete floor. "No."

The word slipped so faintly from her lips that Pudge didn't hear her. "Come on, in you go."

"I'm not sleeping in that coffin," Rachel managed a little more strongly.

"Yes, you are," he insisted. "Get in the coffin. You'll sleep better."

She managed a shake of the head and glared at him, not surprised when frustration immediately crossed his face. Then his expression cleared.

"Get in the coffin or I'll kill Crabbyshaw."

Rachel's shoulders slumped in defeat at that threat and she admitted, "I don't think I can—"

It was as far as she got. Pudge scooped her up and dumped her unceremoniously inside. Rachel wasn't sure if it was irritation or simply that he was too weak to hold her for long, but she landed hard and was left gasping as added pain radiated through her. While she was thus incapacitated, Pudge snapped a new manacle around her ankle.

"The chain's long enough for you to get out and feed on old Crabbyshaw when you get hungry," he explained. "But not long enough for you to get away. Sleep well!"

The lid slammed closed.

Rachel was immediately enclosed in cloying darkness. She reached up weakly, her hand coming up against the satin lining of the coffin. Panic tried to overwhelm her. She had always had a touch of claustrophobia, but it seemed intensified in that moment. Forcing herself to breathe deeply, Rachel let her hand drop weakly back to her chest and tried to calm herself. She would just rest a while. She would rest and regroup, and when he left, she'd slip out and . . .

Her thoughts became fuzzy there. Slip out and what? Would she even be able to slip out? Without blood, she wasn't likely to regain her strength. Instead she would grow weaker and weaker and . . . Dear God, where was Etienne? Why wasn't he here getting her out of this mess? She'd saved his behind by ensuring he was left in his office where blood was readily available; the least he could do was come give her a hand.

It was growing hard to breath. There didn't seem to be enough air in the coffin. She must be using it all up. She would suffocate and die in here.

Rachel forced herself to calm down, telling herself it was just her claustrophobia. She wouldn't die. No one had mentioned lack of air as one of the ways they could die. She just needed to stay calm and wait. Etienne would come.

Etienne frowned and glanced toward the door. He wasn't sure, but he thought he'd heard something. Leaving the mess of burnt circuits he'd been fiddling with for what seemed like hours, he stood and moved to the door to press his ear against it.

"Etienne." The name was very faint through the door, barely audible, but there nonetheless. They'd arrived. Relief welled through him but was quickly followed by confusion as he wondered why his brother hadn't just tried to use thoughts to speak to him. The moment he wondered that, he became aware of several different thoughts hitting his mind at once and realized that they probably had been trying to reach him mentally, but he'd been wrapped up in tinkering with the computer and had unconsciously closed his mind to outside thoughts.

Etienne? Are you all right?

What happened?

We can't get the door open.

The thoughts flooded his mind all at once and were somewhat confusing, but he recognized that Bastien, Lucern, and his mother were all there on the other side of the door.

Pudge wrecked the door panel. He sent the thought back. *I'm all right, but he took Rachel. You have to get the door open.*

How? The word was clear but accompanied by various unpleasant thoughts about Pudge and concern for Rachel. Etienne considered the question briefly. If he were out there he could probably get the door open himself, but the rest of his family wasn't very technical. He could probably talk them through it if he could see the panel to see what was damaged, but without that, the fastest way was—

You'll need an acetylene torch. You'll have to cut through the steel around the door lock. He waited to be sure they had understood and that one of them had left to go in search of the needed torch, then asked, *What time is it?*

A little after six, came the answer, and Etienne closed his eyes. He wasn't positive, but he thought it had been around noon when Pudge had broken in.

That meant he'd had Rachel for more than six hours. God, he hoped she was all right.

It was loud rock music that woke Rachel up. She opened her eyes and stared into unrelenting darkness. Her breathing immediately seemed to come harder, as if all the air in the coffin was gone. Panic swamped her again. This time it worked in her favor; the rush of adrenaline accompanying it gave her the strength she needed to shove the coffin lid up. Rachel was so weak she only managed to lift it a couple of inches; then she had to leave her hand between the top and the coffin itself to prevent it closing. She winced at the pain as the lid pressed down on her hand, but it was worth it to have the added air that was now slipping in to her. Gathering her strength, she eased up, forcing the lid of the coffin upward until she could see out into the room.

The first thing she saw was Mrs. Craveshaw tied up and leaning against the wall. The woman was awake and staring wide-eyed at something at the far end of the room. Rachel tried to see what it was, but all she could glimpse was an open door. The position of the coffin didn't allow her to see much of the next room, only a sliver. She didn't see Pudge anywhere. Half-dragging herself and half-pushing, Rachel began to climb over the side of the coffin, suddenly recalling her first morning in Etienne's house, and the way he had sat up and leapt smoothly out of his coffin. She wished she had the strength to do that right now but considered herself lucky to be able to climb out at all. It was sheer determination moving her, Rachel suspected. She needed blood. She had to get out of there.

A grunt slipped from her lips as Rachel managed to force herself far enough over the edge so that gravity took over and she tumbled to the floor. The rattle and clang of the chain attached to her ankle seemed incredibly loud, despite the music blaring from the other room. She gave herself a chance to catch her breath, expecting Pudge to come stomping up and ruin her escape at any moment.

Rachel opened her eyes and peered toward Mrs. Craveshaw. The woman was now dividing her wide-eyed gaze between Rachel and the other end of the room. Rachel didn't know whether the look on the old woman's face was fear of her or fear for her but knew she had to move.

Not feeling up to standing, Rachel crawled to the woman on her hands and knees, dragging the chain behind her. "Are you okay?"

Mrs. Craveshaw managed a shaky smile. "Yes, dear. But I'm afraid Norman has gone quite mad. He seems to think he's a vampire."

Rachel followed her gaze to the door in time to see Pudge walk past it. The long cape she'd spotted hanging on the wall was now billowing around his body. Fake white fangs flashed at his mouth.

"Crazy as a loon," Mrs. Craveshaw said with disgust,

as Pudge suddenly stopped and whirled back the way he'd come, drawing the edge of the cape up to his chin with one hand as he leered into what Rachel presumed was a mirror out of sight in the room.

"I vant to suck your blood, baby," she could just barely hear him say over the music, in a really bad Dracula impression.

"Yes," Rachel agreed. "Crazy as a loon."

"We can't call the police. What would we tell them?"

Look," Etienne interrupted his brothers, who had been arguing ever since finally freeing him from his office. It had felt like forever but might have only been moments since he had been freed, but every minute wasted was too much to him. He had to get to Rachel. "You can call or not as you like, but I'm heading over to Pudge's house. He must have taken her there."

"You aren't going alone," Marguerite said firmly. "We'll all go."

"What about the police?" Bastien insisted. "This is the perfect opportunity to get Pudge out of your hair. He's actually kidnapped Rachel. They'll throw him in jail."

"Pudge will be dealt with one way or another," Etienne said with determination and started up the stairs.

"You have your cell phone, Bastien," Lucern pointed out. "You can call the police on the way over. It can be an anonymous tip. You saw some guy forcing a woman into his house at gunpoint."

"Good thinking," Bastien agreed as he followed them into the kitchen. "What's his address, Etienne?"

Etienne hesitated. He kept seeing Rachel in his mind's eye, trying to look brave despite her worry as a line of blood beaded on her throat beneath the slice of the knife. For the first time since all this nonsense had started, he wanted to kill the pathetic creature everyone called Pudge.

"Etienne." His mother's voice was firm, carrying a warning. Marguerite obviously knew what he was thinking. He wouldn't put it past her to have Lucern and Bastien restrain him "for his own good" until he released the information, and he cursed himself for not being able to get out of the room on his own. Had he been able to, Pudge would already be dead and Rachel safe.

Before, killing Pudge to get rid of the problem he represented had seemed extreme. He was such a pathetic fellow, motivated by jealousy and anger. Etienne had actually felt sorry for the little weasel . . . until now. Now he heartily wished he'd killed him while he'd had the chance.

"I'll give you the address on the way. I want to get there before the police do. Their presence might threaten her well-being. I want to be there to be sure she's all right," he said as he led the way to the garage.

* * *

Rachel struggled with the rope tied around Mrs. Crave-shaw's wrists, her attention distracted by the idiot prancing around in the next room. He kept swooping past the door, posing and dancing about to what she suspected was the soundtrack from the movie *The Lost Boys.* Fortunately, he was too busy flashing his fangs and testing really bad vamp pickup lines to no-tice that she was out of her coffin and trying to free his neighbor.

Trying. Rachel sighed and returned her attention to the ropes. He had really knotted them good, and she was working with very little strength. She sagged against the wall next to the woman as she worked. The woman's bulk helped keep her out of view of the door, but her position was also the only thing keeping her upright. She was growing weaker with every pass-ing moment, finding it more and more difficult to think. It also left her temptingly near the other woman's throat, where perspiration was shining like the glitter of a diamond. Rachel could smell her anx-iety and fear, but even more overwhelming was the scent of her blood. Rachel was fighting the instinct to bite the woman as she wrestled with the rope, and she seemed to be losing both battles. Tears welled up in her eyes as she glanced at the woman's neck again.

Just a little bite, a nibble, her mind tempted her. Just enough to be strong enough to untie her.

"No," she told herself firmly.

"No, what, dear?" Mrs. Craveshaw asked.

Rachel shook her head, then glanced around frantically when Muffin suddenly let out a bark. Terrified that the animal would draw Pudge's attention, Rachel hushed the pet. "Shhh, Muffin, nice doggie," she hissed.

The little dog sat down, but his gaze was fixed on the stairs and his tail was wagging hopefully. Rachel twisted to see the stairs and felt her heart lodge in her throat at the sight of Etienne descending them. He'd come.

"Thank God," Rachel moaned and sank against the wall. His arrival wasn't a moment too soon. One more second and she might have done something she could never forgive herself for. She doubted Mrs. Craveshaw would have forgiven her either.

"Rachel." She let her eyes flutter open as he pressed a kiss to her forehead.

"Thank God you came," she whispered then fell silent as his lips dropped to press on hers. It was a sweet kiss, almost reverent.

"Of course I came. I care about you."

Rachel's eyes had drifted closed when he kissed her, but now they flew open again. It wasn't a proclaimation of love, but it was nice just the same. "You do?"

He smiled at her expression and brushed her hair away from her face. "How could I not? You're beautiful, brave, intelligent, and stubborn as hell." He grinned at the way her lips twisted, then added, "And you like my games. That shows you have incredibly good taste." He kissed her again.

"Ahem."

Rachel and Etienne pulled apart at that rather loud throat clearing from Mrs. Craveshaw. The woman gave them a pained smile. "Everyone loves a lover, dears, but there is a time and place for everything, and this really isn't the time or . . ." She glanced around with a wrinkled nose. "Or the place, really."

"Sorry, ma'am." Etienne gave her a charming smile.

"I was having trouble untying her," Rachel informed him.

"She's awfully weak, the poor child," Mrs. Craveshaw informed him as Etienne began to untie her ropes. "I don't know how long he's held her here, but he's obviously been starving her. Why, he kept calling her a vampire and trying to make her drink mine and Muffin's blood. Norman has obviously lost his mind."

"Norman?" Etienne paused in surprise. "You mean Pudge?"

"Pudge." The woman tsked in disgust. "He insisted people call him that. His mother hated that nickname, God rest her poor soul. She was a dear woman, you know. And a good neighbor too. It was a dark day when she died and Norman was left to live here alone. Norma—his mother—kept him in line while she was alive, but I knew the moment she was gone he would go bad. I was rather hoping he'd move away, but no, he had to stay. His brother wasn't too pleased and I don't blame him. The house should have been sold and the profits split between them, but it wouldn't sell with the mess Norman keeps it. I think he keeps it that way on purpose, and so does his brother. He—"

"Er—ma'am?" Etienne interrupted. "You're untied now. Maybe you could go call the police while I get Rachel free."

"Oh, I'm afraid you'll never get her free without the key. But, yes, of course, I'll go fetch the police."

The woman had been tied up long enough that she needed assistance rising. Rachel watched as Etienne helped her up and hurried her over to her dog, whom she insisted on taking with her. He watched her go up the stairs, then moved quickly back to Rachel.

"How bad is it?" he asked once he was again kneeling at her side. "I can tell you're in pain. Did he hurt you again?"

Rachel nodded. "It was an accident. The crossbow went off when he hit Mrs. Craveshaw over the head with it, and he staked me in the chest."

A curse slid from Etienne's lips as he slipped a bag of blood out of his shirt. "It'll be warm and won't be enough, but it should ease the pain a little bit at least."

She didn't care if it was bacteria-ridden blood; she lifted it to her lips and slammed her teeth into it. The liquid drained out so quickly, Rachel could hardly believe she'd ingested it. She did feel a little better, though, and right away too, but it was only a little, a slight easing of the ache and perhaps a bit more strength. At least she didn't feel like she would pass out if she didn't bite someone immediately.

Rachel sucked every last drop out of the bag, then crumpled it up and shoved it in her pocket as Etienne snapped open the manacle around her ankle. He did it as easily as if it were made of nothing more than paper. He was obviously back to full strength thanks to the blood in his fridge.

"How did you get out of the office?" she asked as he helped her to her feet.

"Mother, Lucern, and Bastien," he answered. "They had to cut a hole out of the door with an acetylene torch. They're waiting out in the van," he added. "It took some talking to convince them to wait there too, I can tell you. I had to promise not to kill him."

Etienne caught her against his chest as she swayed. Concern flickered on his face, but it didn't hide the fury radiating from his eyes, and Rachel thought it would be a good idea to get him out of there before Pudge noticed their presence and the inevitable confrontation occurred. Promise or no promise, she didn't trust him not to kill the man—or get himself killed trying.

"There's more blood in Bastien's van. I'll take you out there, then come back and see to Pudge."

"No. Let the police handle him, Etienne," she said urgently.

"I have to—"

"Holy shit!"

Rachel and Etienne both turned toward the other end of the room. Pudge was frozen in the doorway, shock on his face as he stared at Etienne and Rachel.

Etienne immediately started toward him, but Rachel clung to his arm desperately, managing to hold him back. Or perhaps she merely reminded him of her presence. Whatever the case, he stopped and peered down at her, then moved her behind him and turned to face Pudge. But there was no Pudge to face. While Rachel had distracted him, the other man had disappeared.

"Where the—" Etienne began, then paused and stood a little straighter. He pushed her backward toward the stairs, his body blocking hers as Pudge reappeared, crossbow in hand. It was armed with a fresh stake and aimed directly at Etienne's heart.

Chapter Sixteen

"He's taking an awfully long time."

Bastien shifted behind the wheel of the van and glanced in the rearview mirror at his mother's face. Her expression reflected the worry and concern that had been in her voice, the same worry and concern he himself was suffering. Bastien had been most reluctant to let his younger brother go into Norman "Pudge" Renberger's house alone. Etienne had been so cold and furious, he'd feared what he might do. But that was Etienne's problem. It was his woman and his battle and, in the end, Bastien had decided to let him handle it . . . until he proved incapable of it.

"It hasn't been all that long," Lucern said from his position in the front passenger seat. "Don't forget he had to— What's this?"

Bastien glanced back to the house in time to see an older woman come rushing out. Short, gray-haired and cherubic, she carried a small furry bundle in her arms. They watched in silence as she rushed across the yard and into the house next door.

"That doesn't look good," Marguerite spoke the thought they all shared. They had expected Pudge to have Rachel here but hadn't even considered that anyone else might be in the house. Now they didn't know what to think. What had the woman been doing there? Had she seen Etienne? Or Rachel? She'd been fleeing as if all the demons of hell were on her tail.

"Perhaps you two should go in and see if Etienne needs any help." Their mother sounded anxious.

Bastien exchanged another glance with Lucern, reading the uncertainty in his brother's mind. Neither of them were sure they should interfere. Etienne wouldn't thank them if he had everything under control. The younger man hadn't said as much, but it had obviously been important to him to be the one to find and rescue Rachel, not to mention deal with the man who had been making his life such hell.

"Why don't we give him another couple of minutes?" Lucern finally suggested and Bastien nodded. They fell silent as they turned their attention back to the house. It was a short, tense wait. The three of them stiffened in their seats and exchanged wary glances when they heard the wail of a siren in the distance. They remained where they were as it drew nearer. It was a big city; the vehicle could be either the police or the fire department, it could be headed anywhere.

Bastien and Lucern reached for their door handles, however, when a police car turned down the street they waited in.

"Wait," Marguerite barked, making them pause. The brothers stayed where they were but unrolled their windows as the cruiser pulled into the driveway of the house next to Pudge's—the one the woman had just dashed into. She ran back outside now, still clutching something small and furry to her chest as she rushed the patrol car. There were two officers in the vehicle, one short and blond, the other a tall brunette. The dark-haired officer was the closest and the one the woman ran to as he got out from behind the steering wheel and slammed the door closed.

"He's gone crazy!" she shrieked. "He thinks he's a vampire! He wanted to eat my Muffin!"

"I certainly hope her muffin is the furball she's carrying," Lucern said with a dry humor that made Bastien laugh and dispelled some of the tension that had been gripping him.

"Who's gone crazy, ma'am?" They heard the blonde officer ask as he rounded the car to join the pair.

"Norman. My neighbor." She pointed toward the house Etienne had disappeared into. "He has a poor young woman chained up in there. I think it's that girl from the news, that hospital worker who went missing a couple of weeks ago. She's pale and doesn't look well at all. He's obviously been starving her. He tried to make her eat my dog."

"Your dog?" the darker officer asked with disgust.

"My Muffin." She lifted her arms slightly, then petted the trembling ball of fur she held.

"Was that before or after he tried to eat your Muffin himself?" the blonde asked with a trace of amusement that made Bastien frown. It was obvious that at least one of the men thought the woman was batty. Apparently, he wasn't alone in gathering that. The woman narrowed her eyes on the officer like a first-grade teacher spotting a troublemaker in her class.

"Don't mess with me, young man. I'm not some dotty old fool. There are two people in that house right now in jeopardy."

"Two?" the second man asked.

"Yes. That pretty redhead from the news and a handsome young man who came in and set me and Muffin free and told me to call you."

The officers glanced toward the Renberger house, then back.

"Why didn't they come out with you?" the blonde asked.

"I was just tied up. He was able to untie me, but the girl was chained to a coffin."

"Coffin?"

"I told you, he thinks he's a vampire," she explained with exasperation. "He's insane! Now stop dawdling out here. Go help that young man rescue the girl. That's your job."

When the two officers still hesitated, obviously unsure what to make of her wild claims, she made a sound of disgust and turned toward the house. "Very well. I'll go get the young man and have him come out . . . if he hasn't already been noticed and killed by that nasty Norman."

She was out of her yard and across Norman's before the officers kicked out of their frozen state and hurried after her. The little woman could really move when she wanted to. She mounted the porch and entered the house before they could reach her.

"Turn me."

Rachel shifted a little to the side to look around Etienne's shoulder at Pudge. After the tense silence that had passed since his reappearance with the crossbow, those weren't the words she'd expected to hear.

"Come on," Pudge whined when both Etienne and Rachel stared at him blankly. "Why should you have all the fun? Turn me. Please?"

Etienne glanced toward Rachel, seeming to ask her whether Pudge's request was for real.

"Turn me and I'll give you rest," Pudge promised.

"Rest?" Etienne echoed with amazement.

"Vampires always want rest," Norman announced solemnly, then frowned. "Well, mostly they do. Once they're staked they look at peace in the movies. Sometimes they even thank their staker. Except for Dracula. I don't think he wants peace, but he's been alive forever." He peered at Etienne curiously. "Have you met Drac?"

"Pudge, do you understand the difference between fiction and reality?" Etienne asked.

"Of course I do," he said with a scowl. Then he added impatiently, "Just turn me already, and I'll put you to rest."

Etienne released a short laugh. "Are you even thinking about what you're suggesting? You're asking me to give you an eternal life . . . and in exchange you'll end mine? Hellooooo. You want eternal life. What makes you think I don't?"

"Oh, come on. You must be tired by now. How old are you? Five, six hundred years old?" he guessed. "You have to be way old. I looked up the Argeneau name and it goes back a long way. There's a reference to a Lucern Argeneau back in medieval days, and that's your brother, right? There was a Lady Marguerite married to some Claude guy too. And I know that's your mom and dad."

Rachel noted Etienne's startled expression. Apparently, he hadn't considered that Pudge might do research. It was obvious he didn't care for the fact, or the possibility that his family might now be targeted as well. She shook her head with disgust. Woe and betide the idiot for bringing Etienne's family into it.

The man was as easygoing as could be most of the time, but he also had a protective nature and that was coming to the fore. His usually smiling face had become a cold, hard mask.

Etienne moved so quickly that he was across the room and grabbing Pudge by the throat in the blink of an eye—far too quickly for Pudge to stop with his crossbow. It did go off as he dropped it, but the stake harmlessly hit the wall. Rachel saw Pudge reach into the front pocket of his black jeans but didn't understand the significance of it. She didn't realize trouble was coming until he pulled out a remote control and pushed several buttons. Light immediately exploded in the room even as a whirring sound filled the air.

Rachel gaped at the sunlamps pouring warm illumination down on her, then her head twisted to the side as the whirring was explained by a huge cross sliding out of a recess in the wall and swinging across the room like a pendulum. Her gaze shot to Etienne to see that he had been startled enough by the sudden explosion of light and sound that he was gaping as well. But he hadn't seen the six-foot cross crashing toward him.

Rachel cried out in warning, but it was too late, merely making him turn toward the large object in time to take a full frontal blow. She cried out again as he was slammed backward and crashed into the far wall. She started to run toward him, but changed direction and ran at Pudge instead when she saw what he was up to now. The moment Etienne had been knocked down, Pudge had bent to retrieve his crossbow. He tugged a fresh stake from his pocket.

Despite her speed, Pudge had the weapon reloaded by the time she reached him. His back turned to her, he didn't see her coming, and she took advantage of that fact and jumped on his back. He straightened with a shriek and attempted to throw her off, but Rachel held on like a monkey as animal rage poured through her. With one arm around his arm and over his chest, she snaked the other around his neck and grabbed his jaw. Rachel wasn't even thinking when she twisted his head sideways. It was pure animal instinct that made her do it, and bend her own head to his neck with every intention of biting the little weasel and draining him dry.

"Freeze!"

Rachel heard that shout and quickly pulled her mouth away from Pudge's neck without drawing any blood. Her head shot up as Pudge wheeled toward the stairs, the crossbow waving wildly. Her eyes widened in shock at the sight of the two uniformed police officers standing at the base of the stairs, their weapons drawn and pointed in her direction. Then the crossbow went off.

"Oh," Rachel breathed as the officers tried to jump out of the way of the whizzing projectile. There was a curse, followed by a thud as the blond officer was hit. At first she thought the man had taken the missile in the arm, but as he began tugging at it, she saw that it had missed flesh and bone and was merely caught by his sleeve, which was now pinned to the wall.

Rachel was still gaping at the struggling man when Etienne suddenly moved. He was at her side, ripping her from Pudge's back and dragging her out of the line of fire before she even considered the need to move. But the officers didn't return fire. The dark-haired one kept his gun trained on Pudge, but his gaze kept returning to the blonde struggling to free himself. It gave Pudge the chance to snatch yet another stake from his back pocket and re-load his weapon.

Pudge had just finished locking the stake into place and turned to aim it at Rachel and Etienne when the trapped officer managed to pull his sleeve free. The two men immediately shifted several feet apart, both aiming their weapons at Pudge.

"Drop it! Drop the weapon, buddy! Just drop it!" the blonde shouted. He sounded pretty angry. Perhaps pissed off was the better word, Rachel thought, as Etienne shifted her behind him and stood like a brick wall between her and the stake Pudge was aiming their way.

She appreciated the concern obvious in this action, but it made it difficult to see what was going on. Rachel ended up having to duck and twist to see past him. She almost felt sorry when she saw Pudge's re-action to finding himself the target of the officers' anger. He was staring at them in dawning horror, his eyes wide and his mouth agape. He obviously hadn't expected this.

"Come on, buddy. Put the weapon down," the dark-haired officer suggested in cajoling tones. "We don't want to have to shoot you . . . but we will."

"Me?" He stared at them in amazement. "Shoot me? I'm the good guy here. I'm like Van Helsing! It's them you want! They're the vampires!"

Rachel caught the glance the two officers exchanged and knew everything was going to be all right. They weren't buying what must sound like nonsense to them. However, she couldn't help but think that, had their entrance been one moment later and had she managed to sink her teeth into Pudge's neck as she'd intended, this whole scenario might be completely different.

A glance at Etienne had her suspecting he was thinking the same thing.

"Really!" Pudge was squealing like a pig. "They're vampires. Both of them."

The officers glanced in Rachel and Etienne's direction out of reflex. Both then started to look away, but the one who had so recently been pinned to the wall stopped midway and swung his gaze back. Rachel felt herself stiffen at the recognition on the blonde's face.

"Dr. Garrett? Dr. Rachel Garrett?" the officer asked. "It *is* you."

Rachel nodded warily but didn't get the chance to say anything. Pudge jumped in there, his voice excited. "Yes. That's her. She was working in the morgue the night I went in to finish him off." He waved the crossbow wildly toward Etienne, making Rachel flinch. It had already gone off once accidentally and could easily do so again. "She jumped in the way when I went to cut off his head and I axed her by mistake. I hit her in the chest. She should be dead, but he turned her. Now they're both vampires," he explained, sounding completely insane. "They're both soulless bloodsuckers, cursed to walk the night forever."

Rachel bit her lip, almost embarrassed for the man. Everything he had said was true, of course. Well, except for the soulless part. But really, where was his common sense? Surely he must realize no one would believe him. She wasn't terribly surprised when the officers began easing farther apart and approaching Pudge in a rather wary manner.

"Okay, buddy," the dark-haired officer said. "We get it. They're vampires and you're the good guy. But we're here now. You're safe. So drop the weapon and put your hands up, huh?"

Pudge frowned, his gaze shifting between his weapon, the police, and Rachel and Etienne. "But what ábout them? You should be pointing your guns at them," he said finally.

"Well, now," the blonde drawled, "guns don't work on vampires, do they? But I'm sure they'll come along

318

peaceable-like." He glanced at Rachel and Etienne. "Won't you?"

They both nodded.

"See?" the first officer said soothingly. "They know they're caught. Now you just need to give up your weapon there, buddy."

When Pudge hesitated, the second officer added, "We didn't come prepared for a call like this. You know, vampires aren't exactly thick on the ground these days. We aren't armed properly. Why don't you give us the weapon so we can take them into custody?"

"Oh, yeah. Yeah." Pudge looked relieved. "You should be armed too." He started to shift sideways toward the nearest officer, making sure to keep the crossbow aimed at Rachel and Etienne. "I have more weapons in the back. You can keep this trained on them while I get more. I have holy water, crosses, and more stakes. I'll get them while you watch them."

"Good thinking," the blonde said agreeably, lowering his gun slightly and holding his free hand out to accept the crossbow.

"Don't take it off them," Pudge warned as he handed it over. "They're super fast you know. And super strong. I— Hey!"

The moment the weapon changed hands, the officer tossed the crossbow aside and raised his gun to aim it at Pudge. Ignoring his wounded expression, the policeman gestured with it. "Against the wall. Come on, against the wall and spread 'em."

"But—" Pudge's protest was cut off as the second officer hurried forward and caught him by the arm.

"Spreadeagle," the dark-haired man barked, all trace of cajolery gone. The blonde kept his gun trained on Pudge while his partner ripped off his cape and proceeded to frisk him. The maniac had a couple more stakes in the back pocket of his jeans that the officer took away.

Rachel and Etienne watched in silence as a protesting Pudge was cuffed and led to the stairs. He was still babbling about their being soulless vampires and he was the hero in this piece and that they were making a huge mistake.

"Well," the officer who had been pinned to the wall said as his partner disappeared upstairs with Pudge. He turned to survey Rachel and Etienne, then his attention focused on Rachel. "I gather this is where you disappeared to from work a week ago?"

Rachel glanced at Etienne as she felt him standing tense beside her. She knew what he wanted her to say. He and his whole family wanted her to claim that Pudge had brought her here that night over a week ago. It wasn't true, though, and she was a lousy liar. She hesitated briefly, considering her options. The man *had* kidnapped her. She certainly hadn't come here from Etienne's place willingly. On the other hand, she couldn't explain where she had been for the past week without there being questions that would be difficult to answer. Rachel decided to be honest but cagey.

"Pudge kidnapped me, brought me here, and held me against my will," she admitted solemnly, and felt Etienne relax beside her. She almost turned to ask him why he was relaxing; they weren't out of the woods yet. But she caught herself as the officer nodded.

"How did he get you here, ma'am?"

Rachel hesitated, then said, "He came into the morgue wearing a trench coat over fatigues. He had a rifle and ax under the coat and was shouting something about vampires and such and . . ." She hesitated and glanced at Etienne again. He seemed to be holding his breath. Swallowing, she turned back and said, "I'm afraid my memory gets rather blurry after that. The next thing I can tell you is that I woke up here today chained to that wall. He was still rambling on about vampires and geeks, and he seemed fixated on Etienne's game."

"Game?" The policeman glanced between them in confusion.

"Etienne is the designer of Blood Lust," Rachel explained. "It's a vampire video game."

"Oh," the man said, but still appeared lost. "Okay, he was fixated on your game," he said to Etienne, then turned his gaze back to Rachel. "But if that's the case, why did he kidnap you and not him?"

"Because she's my girlfriend," Etienne said calmly.

Rachel added, "It was really quite confusing. Half the time he thought I was a vampire and Etienne was one too, then he thought he was one or wanted to be one. The fellow seems quite insane."

"Yeah. It would seem so," the blonde said dryly and shook his head. Then he told her, "Every cop in the city's been looking for you, ma'am. And him." He gestured toward the now empty stairs. "The girl who was supposed to replace your assistant arrived as this guy stormed into the hospital morgue. She went to find security, but they were dealing with another issue at the time and slow getting to your offices. The room was empty when they got there, and it was assumed the fellow had taken you." He shook his head. "She did a pretty good job of describing him too. They did a police sketch and put it on all the news shows. I don't know why no one picked up on it being this guy. He's a dead ringer for his picture."

Rachel nodded but remained silent, afraid to draw any more questions from the man. Fortunately, he turned his attention to Etienne to ask, "How did you end up here today, sir? The next-door neighbor said you came in and set her free, but she didn't seem to know who you were."

Etienne hesitated, then said, "I've been quite concerned about Rachel since she disappeared. I spotted Pu—this guy while I was waiting at a streetlight. He was driving a van. I recognized him from the pictures on the news and followed him here," he lied blandly.

Etienne was very good at lying, Rachel noted with interest. She supposed it shouldn't surprise her. He'd had over three hundred years to perfect his technique.

"You should have called the police at once," the officer said with disapproval.

"I intended to," Etienne assured him solemnly. "But I wanted a closer look at the guy. I didn't want to raise a false alarm. By the time I parked, he was out of his van and had entered the house. I peeked in a couple of windows, hoping to get a better look at him, but he must have gone straight downstairs. I came around the back of the house and found that window—"

Rachel followed his gesture and noted with some surprise that there were indeed windows in the basement. She hadn't noticed them before, but they hadn't been unblocked to allow sunlight in earlier. She supposed one of the buttons Pudge had pushed had uncovered the windows as well as turning on the sunlamps. She wondered what Pudge had made of the fact that they hadn't burst into flames the moment the sunlamps and sunlight hit them as he had no doubt expected.

"When I looked in and saw Rachel chained up down here, all I could think of was getting in to her. I forgot all about calling you. I could see the coffin, and the old lady. Not to mention the fellow dancing around in a cape and fake teeth." Etienne shook his head. "It was obvious he was crazy and I was afraid to leave the women alone. So when the back door turned out to be unlocked, I slid inside and crept down here to free them."

"Well, I guess I can understand your concern, but you really should have called us," the officer grumbled. "The old lady said she was tied up, but that Ms. Garrett was chained and you couldn't free her. How—?"

The question died midsentence and the officer appeared confused for a moment. When he spoke again, his voice sounded almost robotlike. "Well, that's enough questions for now, I suppose. You've been through enough. We should get you out of here."

Rachel arched an amused eyebrow at Etienne. It was pretty handy to be able to control people's minds. She really had to learn that skill, she decided.

"After you." Etienne's grin was unrepentant as he gestured for her to lead the way upstairs. He obviously felt no shame at using his skills so shamelessly. And frankly, she couldn't blame him. She was exhausted and starving. The sunlamps, on top of her original hunger, were making her body cramp with need. Getting back to his place and partaking of blood was the only thing on her mind right then.

Rachel managed the stairs on her own, but it was slow and wearying. By the time they left the house she was swaying slightly on her feet, and Etienne put out his hand to steady her as they crossed the lawn.

"We'll have to call an ambulance to take you to the hospital, Ms Garrett. You look in pretty bad shape," the officer said, taking in her weakness and pallor. "Has he fed you at all since taking you?"

"No," Rachel answered, grateful she was able to be honest.

"I'll see her to the hospital," Etienne announced and the hypnotic tone of his voice told Rachel he was digging inside the officer's mind again. He was probably planting the suggestion that his seeing her there was the better option, she thought.

"That will be fine, sir," the officer agreed. "My partner should have already called for backup to come and collect our friend there." He gestured toward the vehicle where Pudge stood, still vehemently trying to convince the dark-haired officer that Etienne and Rachel were the bad guys, while he was trying to save the world from their soulless selves.

"We'll meet you at the hospital. If the doctor says you're okay, you might have to come to the station while we type up your statements."

"That'll be fine," Etienne agreed, as if he had some say in the matter. Which, she supposed, he did. He could probably wipe the memory of their presence from their thoughts had he wished, but then, this all worked to his benefit. Pudge was no longer going to be a threat to him or any of his clan.

Including herself. The thought ran through Rachel's mind, and she recognized at once that it wasn't her own. Her gaze slid to the van parked on the street as Etienne finished talking to the officer and took her arm to lead her toward the vehicle. She recognized his brothers sitting in the front seat but was sure neither of them had been the voice in her head. It had been a woman's thought placed there. Rachel wasn't terribly surprised when Etienne slid the side door open to reveal Marguerite seated on the bench seat.

"Come in, dear. You look terribly dehydrated. Etienne, fetch the poor girl some blood from the back," the Argeneau matriarch ordered. "She's in terrible pain."

Etienne helped Rachel into the van, then followed and slammed the door closed before crawling into the back to retrieve several bags of blood from the medical cooler there.

"How are you?" Bastien asked solicitously as Etienne settled on the bench next to her, sandwiching her between himself and his mother.

"I'm fine," Rachel murmured as she accepted the first bag of blood. She was hungry enough that she didn't bother with the straw business, but merely opened her mouth and punched the bag into her teeth to let them do the work.

"You'll have to tell us what happened. Don't leave out any details," Lucern said from his seat.

Rachel stared at the man, the bag still affixed to her teeth, as he drew a small pad and pen from his pocket. He obviously intended to take notes, and she was aware that he had done this the other times he had come around Etienne's home. When she had asked

Etienne what his brother was doing, he had muttered something about Lucern being a scribbler, whatever that meant.

"Later, Lucern," Marguerite said quietly. "Let the poor girl recover a bit before you bombard her with questions."

"I take it we're to go to the hospital?" Bastien asked, turning in his seat to start the engine.

"Drive slowly, Bastien. Rachel needs a lot of blood and the time to consume it," Marguerite said by way of an answer. "You'll have to go in with Etienne to help at the hospital. We all will. Between her working there and the fact that she's big news, she'll draw a lot of attention. Etienne will need all the help he can get."

"Help with what?" Rachel asked as she pulled the now empty bag off her teeth and accepted the next one Etienne held out.

"They'll want to examine you," Etienne explained.

"And we simply can't allow that, dear," Marguerite pointed out. "Bastien, Lucern, and I will go in with you to make sure the doctors and nurses think they've examined you and found you dehydrated and under-nourished, as you should be after being kidnapped and starved. We'll attend you to be sure all goes smoothly."

Rachel nodded her understanding, silently allowing her teeth to soak in the blood her body needed so badly. She was exhausted enough to let them handle it whatever way they saw fit. Rachel was even starting to think she should have listened to them regarding the issue of Pudge and agreed to lie about him, bad at it or not. They had all lived an awfully long time. No doubt the collected wisdom they had gained over the centuries was monstrous. The very thought of what might have happened to Pudge's neighbor, not to mention Etienne and herself, because of her stubborn insistence on telling the truth was frightening. Perhaps there were times when honesty wasn't the best policy and a small lie might save a bad situation.

"You'll learn," Marguerite said quietly, obviously having read her thoughts. "Time is not the great teacher. Experience is. A man may live a whole life, but if he never leaves his home to experience that life, he dies knowing nothing. A mere child who has suffered and lived can be the wiser of the two."

Chapter Seventeen

"They're vampires, I tell you!"

Pudge was beginning to sound more whiney than adamant, Rachel decided, as she watched him run his fingers through his greasy hair and tug on the ends with frustration. She couldn't really blame him. They had been questioning him for hours now. They'd apparently brought him straight here to the police station, booked him, and settled him in the small square room where they were now grilling him. And they had kept him there ever since.

Rachel and the Argeneaus had missed the first two hours of the interrogation. It had taken that long to get her through emergency and out of the hospital. Despite her being an employee at the hospital—not to mention her being something of a celebrity, thanks to the fact that she had been "kidnapped" from work—they'd had to wait quite a while to be seen by a doctor. When Rachel had asked why they simply didn't put the whammy on the nurses and move them to the front of the line, Marguerite had seemed surprised at the very idea. Her case wasn't urgent, she had pointed out, and they could manage the wait.

Rachel had felt a moment's shame that she hadn't thought that herself, but Marguerite had immediately reached into her mind to soothe her with the words that she "would learn." Frankly, Rachel couldn't wait to learn. She had marveled at the family as they escorted her everywhere uncontested. There were definitely benefits to being able to control the thoughts and minds of those around them. She hadn't been examined, but as far as the hospital staff could recall she had been. And as Marguerite had promised, the reports all read what would be expected: She was suffering dehydration and malnutrition. The Argeneaus had been astounding to watch in action, and Rachel was quickly beginning to realize the power Etienne had gifted her with.

"They're vampires, are they?" Officer Carstairs, the blond officer asked. He stood to the side of the table where his partner and Pudge sat facing each other. "You're the one with the coffin and the vampire teeth, Norman. Yet you claim Ms. Garrett and Mr. Argeneau are the vampires?"

"They're fake teeth, I tell you," Pudge muttered,

sounding harassed. "If you'd uncuff me, I'd take the damn things out. Mine are fake, but theirs are real."

"Sure they are, Norman," the darked-haired officer, Treebech, agreed soothingly.

"Stop calling me that!" Pudge snapped. "Norman. God, I hate that name. It makes me sound like a geek." He glared at them briefly, then said, "I tell you, Etienne Argeneau is a vampire. So is the woman. Hell, she bit me!"

Rachel grimaced. She hadn't really bit him, but she'd gotten closer than she'd realized, and the man had a scratch where one tooth had caught him. It was a nick really, and not even recognizable as a bite. Still, it was closer than she ever hoped to get to biting some-one again. Well, except perhaps for Etienne. She rather enjoyed giving him love bites when they— Love bites? Rachel gave her head a shake. Sex bites, she meant. Not love bites. She didn't love Etienne. Did she? The question ran around and around through her mind, followed by a welling of confusing thoughts and feelings. Warm, gushy feelings that rather alarmed her. Dear God, she *couldn't* love him.

Rachel was suddenly aware that Lucern was staring at her with interest. Then it occurred to her that any one of the people standing protectively around her could be reading her thoughts. She forced her run-away thoughts and feelings into a dark corner of her mind and turned her attention back to what was taking place beyond the one-way mirror. Pudge was glaring at the officers, closemouthed.

"Okay, so say she did bite you," Carstairs commented. "Do you think you'll be a vampire now too, Norman?"

"Don't call me Norm—" Pudge paused abruptly, his eyes widening. He suddenly looked less harassed. Excitement and wonderment filled his expression. "She *did* bite me. Do you really think I'll become a vampire?"

"I don't know, Norman. You're the expert. Why don't you tell us?"

Pudge pondered for a minute, then reasoned, "I guess it's possible. But Renfield didn't turn into a vampire after one bite. He . . ." His expression became horrified. "Oh, man! Renfield became Dracula's servant for life after one bite. He was his slave."

"So, does that make you Ms. Garrett's slave?" Treebech asked.

Pudge wasn't listening. His mind was preoccupied. "Jeez, and he ate bugs and stuff too. Man! I don't know if I can eat bugs."

The officers exchanged glances as Pudge shook his head in despair.

"I think that's enough. I'd like to question him now."

Rachel glanced at the man who had spoken: Dr. Smythe, a psychiatrist from her hospital. He had been called into the police station to assess Pudge's mental state. He'd asked to first be allowed to simply observe Pudge while he was being questioned. He claimed that subjects tended to respond differently to mental health professionals than to lay persons, even police. Now, it appeared he wanted to ask some questions himself.

Captain Rogers—Carstairs' and Treebech's superior—nodded and stood. "Certainly, Doctor. Come with me."

Rachel watched them leave the viewing room. A moment later the door of the interrogation room opened and Dr. Smythe and Captain Rogers entered. The police captain gestured Carstairs and Treebech to his side, held a brief whispered consultation and then left the room. The moment he was gone, Dr. Smythe introduced himself and took possession of the chair Treebech had vacated. He smiled at Pudge and asked, "Norman, do you understand the difference between fantasy and reality?"

Rachel smiled slightly at the question. It was the same one Etienne had asked at the house. Her gaze darted to the viewing room door as it opened to admit Captain Rogers but quickly shifted back to Pudge, who was staring at the doctor as if he were an alien. "Huh?"

"Do you understand the difference between fantasy and reality?" Dr. Smythe repeated patiently.

"Sure." Pudge scowled. "I'm not crazy, you know."

"No, of course you aren't," Dr. Smythe said soothingly. "Could you explain the difference between fantasy and reality for me?"

"Sure. Fantasy is . . . well it's like that wizards and warriors game. Magic and stuff. It's not real."

"Ah. Huh." Dr Smythe pursed his lips and nodded his head. "And could you give me an example of reality?"

"Blood Lust," Pudge said firmly.

"Blood Lust?" Dr. Smythe asked in confusion.

"That's the game Mr. Argeneau created," Carstairs explained. "Vampires and stuff."

"Ah." Dr. Smythe glanced back at Pudge. "And that would be reality?"

"Oh, yeah," Pudge assured him. "Magic, well, that's a bunch of nonsense—but there really are vampires. Chicks dig them, and they're super strong and super fast and live forever."

"And which is most important?" Dr. Smythe asked.

Pudge didn't have to think long. "Living forever . . . and the chicks," he decided.

"Women and immortality are most important, you say?" Dr. Smythe nodded, then added, "It seems to me you mentioned at some point that your mother died recently—didn't she, Norman?"

"Yeah." He nodded, then his attention drifted from the doctor and followed the table as if trailing something. Rachel gave a start when he suddenly raised his arm and slammed it down on the tabletop, apparently

squashing a bug. She wasn't the only one to jump.
The doctor and police officers did too.

"Excuse me a moment." Dr. Smythe stood and left
the room. Rachel wasn't terribly surprised when he
stepped back into the viewing room. He didn't say
anything at first, but simply stood beside the captain
to view Pudge through the window. They all watched
in silence as Pudge picked up the bug he had
squashed and examined it with seeming fascination.
Rachel grimaced with distaste when he suddenly
popped the squashed creature into his mouth and
chewed experimentally. After a moment, he shrugged
mildly and muttered, "Not bad. A bit nutty."

"We have a very confused young man here," Dr.
Smythe said. "I've already talked to his brother, and
he claims Norman has become obsessive and strange
of late. He thinks he should be locked up for his own
safety. I'll need to do extensive testing, of course, but
Norman has already proven himself a threat not only
to himself but to the public at large; specifically anyone he decides is a threat."

The psychiatrist's gaze slid meaningfully to herself
and Etienne before he continued. "That's enough to
commit him for seventy-two hours of testing."

"Thank you for coming, Doctor," the captain said.
"We'll have to process the paperwork, but I think you
can expect to have Mr. Renberger in your custody
rather quickly."

"I'll have a bed ready when he is," Dr. Smythe assured him solemnly. They shook hands, then the gentleman left them alone. The captain glanced toward the viewing room and shook his head as Pudge slammed his hand on the table again, then picked up whatever he had killed to examine.

"Nutty as a fruitcake," the cop muttered as Pudge popped the bug into his mouth and chewed. Pushing one hand across the top of his balding scalp, the captain shook his head, then sighed and moved to the door when a soft knock sounded. He spoke briefly with someone Rachel couldn't see, then turned back to them.

"Your statements are ready to sign. If you'd like to follow Officer Janscom, she'll take you to do that."

"Fine. Thank you." Etienne took Rachel's arm and urged her toward the door. She went silently, aware that the rest of the Argeneau clan were following.

Signing the papers was a relatively quick ordeal, at least for Rachel. She had been separated from the Argeneaus and led to a different room from Etienne and his family to sign papers in front of a witness. Rachel felt a bit lost when she finished and stepped out into the hall to find it empty. The Argeneaus had stuck protectively close to her since retrieving her from Pudge's house. She felt a bit disconcerted to suddenly be alone.

She paused in the hallway briefly, considering what she should do. Should she wait? Should she go? The officer had said she was free to leave now that her statement was signed. Rachel was debating her next move when it suddenly occurred to her that there might not be anyone to wait for. Etienne may have already finished with his paperwork. He might have already left. After all, there was really no need for them to hover over her now. She had learned to feed herself and to control her teeth, and working in a hospital, it wasn't as if she would have trouble getting her hands on blood. It wouldn't be easy, but she could manage it, and they probably realized that. Perhaps they were relieved to be free of the responsibility for her.

That thought was distressing. Rachel was almost gasping under the impact it had on her. It was surprisingly hurtful.

"Rachel?"

She turned abruptly at the sound of her name. Relief coursed through her when she recognized Lissianna hurrying up the hall toward her, Gregory Hewitt on her heels.

"Are you all right?" Lissianna asked with concern. "The message Mother left on my answering machine was rather garbled. All I understood was that you had been kidnapped."

"I'm fine." Rachel forced a smile.

"Oh, good." Lissianna smiled, but the worry didn't completely leave her eyes. "Where is everyone? Is Etienne all right too?"

"Yes. He's fine. I'm not sure where they are though,"

Rachel admitted. "For all I know, they may have finished with their paperwork and left all ready."

Lissianna frowned at this news, then glanced around. "I'll go ask someone."

She was gone as quickly as that, hurrying up the hall in search of someone who could answer her questions.

"I'm sure Etienne wouldn't leave without you," Gregory said in a solemn voice.

Rachel turned and forced a smile for his benefit. "Well, there isn't any real reason for him not to. I've gained control of my teeth and can feed myself now. He doesn't need to baby-sit me anymore."

Gregory frowned at her words, his handsome face troubled. "Rachel, has anyone told you about the life mate rule?"

Rachel blinked in confusion at the question. It seemed to her to be completely unrelated to anything going on at the moment. "I—No. I'm sorry. No one has mentioned this rule."

He nodded slowly. "I didn't think so. But I feel it's important you understand. It will help you to comprehend where you stand with Etienne."

Rachel's eyebrows rose. It would be a relief to have some idea of where she stood. She was starting to realize that her feelings for Etienne went deep and could be potentially painful.

"Because our people feed on the general population," he began, "it's important—of course—that our numbers be kept small, so as not to outgrow the potential of our food source."

Rachel nodded. That made perfect sense to her.

"So there are certain rules. For instance, each couple can only have one child every hundred years."

"Marguerite mentioned that," Rachel said with a nod.

"I'm not surprised. But what she might not have mentioned is that each vampire is allowed to turn only one human."

Rachel shook her head. "Excuse me? They're allowed only one mate?"

"Oh, no. Divorces do happen. We are speaking of hundreds of years of life here, so of course divorce happens, although I understand it's much less frequent than in the general population," he informed her. "I mean they are literally allowed to turn only one person. This person is usually a life mate, though it can be something else altogether, and then that vampire can't turn anyone else. They can't turn a life mate if they should find one."

"But Etienne turned me," Rachel said.

"Yes." Greg nodded solemnly.

"Rachel!"

This time Rachel was slower to turn toward the voice calling her name in strident tones. Her head was spinning, and it took several moments for her to recognize the older woman rushing toward her. It was the sight of the gray-haired man hurrying along behind her who made her realize that these were her parents hurrying up the hall. Then her mother's arms closed around her, and Rachel found herself enveloped in Poison, the perfume her mother favored.

"Thank God, baby. I was so worried. I couldn't believe it when Officer Janscom called to say that you had been found and were safe. Oh, honey, we were so scared we'd never see you again. Thank God." She paused to clasp Rachel's face in her hands and kiss her on each cheek. Then she studied her and frowned. "You look different. And terribly pale. You need a nice home-cooked meal and a nap."

"Yes, we'll take you home," her father said gruffly, putting his arm around her in a half hug as he turned her back the way they'd come.

Rachel remained silent as her parents herded her from the building. She shouldn't be pale; she had ingested more than enough blood in the van on the way to the hospital. Her pallor was no doubt due to the news Greg had given her, and the impact it had made. Etienne had given up his chance to turn a life mate by saving her, she thought faintly. Dear God, he had turned her, taken the time and care to train her to feed and to control her teeth, yet he could never have a life mate. He had given up any chance at a life partner for her.

All she could think was that he must hate her. And if he didn't, it was only because he hadn't yet had the chance to think about the sacrifice he'd made. The moment he realized all he had given up, he would definitely hate her. A lifetime without someone to love him, the equivalent of several lifetimes really. He'd lived hundreds of years and would live hundreds more without love. Or he would find that love, only to be forced to watch her age and die while he stayed young forever.

Etienne signed the last copy of the statement set before him and pushed it impatiently across the desk to be witnessed. He was eager to get this done and get out of there. No one had gone with Rachel. It had all happened so fast, they hadn't been given the opportunity. They'd all been led into this room and then Officer Janscom had asked Rachel to follow her and had taken her away. He didn't like the idea of her being alone. It wasn't that he was concerned that anything might happen to her; Pudge was no longer a threat so she was safe enough. But what if someone asked her an uncomfortable question and no one was there to erase the mind of the asker? Rachel was a lousy liar. Besides, he had the nagging fear that she was going to disappear on him. She could feed on her own now. She'd even fed straight from the bag in the van. She could control her teeth as well. And with Pudge removed, the final excuse for keeping her in his home was gone. What if she decided to leave, or refused to return to his home with him? He didn't want her to leave. Etienne had grown far too used to her presence. He enjoyed her. He wanted to spend his life—

"There we are then, sir," Officer Janscom said as she stacked the copies of the statement in a neat pile. "All done. Someone will contact you if we need anything else, but you're free to go now."

Etienne was out the door almost before she'd finished speaking. He had to find Rachel. They needed to talk. He needed to know how she felt about him. If she thought she might someday come to love him as he was quickly coming to love her.

"Etienne!"

He whirled at that exclamation as he came out into the hall, but it was only his sister. Etienne nodded at her, then turned to glance expectantly around. Unfortunately, there was no sign of Rachel anywhere.

"Have you seen Rachel?" Etienne asked his sister as she reached his side and enveloped him in a hug.

"Yes. She was here with Gregory when I left to ask about your whereabouts." Lissianna pulled back and glanced toward her husband in a silent question as he slowly approached. "Where did she go, honey?"

"Her parents arrived. She left with them," he explained, but there was a look on his face that made Etienne wary.

"What is it?" he asked.

Gregory hesitated briefly, then admitted, "I think I might have made a mistake."

"What kind of mistake?" Lissianna asked, slipping her hand reassuringly into his.

"I explained the rule about only being allowed to turn one person in a lifetime and that it was usually a life mate," he admitted.

"You explained the sacrifice Etienne made for her and she still left without a word to him?" Lissianna asked with disbelief. "Knowing *that*, she couldn't even take the time to say good-bye? Or even offer a thank-you?"

Etienne heard Lissianna's words, but in truth he couldn't comprehend them. He would later. In the meantime, he was simply standing there feeling lost and abandoned. She'd done exactly what he'd feared. Rachel had left him.

His mother was speaking to him now, but Etienne wasn't listening. He felt as if he had cotton wool in his ears. Actually, it felt rather as if his entire brain were stuffed with cotton wool. He nodded his head absently every once in a while as they were walking out of the police station. Etienne doubted he was fooling anyone; they all were probably reading his mind, though he couldn't seem to read his own thoughts. But he must have nodded at the appropriate places because no one called him on it. They all simply talked away as they walked out to Bastien's van and got in for the ride home.

Someone suggested they come in with him when they reached his house, but Etienne muttered something about work and quickly hopped out of the van, slamming the door behind himself. He didn't want company right then. He didn't want to talk or even think. He just wanted to crawl into a hole and escape his life, however briefly. To him that meant working.

Etienne entered his house, suddenly aware of how large and empty it was. Too large for one person, if you got right down to it. He should sell it and get an apartment. He didn't need much space; an office, a bedroom, a fridge . . . It wasn't like he entertained much.

He winced as memories of Rachel flooded his mind; playing video games, reading quietly together by the fireside in the library, laughing over her trying to consume the reject blood he had fed her, their moonlight picnic . . . He closed the door on those memories as loss and fear crowded in behind them. But he didn't manage to do so before questions assailed him. Had he lost her forever? Did she feel anything for him at all? Or had it all just been a fun way to pass the time?

Not bothering to lock the door behind himself, Etienne strode straight down the hall, through the kitchen and jogged downstairs to his office. The mess they had made trying to get him out of it confronted him as soon as he reached the bottom of the stairs. He ignored it, stepping over the debris on the floor and striding on into his office. He would have to see to it that the door was replaced eventually. There was a deadline on finishing Blood Lust II and he really wanted to meet it. Life had been so chaotic lately that, between the trouble with Pudge and the advent of Rachel in his life, Etienne had fallen behind on finishing the project. He'd concentrate on that now. Work had always been his refuge, and it would be again now.

Etienne settled in at his desk and stared at the mess that used to be his computers. Pudge had truly ruined them when he'd shot up the room. Fortunately, Etienne had learned long ago that making backups of everything was a smart thing to do. He hadn't lost any of the work he'd done so far, but he couldn't continue on these computers.

His gaze slid to the phone, but he already knew it too had been destroyed. Turning away from the mess, he strode back out of his office and out of his house to get into his car. He'd have to buy new computers— four of them to replace those he'd lost—and then he'd work like a demon to meet his deadline. Once that was done he would consider what to do about Rachel. If there was anything *to* do.

"What are you going to do about Rachel?"

Etienne scowled at that question from his mother. It was one he had asked himself repeatedly over the week and a half since Rachel had walked out of the police station and out of his life. It was a question he didn't have an answer to. It seemed obvious she didn't want him. She'd walked away without a backward glance and hadn't tried to contact him since then.

"Have you tried to contact her?" Marguerite asked, obviously reading his thoughts.

Etienne didn't bother getting upset at her intrusion into his mind. What was the use? Besides, he didn't seem to have a lot of energy lately. Certainly not enough to bother with a battle he had been losing all his life. His mother had read his mind despite his protests and would no doubt continue to until one or the other of them died.

"Of course you don't have energy; you haven't been feeding right. You're dehydrated right this minute," Marguerite snapped. "And look at you: You haven't bathed or changed your clothes since leaving the police station. You should be grateful that Rachel hasn't tried to contact you. She'd take one look at your sorry state and turn around and walk away, glad to make her escape."

"I've been busy," Etienne snarled. He wasn't the sort to snarl as a rule; that was more Lucern and Bastien's bag. They were the grumpy ones in the family. But he had been feeling rather snarly of late.

"Hmm." Marguerite stared at him, and at first he felt sure she was going to let the subject drop. Then he became aware of her sifting through his mind. He tried to close his thoughts to her, but he had never been able to do that. Besides, she had already found what she was looking for. "You never told her that you loved her."

Etienne winced at that accusation, then scowled. "I didn't know I loved her. I knew I cared for her, though, and wanted to keep her with me, and she no doubt knew that. Obviously she didn't care to."

"How did she know that?" she asked dryly. "Did you tell her?"

"No."

"How did I raise such stupid children?" Marguerite asked the room at large with disgust.

"We could read each other's thoughts when we were . . . intimate. She knew I cared and wanted a relationship with her."

"What?" The expression on her face suggested he was an idiot, Etienne noted, feeling uncomfortable. "How could she read your thoughts? She was no expert. Dear Lord, the poor girl couldn't even control her teeth until the last day or so that she was here. Reading thoughts is an advanced skill that takes years to learn." She frowned at him. "Did you read her thoughts while you were intimate and her mind was open to you?"

"No. Of course not. I didn't want to intrude."

"But you think she was somehow able and willing to intrude on your thoughts?" she asked, then snorted with derision. "Of course she didn't. You're going to have to gather your courage and tell her, son."

Etienne remained silent, but Marguerite could read

the fear in his mind and heart. He wanted to go after Rachel but feared rejection. She knew her son and was positive that he would go after the girl eventually. Marguerite just feared it might be too late by the time he did. It seemed to her that if she didn't want to watch her son mess up his chance at happiness, she would have to utilize a little motherly interference.

Good Lord, she thought with exasperation. The boy was over three hundred years old. A mother's job never ended.

Chapter Eighteen

Rachel sat back and capped the bottle of nail polish before holding her feet out and examining the results of her labor. She now had ten dark red toenails. This was a new experience, but she'd had a lot of new experiences since Etienne Argeneau had made his first appearance in her morgue.

Frowning, she forced that thought away. It wasn't good to think about Etienne. She tended to grow morose and depressed when she allowed herself to think of the man and their time together. Rachel missed him. She had only spent a short time in his home, yet it had felt like both an eternity and a mere minute at once. It was as if she had known him forever and experienced a lifetime in a heartbeat. She missed him horribly.

Sighing, she set the polish on the table and stood up. Rachel lifted her jeans so that the cuffs wouldn't ruin all her hard work, then crossed the living room of her apartment and walked into the kitchen. She really should let her nails dry properly before trying to walk, but if she continued to sit on the couch there was no doubt she would just depress herself with thoughts of Etienne and their time together. Rachel had learned that quickly once ensconced back in her own life. Thinking of Etienne was a no-no likely to sink her into deep depression and make her eat ridiculous things like ice cream that her body didn't need and she really had no taste for anymore.

Realizing that she had walked straight to the fridge and opened it to examine its contents, she closed the door with a disgusted sigh. Then she propped her hands on her hips and turned to examine the room. It was spotless. She had cleaned it, as well as the rest of the apartment, before settling down to paint her toenails to pass the time. Rachel still had trouble filling her nights off. She had returned to her life to find that the day position had been given to someone else while she was missing. Her boss had apologized profusely, explaining that they had feared the worst when she had disappeared. The position had needed to be filled at once, so he had given it to Tony, who had also applied. Rachel had assured him she understood, and she did. In fact, much to her own surprise, she hadn't really minded. Her experiences in that one short week had definitely turned her into something of a night person. She now loved the nights and was happy to work through them. Oddly enough, her noisy neighbors no longer disturbed her sleep. She was somehow able to block them out and slept like the dead.

Her only problem with the night now was that it reminded her so much of her time with Etienne, which was wonderful and sad at the same time. She missed him.

A knock at her door saved Rachel from dwelling on Etienne and sinking into sadness and depression again. Pasting a smile on her face, she left the kitchen and walked down the hall to answer it, wondering which of her neighbors would be knocking at this hour. It was well past midnight, but no one had buzzed to be let into the building, so she was sure it had to be a neighbor.

Rachel didn't bother to check the peephole before opening the door. Her strength and speed had continued to grow in the weeks since she'd been turned, and she wasn't really afraid of anyone anymore. It was a new and rather empowering way to live. She pulled the door open and glanced out, then stilled briefly before stepping through the door and glancing up and down the hallway with bewilderment. She was sure she had heard a knock, but there was no one at the door. And there was no one in the hall.

"I must be losing my mind," she muttered as she

stepped back inside and automatically locked and bolted the door. Rachel had turned and taken two steps away from the door when the knock sounded again. She stopped walking but didn't turn back to her apartment door. The knocking hadn't come from there. It was coming from down the hall, in the vicinity of the living room. More curious and confused than anything, she continued down the hall, and into the large, comfortable room, her gaze sliding over her overstuffed furniture before another knock drew her gaze to her balcony window.

Rachel gaped at the man who stood on the other side of her sliding glass doors, then rushed forward when he grinned and waved.

"Thomas!" she greeted as she pulled the door open to allow him in. "How did you get up here?"

"I climbed, of course," he said with a shrug.

Rachel stared at him, then stepped out onto the balcony and peered over the edge at the front of the building and the six balconies below her own. She turned back to ask with disbelief, "You climbed that?"

"Sure." He shrugged with amusement. "I like climbing."

Rachel peered back down the building again. It wouldn't be impossible to climb, she supposed, if you were strong and agile and weren't afraid of falling to your death. All of which were no doubt true of a two-hundred-year-old vampire. Heck, give her a couple of hundred years and she might be doing things like that herself.

A little laugh slipping from her throat, she turned back and led the way inside again. "Why didn't you just buzz? I'd have let you in, you know."

Thomas shrugged again as she closed the balcony door behind them. "I wanted to surprise you."

"Well, you succeeded at that," she said dryly, then smiled. "To what do I owe this visit?"

"I wanted to wish you Happy Valentine's and invite you to the Night Club," he said easily—but his words merely confused Rachel again.

"Umm . . . Thomas, Valentine's is in February. This is September," she pointed out.

He laughed at her wary expression. "We don't follow the regular calendar all the time, you know. After a few hundred years you realize that Valentine's is whenever it is, and Cupid shows up when needs must."

"Oh," Rachel said uncertainly. She really didn't have a clue what he meant, but she was so happy to have company and the chance to do something on her night off that she decided not to question it.

She'd thought a couple of times about going to the Night Club on her own but hadn't had the courage to for fear of running into Etienne. Rachel was afraid she'd throw herself at him or something embarrassing like that. Or that he'd turn away from her in anger. Did he realize yet what he'd given up to save her? Did he hate her? The fact that he hadn't even bothered to call suggested that he might.

"So." Thomas clapped his hands together, startling her out of her thoughts. "Go get changed, Dudette, and we'll hit the club. It should be a happening place tonight."

Rachel didn't even bother to think about it, just nodded with a grateful smile and hurried out of the room and into her bedroom. She was wearing the tight jeans Marguerite had fetched her from her apartment when she was staying at Etienne's. Rachel usually wore them on her days off; they were comfortable and comforting to her now, and reminded her of her time with him. She knew she'd eventually have to replace them but didn't look forward to the day.

She took them off now and donned a short tight black leather skirt she'd purchased recently in one of her weak moments, when she'd hoped Etienne might contact her. Rachel had hoped to wear it out on a date to drive him crazy. He'd never contacted her, however, and she'd let go of that fantasy. She had no desire to drive Thomas wild with it; he was nice, but Etienne had already stolen her heart and she doubted she'd recover for a long while. But there was always the possibility that they might run into Etienne. If so, she wanted to look her best. If nothing else, he would at least see what he was missing out on.

Rachel finished doing up the skirt, then whipped off the large T-shirt she was wearing, exchanging it for a dressy white blouse that she tucked into the skirt. Then she donned sandals that would show off her newly painted toes and hurried into the bathroom to apply a little eye shadow and lipstick. After running her fingers lightly through her hair for a sexy, slightly tousled look, she squirted some perfume on her throat and wrists and hurried back out.

"That was quick. And you look *good*," Thomas said with admiration as she rejoined him in the living room. "Let's go, Dudette. The night awaits."

Much to her relief, he didn't head for the door to her balcony, but started down the hall to her front door. Rachel didn't think she was ready to start climbing buildings yet. She grabbed her purse and followed him out of her apartment, her step suddenly lighter. She liked Thomas. Not in the same way she liked Etienne, of course. But he was fun and made her laugh, and she knew he would make sure she had a good time tonight. An evening at the Night Club would be fun, much better than sitting around her apartment, moping over what might have been.

Besides, she might gain some information about Etienne from Thomas. He would know how his cousin was doing and what he was up to. Rachel was embarrassingly hungry for information about Etienne.

Etienne packaged the discs for Blood Lust II, addressed the label, and set it aside with a sigh. He'd finished. Finally, it was done. He stared at the envelope for a moment, his mind blank, then stood restlessly and left his office. He'd been working on the game nonstop, not allowing thoughts of Rachel to intrude and interrupt him, except for the night that his mother had come by to harass him. Now that he was done, however, his first thought was of Rachel. He wondered what she was doing as he walked upstairs.

Was she at work? No, he decided. She'd learned she'd been given the day job the night he'd turned her. It was after midnight. No doubt she was sleeping right now, tucked up nice and comfortable in a big warm bed, he thought, and felt longing rise up within him. He wished he was there in that bed with her. Of course, she wouldn't get much sleep if he were there. He wouldn't be able to resist touching her, caressing her—

Etienne killed his own thoughts there. Fantasizing about making love to Rachel wasn't the most productive thing in the world. Besides, he had more important things to do, like figuring out a way to approach her. He had decided his mother was right. He had to tell her of his feelings and find out what hers were. The only question was how he should go about doing it.

Etienne was halfway through the kitchen when the phone began ringing. He immediately turned to the door to the basement, then recalled that he'd had phones placed throughout the house when the repairman had been in to fix the one in the basement.

Turning back, he walked to the phone on his kitchen wall and grabbed it up to bark "hello?" into it.

"Hey, dude!" Thomas's cheerful voice greeted him. "Guess where I am?"

Etienne grimaced. The sounds of loud music and talk nearly drowned out the man. It didn't take a genius to figure this one out. "Night Club."

"Got it in one, dude." Thomas laughed. "Yeah, I'm here with this nuclear babe. You might know her. Rachel?"

"What?" Etienne stiffened, his fingers tightening reflexively around the receiver.

"Yeah." Thomas sounded smug. "She wasn't doing anything. I wasn't doing anything . . ."

"Thomas," Etienne growled. Cold fury rose within him at the suggestive pause.

"She's in the ladies' room now and doesn't know I'm calling you. If you want her, you better come on out here and join us," his cousin said with amusement. Then, in more serious tones, he added, "And you'd better get it right this time, dude. I'm not playing Cupid for you two again. If you mess up now, I'm taking her for myself. Happy Valentine's."

The click of the phone was followed by a dial tone. Etienne listened to it for at least a full minute as his mind raced. Thomas was playing Cupid. He was interfering again. God bless him, he thought, and slammed the phone down. Then he spent a moment dithering about what he should do first. He needed a shower and to change his clothes. He had to shave. Dear God, he had a beard growing on his damned face, he'd gone so long without shaving. Maybe he should bring her something. Flowers maybe. Where the hell was he going to find her flowers at this hour? Why did everything have to close at night? Didn't anyone out there want to make any money? he thought irritably as he hurried out of the kitchen.

"You're a happening chick, Dudette!"

Rachel laughed at Thomas's compliment as she danced to the rock tune blaring at them on the dance floor. She was having fun. Really. Lots of fun. And she'd only thought of Etienne about two thousand times in the two hours that they'd been there. That was less than usual.

"I'm pooped, Dudette. Let's sit." Thomas didn't wait for her agreement, but caught her by the hand and dragged her off the dance floor. Rachel followed without protest. She was enjoying herself but could do with a rest.

"Good, our drinks are here," Rachel said with a pleased sigh as she dropped into her chair. She'd decided to be brave and let Thomas order for her again, stating only that he couldn't order her a Sweet Ecstasy. He'd ordered her an Ever Enduring. That hadn't sounded too risky. Still, she'd asked what it was, and he'd merely smiled and said she'd see. Rachel tried it curiously, surprised that it wasn't bad. Not bad at all. She no longer needed straws to feed.

"Oh, look who's here."

Rachel glanced up and froze at the sight of Etienne making his way through the crowd toward them. For a moment, happiness filled her heart, but then worry replaced it. He didn't look happy to see them. In fact, he looked rather irritable, she decided as she watched him walk the last couple of feet to the table and pause there to stare at her. She was just deciding that he had realized what he had given up and did hate her when he suddenly whipped his hand out from behind his back and held out a bouquet of limp flowers to her. Rachel stared blankly at the sad bouquet before reaching out uncertainly to take them. Her hesitation was obviously too long, because Etienne immediately began to apologize for their state.

"I wanted to get you flowers, but none of the flower shops are open at this hour. I checked six all-night variety stores before finding any at all, and this was the best of the—"

"They're lovely," Rachel interrupted as she took the flowers. Limp and sad-looking as they were, they truly were lovely to Rachel. They represented hope, and she accepted them gladly, offering a shy smile as she lifted them to her face and sniffed the delicate bouquet of—"Salami?"

"They were kept in the deli fridge," he muttered, looking embarrassed.

Rachel bit her lip to keep from laughing, then smiled at him widely. "How have you been?"

"Miserable," he answered simply. "You?"

"The same." They shared a smile and both relaxed.

"Well, it looks like my job here is done," Thomas announced and got to his feet before explaining to Rachel, "It was fun, but I'm just the delivery boy, Dudette. Aunt Marguerite asked me to play Cupid and I like you, so I agreed."

"Cupid, huh?" Etienne asked with amusement.

"Yeah, you can laugh," Thomas said good-naturedly. "Enjoy it while you can. But don't mess up with Dudette this time. Once every hundred years is my limit on the Cupid gig."

Moving to Rachel's side, he bent to hug her and murmured, "Welcome to the family."

Rachel wanted to ask what that meant, but Thomas walked away too quickly for her to get the chance. She watched him disappear into the crowd, then turned to glance at Etienne as he took the seat his cousin had just vacated.

"I missed you," he announced the moment her gaze met his.

Rachel's eyebrows flew up at this claim. The thought "You could have fooled me" flew through her mind, and Etienne smiled wryly.

"I heard that," he said with amusement.

"I thought you couldn't read my mind," Rachel said suspiciously.

"I can't," he assured her. "Well, except when we're intimate. Your mind opens to me."

"Then how did you—?"

"You actually projected that thought to me."

"Did I really?" she asked.

"Yes. It was most likely accidental, but with practice you'll be able to do it at will."

"Really? Can you teach me how?"

He was silent for a minute, then said, "I have a better idea. I'll project a thought to you and you try to read it."

"Okay," she agreed, then tilted her head. "How do I do that?"

"Just open your mind to me and I'll do the rest," he told her, then went silent, his eyes narrowed with concentration. A bare moment passed before Rachel heard his thoughts as clearly as if he were speaking in her ear.

I miss you. I ache for you. Something is missing from life when you aren't there. I want you back in my life, my home, and my bed. I want to wake up each evening beside you. I love you, Rachel.

Rachel stared at him, hardly able to believe she had heard correctly. "Then why haven't you called? If Thomas hadn't brought me here tonight—"

"I would have found another place and way to approach you," he assured her solemnly. "I just wanted to get my deadline out of the way so I could concentrate solely on you."

Rachel thought that sounded rather lame. He'd wanted to get his work out of the way first? She came after work, after his video game? Well, that was flattering.

"You must be really pissed," he said wryly. "You're sending your thoughts out clear as a bell."

When she didn't smile or react in any way that might let him off the hook, he sighed and said, "Perhaps we should go somewhere quieter."

Rachel nodded solemnly, downed the last of her drink, and stood. They were both silent as they exited Night Club and made their way to his car. She didn't demur when he opened the passenger door for her to get in and didn't ask where they were headed. Neither was she terribly surprised when they pulled up in front of his house. It was where most of their relationship had taken place. It seemed the most logical place to resolve it.

Rachel followed him inside and into the library on the main floor. She felt calm steal over her on entering the room. They had spent several quiet evenings together in this room, simply reading together.

"Okay," Etienne said as they sat on the love seat and he settled his arm around her, drawing her against his chest. "It wasn't work. That was an excuse."

She wasn't terribly surprised at this admission but remained silent and was rewarded when he added, "I was afraid."

Now that *did* surprise her, and Rachel sat up and turned to peer at him. "Afraid of what?"

"Of being hurt, Rachel," he said quietly. "I've never thought of myself as a coward, but this was an entirely new experience for me. I've never met a woman I was attracted to and whose thoughts I couldn't read. It was a new experience and not very comfortable. I felt vulnerable from the start. And confused too, I suppose. You should remember, I've managed to live three hundred years without falling in love. The feelings you brought about in me took me by surprise."

"I was rather taken by surprise too," Rachel admitted quietly and settled back into his embrace. "And scared of being hurt. Actually, I was afraid you would realize what you had given up to save me and would come to hate me, which was—"

"Never," he interrupted firmly, giving her a squeeze. "I knew what I was doing right from the start. I was attracted to you from the beginning, even when you were sick and pale and looked ready to keel over." When she glanced up at him, he smiled to soften the description. Then he caught her chin in his hand and said, "Rachel, I can't imagine spending my life with anyone but you. I can't imagine a life without you. You have my heart, and I realize I may be rushing you and that you might want more time to consider it, but—"

"I don't need more time, Etienne," she interrupted quietly. "I know this is all happening quickly, but you're the man I've wanted all my life. If I had taken the time to imagine what the man I loved looked like and the qualities he would have, you would have been who I dreamed of. I love you," she said simply, and smiled when he released a long drawn-out sigh.

"Then marry me," he blurted.

"Yes," Rachel said at once, but he shook his head.

"You have to think about this, Rachel. This isn't a piddling twenty-five to fifty years I'm asking for. Marriage among my people—at least the people in my family—is for life. And life for us can be a very long time."

"I hope it's an eternity," she said solemnly. "I love you, Etienne. I would spend eternity with you. You have my heart too."

A slow smile spread wide across his face. "Thank you. I will guard your heart all the days of my life." The words were a bare whisper before he leaned forward and claimed her lips in a kiss.

Rachel sighed into his mouth as her lips opened. His kiss felt like coming home, and she had been away for far too long. Meeting his invading tongue with her own, she twisted where she sat and slid her hands up his chest. She allowed one to continue up around his neck and into his hair to catch in the silken strands there. With the fingers of the other she caught at his shirtfront to tug him closer. Her body arched into his of its own accord and desire was a sudden rush through her body, making her hungry and bold. Rachel wanted him under her, on her, and in her all at once. She wanted to join with him and feel his body fill her. She wanted to hold him and be held like this forever.

And you can. The words whispered through her brain, a message from him to her that brought a chuckle from deep in Rachel's throat. But her happy amusement died and the chuckle ended on a growl as his hand found her breast through the cloth of her blouse. Things were suddenly quite serious.

Rachel allowed herself to fall backward on the love seat, tugging more insistently at the cloth of his shirt as she did so and forcing him to follow her down. Etienne shifted and came down on top of her, his lips and hands becoming more demanding. Within moments, Rachel's white blouse was open and the hooks that fastened the front of her bra were undone. She shivered in anticipation and arched beneath him as he pushed the silky material of her bra aside, revealing her naked breasts. When he bent his head to capture one already erect nipple, she clasped his scalp in both hands and held him close, then suddenly released her hold on his hair and pushed him away.

The startled expression on his face as he raised up away from her was priceless, but Rachel was too busy working at his shirt buttons to take much notice. She quickly undid them until his shirt gaped open as he leaned over her, then spread her hands over the wide expanse of bare skin. Rachel loved his chest, the hardness, the strength. She stopped when her palms ran over his nipples and caught them between her thumbs and forefingers to fondle them with interest.

Etienne released a low growl at the caress, then lowered himself over her to claim her lips once more. Passion burst between them, hot and unstoppable, and the time for exploration was over. It felt as if they had been apart forever and the need between them wouldn't be denied. It was like a brushfire, burning bright and furious. Their kisses became almost rough, and she scraped her nails up his back as his hands roamed her body, then dug them into the backs of his upper arms and arched beneath him as he slid one hand between her legs to press against the leather of her skirt.

"I need you," she gasped. It was a demand, not a plea, and was accompanied by Rachel reaching between them with one hand to clasp him through his jeans.

Etienne's reaction was immediate. He lifted himself briefly to kneel between her legs on the couch, pushed her skirt up the few inches necessary, grasped her panties and, rather than draw them down, simply snapped the sides of the flimsy silk so that it fell away like so much flotsam. He was undoing his jeans as he came back down on top of her, then he slid one hand under her bottom, lifted her slightly, and slid into her as she wrapped her legs around his hips.

Rachel groaned with relief as he entered her, her

body welcoming and holding him tightly as he groaned at her ear. Then he began to move, and they were both swept up in the moment; striving, almost fighting for the release they needed. Etienne made sure Rachel found hers first, but the moment she cried out and clenched around him as it claimed her, he said, "Thank God" through clenched teeth and allowed himself to join her. Then he collapsed on top of her and they lay panting together.

Etienne was the first to stir. Releasing a wry, still breathless laugh, he shifted them on the couch so that he lay flat on his back and she now lay splayed on top of him, limp as a rag doll.

"Well, that was . . ." His voice was husky and he let the words trail off.

"Hmmm . . ." Rachel murmured, then lifted her head to grin at him lazily. "Want to do it again?"

Chuckling, he clasped his arms around her and hugged her close. "Love to. You good to go?"

"Oh yes, I—" She stopped abruptly and lifted her head again, her eyes wide.

"What?" he asked with concern.

"I didn't faint," she said with amazement. "That's the first time I haven't fainted."

"Then I definitely didn't do it right," Etienne decided and sat up, forcing her up with him.

"Oh, but I . . . er . . . enjoyed it as much as usual," Rachel said, aware that she was blushing but unable to stop it. "Maybe more. It was pretty hot."

"It was, wasn't it?" He was grinning rather smugly as he scooped her up in his arms and stood to carry her across the library.

Rachel shook her head at the male ego and laid her head against his chest as he carried her into the hall. They were halfway up the stairs to the second floor when Etienne suddenly asked, "What were you drinking at the club?"

"An Enduring something," Rachel murmured, toying with the hair at the base of his neck.

"Ah." Etienne nodded.

"Ah what?" Rachel asked raising her head off his shoulder to peer at his face curiously.

"You won't be fainting tonight," he informed her with amusement.

"Oh?"

"Hmm." He chuckled. "In fact, Thomas has arranged it so that I'm in for a real workout."

"Really?" She asked with interest as he carried her into the bedroom. "I think I like your cousin."

"Right now, I do too," he said with a laugh. He kicked the bedroom door closed behind them.

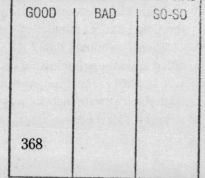

GOOD	BAD	SO-SO

368

Epilogue

Marguerite gave a wide smile to Bastien's secretary as she passed her desk and sailed into his office unhindered. "I received a postcard from Etienne and Rachel. They're having a wonderful honeymoon in Hawaii."

Her serious son glanced up from the report he'd been reading to eye her with resignation as she crossed the large room toward him. "They are, are they?"

"Yes." She bent to press an affectionate kiss to his forehead and handed over the postcard in question. While he read, Marguerite walked back around his desk and dropped into the chair positioned in front of it.

"I don't know why they chose Hawaii," Bastien said

with a wry smile. He finished the postcard. Standing, he leaned over his large desk to hand it back.

"Balmy breezes and moonlit beaches." Marguerite took the card and tucked it into her purse. "Besides, Rachel had planned a trip there before she was changed. She'd never been."

"And Etienne wanted to please her," Bastien finished as he reclaimed his seat. "They'll be happy."

Marguerite heard the wistful note in Bastien's voice and eyed him speculatively. At over four hundred years old, Bastien was her second oldest son. He was also the most serious. Too serious at times. He always had been. Even as a boy he'd been the more responsible of her four children. It hadn't been terribly surprising to anyone when he had taken over as head of the family after Claude's death. Lucern would have been capable of the task but would have hated every minute. Bastien relished the challenges and enjoyed solving problems and helping people. He was a good man. He needed a good woman.

"Why are you looking at me like that?"

His wary question made Marguerite relax and shrug. "I was just thinking that perhaps it's catching. Lissianna and Etienne are now both married and settled down. I have great hopes for Lucern and his little Kate . . . if they don't kill each other at that conference she's dragged him to. Perhaps you'll find someone soon too."

Bastien fell silent as he thought of Lucern and Kate.

His oldest brother had managed to be tricked into attending a romance conference with his editor. He hadn't wanted to go, but Kate was a persuasive little bundle, and once she'd teamed up with their mother, Lucern hadn't stood a chance.

On the other hand, Bastien thought, perhaps his brother hadn't ever stood a chance against Kate, with or without their mother's help. Having seen the two of them together at Etienne and Rachel's wedding, Bastien suspected his mother's hopes for the pair weren't misplaced. Lucern was in love. Whether he knew it or not, the man had found his life mate. Bastien hoped for his sake that he didn't mess it up.

His gaze drifted to his mother, who watched him with interest. Knowing she could read his thoughts, he didn't bother to deny a desire for a life mate of his own. He would like a partner to stand at his side to meet life's trials. But he had been alive for over four hundred years and met only one woman he had thought he might love in that time. Unfortunately, she had not reacted well to learning what he was and had refused outright to join him. Despite that, Bastien had never stopped loving her. He had watched over her throughout her short life, always from a distance. He had watched her age, fall in love with someone else, have children, then grandchildren, and finally he had watched helplessly as she died.

Those had been the most painful years of his life. They had taught him that, thanks to what he was, he would always be the child standing alone on one side of the fence, watching all the other children laughing and having fun at the party taking place on the other.

Aware that his mother was still watching him, he shrugged and looked at his report. He said simply, "Some people aren't meant to find love and keep it."

"Hmmm." She was silent for a moment, then apparently decided to change the subject. "Oh, by the way, Bastien, Dr. Bobby wants to talk to members of my family, and since Etienne and Rachel are on their honeymoon, Lissianna and Gregory are vacationing in Europe, and Lucern is at that writers conference, the only one available is you. Can I say you'll come?"

"Hmm? What?" He glanced up with bewilderment. "Who is Dr. Bobby?"

"My therapist, dear."

"Therapist," he echoed with shock. Then alarm quivered through him. "You're seeing a therapist?"

"Yes, dear. It's all the rage right now. Besides, Gregory was so helpful with Lissianna's phobia, I thought I might benefit from a little counseling myself."

"Why? You don't have any phobias."

"No. But I do have some issues—one in particular I wanted to address."

She wouldn't meet his gaze. Bastien couldn't help but wonder. "And this therapist wants to talk to members of your family? Why?"

Marguerite shrugged. "I'm not sure. Dr. Bobby just

mentioned wanting to talk to members of the family. You will come, won't you?"

Bastien frowned, but finally nodded his assent. It seemed a good idea to go find out just what *issue* his mother was dealing with and how much of their lives—not to mention what they were—she had revealed to this Dr. Bobby.

"Good. I'll leave you to your work then." Marguerite beamed at him and stood to leave.

Bastien started to relax but then stiffened as she added, "Don't worry, son. There's a woman out there for you too. And I intend to help you find her."

He gaped in horror as the door she closed behind her. Those words had sounded suspiciously like a threat.